"Lynette has written another fast-paced book—lace up your tennis shoes and grab a water bottle. It's a race against death."

—**DiAnn Mills**, author of *Deadlock*

"Eason's *Always Watching* had me 'always reading' until I devoured it. Riveting suspense, complex characters, and a twisty, turning plot kept me up until I finished it at 2 a.m. This is one of the best romantic suspense novels I've read in a long time. Highly recommended!"

—**Colleen Coble**, author of *The Inn at Ocean's Edge* and the Hope Beach series

Praise for the Hidden Identity series

"Being the first novel in a brand-new series, all that can be said for this author is that she certainly started out with a 'bang'! For any reader looking for 'edge-of-your-seat' thrills, this series is the perfect gift."

—*Suspense Magazine* on *No One to Trust*

"The author doesn't let up until the end, making *No One to Trust* extremely difficult to set down. I enjoyed her Deadly Reunion series, but this book surpasses those by far, and I hope this is only a glimpse of what we can expect from the Hidden Identity series. Fans of Eason's and readers of Christian suspense will definitely want to check out this new series. I, for one, cannot wait to get my hands on the next installment."

—*Fiction Addict* on *No One to Trust*

"Readers will be on the edge of their seats till the final chapter."

—*Publishers Weekly* on *Nowhere to Turn*

"Eason has written an exciting nail-biter that readers are sure to enjoy."

—*Booklist* on *Nowhere to Turn*

"The third book in Eason's Hidden Identity series starts off with action and doesn't let up until the end. Fast-paced and intriguing, the romance between Jackie and Ian develops naturally. The mystery is not easy to figure out; even astute readers may be fooled."

—*·ook Reviews*, 4 stars on *No Place to Hide*

Books by Lynette Eason

WOMEN OF JUSTICE

Too Close to Home

Don't Look Back

A Killer Among Us

Gone in a Flash (ebook short)

DEADLY REUNIONS

When the Smoke Clears

When a Heart Stops

When a Secret Kills

Retribution (ebook short)

HIDDEN IDENTITY

No One to Trust

Nowhere to Turn

No Place to Hide

ELITE GUARDIANS

Always Watching

ALWAYS WATCHING

A NOVEL

LYNETTE EASON

Revell

a division of Baker Publishing Group
Grand Rapids, Michigan

Published by Revell
a division of Baker Publishing Group
P.O. Box 6287, Grand Rapids, MI 49516-6287
www.revellbooks.com

Printed in the United States of America

Library of Congress Cataloging-in-Publication Data
Names: Eason, Lynette.
Title: Always watching : a novel / Lynette Eason.
Description: Grand Rapids, MI : Revell, a division of Baker Publishing Group.
  [2016] | Series: Elite guardians ; 1
Identifiers: LCCN 2015037005 | ISBN 9780800723262 (softcover)
Subjects: LCSH: Bodyguards—Fiction. | Celebrities—Fiction. | Stalkers—Fiction. |
  GSAFD: Suspense fiction. | Mystery fiction. | Christian fiction.
Classification: LC PS3605.A79 A79 2016 | DDC 813/.6—dc23 LC record available at
  http://lccn.loc.gov/2015037005

Published in association with Tamela Hancock Murray, The Steve Laube Agency, 5025 N. Central Ave., #635, Phoenix, AZ 85012

16 17 18 19 20 21 22   7 6 5 4 3 2 1

As always, this book wouldn't be possible without the love and support of my family, so I dedicate it to you. Jack, Lauryn, and Will, I love you like crazy.

[1]

The music played in the background while the charity's benefactors finished their dinner. A few danced, some chatted. Others looked slightly bored with the whole thing.

But one person caught her eye.

She watched the elegantly dressed female from across the room. She fit in nicely with the crowd, blended well. But stood out in one regard.

"He's mine," she whispered. "He's mine and you can't have him. Go away." No one knew what it had taken for her to get here tonight. No one knew the work she'd put in to making sure she was at this event. No one. And no one was going to ruin it either.

So what should she do? She had seen the woman following him, watching him, her eyes tracking his every movement, never leaving him alone. Even following him to the bathroom and back. Oh, she was discreet. She never made a move to approach, but she watched.

Her heart thumped in time with the upbeat music. How could

7

she get him to see her? Truly see that they belonged together and had belonged together . . . forever?

Grudgingly, she admitted that the woman was pretty. Dark hair and eyes. Just the kind of woman he would be attracted to. "Well, you can't have him." She paused to draw in a deep breath and take another bite of her orange-glazed duck.

It would be fine.

She chewed, swallowed, and looked up. And met the eyes of the woman across the room. She dropped her gaze back to her plate. Why was she looking at her? Did she see something? Could she know what she was thinking?

Another deep breath. Of course not. She couldn't get stupid now. She glanced at the man who'd stolen her heart. And some fat cow at his side. Why had he brought her? She reached for her glass.

"Are you all right? You look like you're agitated."

She nearly choked on the sip of tea. "Agitated?" As good a word as any, she supposed. She placed the glass back on the table and forced a smile. "No. I'm just fine, thank you."

"Good, I'm glad." He took the seat next to her. "You look beautiful tonight."

She swallowed, despising the lump in her throat. "Thank you."

"I'm glad you could make it."

Was he? She glanced at the woman across the room again. "I wouldn't have missed it." Good, she was getting her composure back.

"Of course not. You deserve this."

She stared at him. "I do?" Then blinked and gave a small laugh. Thankfully, it came out low and amused, not coarse and nervous like she felt.

"You do. I think you deserve to have whatever makes you

happy." He smiled and his white teeth flashed bright in his tanned face.

She tilted her head. "Are you flirting with me?" Because if he was, he was out of luck. Her heart was already taken.

He chuckled. "Would you like to dance?"

"You want to dance? With me?"

"I asked, didn't I?"

"Then I'd love to." Maybe *he* would see and would take note. She rose and placed her hand in his. Then glanced back at the woman across the room. The other woman's eyes were back on Wade.

The fury renewed its desire to come out, to spill over onto the woman. But she held it back.

"Is there a problem?" her dance partner asked.

"What do you mean?"

"You seem tense."

"I'm fine."

He nodded in the woman's direction. "You don't like her?"

She stiffened. "I don't know her."

"At least you didn't pretend to misunderstand who I was talking about. I like that."

She was in control. She could handle this. She smiled up at him. "Forget her. I already know what you do. Why don't you tell me something about yourself that I won't read in the papers." She listened with one ear while her gaze drifted back to the woman who couldn't seem to keep her eyes off Wade. Yes, it might be time to do something about her. But that was fine. She'd killed for him before, she'd have no trouble doing it again.

[2]

Madelyn McKay swept her eyes over the radio station door, down the length of the building and back, tapping her fingers on the steering wheel. She kept the car running, only slightly concerned about the gas she was wasting. It was sweltering outside even at this time of night, and she wasn't going to bake. The air conditioner blew in her face and helped keep her awake.

"August in the South. Gotta love it," she muttered and turned the volume up a notch on the radio.

She had to admit, even though she had no trouble sleeping at night, her client's soothing voice could have lulled her into sweet dreams if she'd been suffering from insomnia.

As far as she was concerned, Wade Savage had the perfect radio voice. Sweet, smooth . . . and silky. But more important, he sounded like he really cared. More than once Maddy had reached for the phone, thinking she'd call in and ask him a question. Professionalism held her back. But she really liked his voice.

As did everyone who listened. Including one rabid fan. Wade's stalker. A stalker who seemed to be escalating the hunt.

That was why Maddy found herself sitting in her car watching the building and everyone entering and leaving. Which wasn't anyone at this time of night. Wade was in the building alone. Maddy had her laptop mounted on a special dash stand, allowing her to monitor every area that had a camera on it. Her computer screen was divided into six squares with a view of the six areas. The back door, the front door, Wade sitting at the console speaking into the microphone, the door to the storage room in the back of the building, and the two hallways.

She wished she could see down the back of the building. The station was part of a strip of businesses, but held the coveted end spot in the row. None of the other businesses were open. Night-lights glowed from behind the glass doors, the employees long gone.

Patching in to the station's security system had been ridiculously easy. After this case was over, she planned to help the station upgrade its software and firewall. Until then . . .

Maddy checked her watch one more time. Wade had left the charity dinner and bolted to the station to do the show. He would be finished with it in about another fifteen minutes, then she would follow him home, report in, and go home to get a good night's sleep.

So she could do this all over again tomorrow. Boring? A bit. But she liked it that way. She thought Wade had looked tired, though. But who wouldn't be, keeping his schedule?

A flash of light shot through the driver's window, then was gone. She sat up straighter and looked in the direction the light had come from. When nothing else happened, she didn't relax. Instead her nerves began that little hum they did whenever she needed to be on alert. Aware. The light flashed again, farther away and not hitting the car, but still there.

Ignore it? She continued her rhythmic tap on the steering wheel, debating. Then grabbed her phone and sent a text requesting some backup. She didn't know if she'd need it or not, but it never hurt to be prepared. Maddy had a good view of the front door of the radio station from her strategic position. She'd backed up and parked next to the building just across the lot from the building Wade had entered almost three hours earlier.

When the light swept across the front of the station doors, Maddy's pulse picked up speed and her nerves hummed faster.

Her fingers curled around the handle of the driver's door.

The glass to the passenger window exploded. Maddy ducked, flinched away from the shards hitting her, reached for her weapon. Felt a prick in her upper arm. Looked down to see a small dart sticking out. She grabbed for it and pulled it out. What? Her head began a slow spin and nausea climbed up the back of her throat. Weakness consumed her and she felt the darkness start to grab at her consciousness. She fought it, struggled to get her fingers wrapped around the door handle, her only thought to get out, get help. But her eyes wouldn't stay open. Her phone. She needed her phone to call for help. But her hand was too heavy. She couldn't lift it.

She forced her eyes open and saw a masked figure slide into the passenger seat, the knife glinting in her attacker's right hand.

"Why?" she whispered.

Felt the blade against her throat.

Then nothing.

[3]

3:15 AM

The air held a malevolence. An . . . evil. Wade Savage hesitated as the radio station door shut behind him. The parking lot stretched before him. Goosebumps pebbled his skin, a stark contrast to the sweat beading on his forehead.

Someone was watching him.

Again.

He could *feel* the eyes on him. He stood still, frozen with indecision, as the early morning darkness pressed down on him. He tried to pull in a deep breath, but the August humidity made it hard to find the oxygen in the air. A soft light from the building spilled through the double glass doors behind him.

Wade shivered in spite of the heat, felt a rivulet of sweat slide down his temple. He swiped it away even as a fine mist broke out on the back of his neck. A mere month ago, if anyone had said anything about *feeling* the presence of evil, he would have laughed. But not now, not tonight. For a brief moment, he regretted his refusal to listen to his father's recommendation that he hire a bodyguard. It would be nice to know he had someone watching his back right now.

His phone buzzed and he glanced down at it. Cameron Short, one of the directors on the board of the charity Wade had founded six years ago.

I know your show is over and you're probably on your way home. Call me. I'm up and have a couple of questions about the charity dinner on Thursday.

Wade shook his head. It was the middle of the night for the normal person, but Cameron never seemed to sleep. Ever since his wife, Gina, had died of cancer two years ago, the man used his insomnia to further the cause of the charity he helped run.

Wade would call him when he could. Right now, he kept his focus on the area around him. The night sounds didn't comfort him. A lone car swept past the station and the taillights disappeared round the curve just ahead. He'd never really noticed before how deserted the place could be at almost 3:30 in the morning.

Tonight he noticed.

The hair on Wade's neck spiked.

The fatigue that had dogged him since leaving the charity dinner to head for the radio station lifted and his adrenaline surged.

He hesitated again and let his gaze scan the parking lot, the areas beyond, the lighted places nearby, and—especially—the dark ones. He wondered what—who—lingered in the shadows? Unfortunately, he couldn't see anything.

His Nissan Armada sat just ahead. It was a straight shot across the parking lot and sat innocently under a light, facing the six-lane road that lay just beyond the sidewalk. A mostly empty six-lane road at this time of early morning.

No one in the building behind him.

Someone in the dark in front of him?

Possibly.

He took two more steps toward his car. The sense of danger intensified. With a bit of shock, Wade realized he was truly afraid.

The building doors were locked, the alarm armed. It would take him several minutes to get back inside. His car was most likely his best bet for quick safety.

If he could make it.

While his car was only about twenty yards away, in his mind it was too far. He would be open, exposed to whoever watched. He shifted, pressed his back against the building. Then pulled his phone from his pocket and dialed 911.

A sudden pulse of anger took him by surprise. He wouldn't let whoever was out there do this to him. He started to cancel the call, then let it go through. He gripped his keys. Wade scanned the area one more time and started for the car, his long strides eating up the distance. He ignored the swift beat of his heart, the second surge of adrenaline, the lack of air in his lungs. The *fear* . . .

"911, what's your emergency?"

Within seconds he arrived at his vehicle and inserted the key into the lock. "Yes, I'm—"

He heard the footfall at a distance behind him.

And felt the sharp prick in his lower back. He spun even while his hand went to the area where he felt the pain. He pulled out what was lodged there and looked down to see a small dart in his hand. He'd been shot with a dart?

The movement to his left caught his attention. He looked and saw the shadowy figure of the person dressed in black. Black clothes, black mask, black eyes—

Wade's legs trembled, refused to hold him. The phone and

the dart slipped from his fingers. He heard them hit the ground. Weakness invaded him and his knees landed on the asphalt next to his phone. He tried to reach for the device, but his fingers wouldn't work for him.

He thought he saw the glint of a knife blade before a blanket of black covered him up.

[4]

Olivia Edwards punched the button on her phone one more time. And one more time Madelyn McKay's voice mail picked up after the first ring. "Maddy? Where are you?" Olivia muttered. "Pick up the phone." Maddy had texted her less than twenty minutes ago, saying she might need backup, but would be back in touch to let Olivia know for sure. Going on instinct, Olivia hadn't hesitated, she'd just gone straight to her car and headed for the station. And now Maddy wouldn't answer.

Olivia pressed the button on the Bluetooth device in her ear and hung up. Her fingers curled around the wheel as she turned into the radio station's parking lot.

Her gaze landed on someone on the ground by his car.

The figure bending over him looked up and Olivia slammed on the brakes, pulled her weapon from her shoulder holster, and threw open the driver's door. "Wade!" The masked individual raced away, crossed the street, and disappeared into the shadows beyond. Olivia pulled her cell phone from her pocket and dialed 911. She identified herself. "I need an ambulance."

She gave the address as she moved toward the man sprawled

facedown on the asphalt. "Oh please, please, please, don't let him be dead." She knelt and pressed her fingers against his neck. A pulse beat and she breathed a small sigh of relief. At least he was alive. "Suspect is on foot," she said into the phone. "Crossed Hampton Boulevard, headed north."

"Male or female."

Olivia blinked. "I don't know. Whoever it was is dressed all in black and has on a black ski mask." She hung up and ran her hands over Wade, looking for anything to account for his unconsciousness. When she couldn't find anything, she frowned. His breathing worried her, slow and shallow. She felt he went too long between breaths. Drugged? She hesitated to move him in case of a head injury she couldn't see. A siren screamed in the distance.

Olivia looked around. Where was Maddy? Worry for her friend and partner ate at her, but she couldn't leave Wade. She checked his pulse once again. Slow but still there. She looked up, catching sight of the blue light moving closer. Soon the red ones of the ambulance blended with the blue of the police cars as they turned into the parking lot one after the other.

Two police cruisers whipped past the station and Olivia figured they were going after the suspect. Another entered the parking lot.

She waved the EMTs over. "His name is Wade Savage. I'm not sure what happened, but I think he may have been drugged." They took over and Olivia got on her cell phone. She needed to find Maddy. The woman would never leave her client exposed. The fact that someone got to him scared her. Not just because Wade could have been killed, but because it meant Maddy was most likely incapacitated.

Maybe even dead.

One of the EMTs looked up. "I can't find any obvious injury, but we'll get him to the hospital and checked out. If he was drugged, no telling what it was with. Respirations are slow, pulse is slow. We'll monitor him closely to make sure he doesn't stop breathing. Other than that he just appears to be in a deep sleep."

"Fine. I'll follow behind you." She flashed her badge that identified her as a bodyguard.

She called Maddy's number again. Her fingers tightened with each passing ring. Finally, she hung up and dialed another number. Katie Singleton, another partner with the Elite Guardians Bodyguard Services, picked up. "Hello?"

"Have you heard from Maddy?" She didn't have to bother with small talk or pleasantries. Katie would hear and understand the urgency in her voice.

"No." Katie's sleepy voice went on instant alert. "Why?"

"I can't get in touch with her. Wade Savage was attacked tonight and is on the way to the hospital."

"Attacked? Where are you?" Katie asked.

"At the radio station, but I'm going to the hospital to be with him and to make sure the person who did this isn't there waiting on him to finish the job. I'll explain everything later."

"I'm on my way to the radio station to help search for Maddy."

"Better alert Haley too." Haley Callaghan, the fourth member of their team. Her Irish blood would be pumping until they found Maddy.

"Will do. Check in when you get there."

"Find Maddy, Katie, I'm really worried about her."

"I'm on it. You stick with Savage."

She hung up and turned to find an officer at her side.

"I'm going to need a statement from you," he said.

"Can you follow me to the hospital?" She nodded to the ambulance. "That's my client and I'm going to need to follow him."

"Client?"

"I'm his bodyguard." Technically Maddy was, but since Maddy wasn't around, the job now fell to Olivia.

The officer, whose name plate read Hartman, raised a brow. "Bodyguard?"

"Yes. And I'm not leaving him alone. Especially after this incident. I'm sure you can understand that." The officer's gaze flicked to the ambulance, then back to her. She read his thoughts and gave an impatient sigh. "This didn't happen on my watch. That starts now." The ambulance started to pull out. "Come to the hospital if you want a statement." Olivia raced to her car and climbed in. The ambulance took off and she followed it. She tried Maddy's number again. And still nothing. The officer followed her.

When the ambulance pulled into the Emergency slot to unload Wade, Olivia swung into a nearby "official vehicles only" spot and placed her card in the windshield. A card provided to her by the mayor that identified her as a VIP.

She raced into the lobby of the hospital and went to the triage desk. Again, she flashed her special credentials, hoping she didn't have to go into an explanation of who she was and what she did. The nurse's brow lifted, but she buzzed the door and, within seconds, Olivia was in the treatment area of the Emergency Department. She approached the desk. "I'm with Wade Savage."

"Room 4."

Olivia nodded and walked back to the room. She peeked into the window and saw a nurse drawing blood and another hooking up an IV line.

Wade was being taken care of. He was unconscious and couldn't answer any questions at the moment, but he was alive. Olivia breathed a sigh of relief that he was most likely going to be all right, then pulled out her phone to call Bruce Savage,

Wade's father. The one person she had no desire to break this news to. The man who'd hired her agency to keep his son safe.

Before she had the chance to hit the speed-dial number, her phone vibrated. Katie. Had she found Maddy? "Please share some good news with me."

"We're still looking for Maddy. She and her car are both missing, so it's not looking good. I've gone ahead and called Quinn. I'm hoping he'll get things stirred up." Quinn Holcombe, Maddy's "potential" boyfriend and a detective with the local police department.

"Good." Olivia pinched the bridge of her nose and forced herself to process what she needed to do by priority. "I'm calling Bruce. He'll want to come by the hospital."

"You think he'll pull us from the detail?"

"I don't know."

"Good luck. I'll be praying about that call."

"Not sure prayers will do much good," Olivia grunted, "but guess they can't hurt."

"No, they can't hurt." Katie's soft voice conveyed her sadness over Olivia's lack of faith.

Olivia grimaced. She believed in God, she just didn't like him very much. But now wasn't the time to go into that. She hung up, thought about Maddy.

And almost wished she prayed too.

[5]

Wade tried to push the thick blanket away. Somehow he'd managed to cover his face and now it felt like he would smother. But it was heavy and his arms were tired. No, it wasn't a blanket. His eyes wouldn't open. He tried again. And again. Finally, he saw a sliver of light.

"Dr. Savage?"

He tried to speak and couldn't get past the dryness in his throat. The wave of nausea took him by surprise and he simply lay still.

"Wade? Can you wake up?"

He felt something slip between his lips. A straw? He sipped and the cool wetness slid down the back of his throat. "Yes," he whispered. "Give me a minute."

"He's coming back to us."

"Where's my son?" The smooth bass voice was filled with concern. And fear?

Wade's sense sharpened. His dad? Why was he here? Where exactly was here? The fog shifted and his mind started to clear. He'd been trying to get in his car and felt the sting in his lower back. A person with a knife? Then blackness. Or was it all a dream? He had no memory of anything from then until now.

A chill sliced through him and he struggled against the lure of the darkness once more. The smells and sounds hit him. He was in a hospital? He heard his father's voice. "Wade? Son? Wake up and tell us what happened. Who did this to you?"

He finally managed to pry his eyes open. Glanced left, then right. Yes, a hospital. "I don't know." He licked his lips and took a deep breath. "I knew someone was there. I could feel it."

His father frowned and exchanged a look with someone on the other side of the bed. Wade turned his head and let his eyes land on a beautiful woman. Straight blonde hair, concerned blue eyes. Smooth complexion, oval face. Beautiful. Intriguing. "Who—?"

"My name is Olivia Edwards. I . . . found you in the parking lot of the radio station."

"Found me?" He licked his lips.

"Where was Ms. McKay?" his father asked.

"Who—" But his father wasn't talking to him. He had his laser intense gaze on Olivia's face. Wade let his eyes drift shut, then forced them back open.

"I don't know. She's still missing."

What were they talking about? Who was missing? He tried to form the words to ask, but couldn't seem to wake up any further. He drifted, their voices still echoing in his head.

When reality intruded again, Wade forced himself to wake up. He rolled to his side and pushed his eyelids up. His gaze landed on his father seated in the one available chair, head back, light snores filling the air. Wade rubbed his eyes and sat up, the bed crinkling beneath his weight.

His father stirred. "Son?"

"Yeah."

His dad leaned forward. "You going to stay awake this time?"

"I think so." His head felt less clogged and foggy. He reached for the cup on the table near him and chugged back the rest of the lukewarm water. "How long was I out this time?"

"About thirty minutes."

"What time is it?"

"Six in the morning."

Wade's stomach growled in agreement. "I need to check on Amy." His twelve-year-old daughter with more than just a penchant for worry. He reached for his phone and couldn't find it in its usual spot, clipped on to the side of his belt.

His dad held it up. "Amy's fine. She doesn't know anything about what happened. Martha's going to take her to school just like any other day."

Martha, his sister-in-law and live-in nanny for Amy. Wade thought. What day was it? Oh right, Friday. "She'll wonder why I don't come down for breakfast."

"Martha plans to tell her you had an errand to run and will see her when she gets home."

Even though he worked until three in the morning, he was always up at six-thirty to eat breakfast with Amy before she went off to school. "I guess she'll have to be all right with that."

"She'll be fine. It's not the first time you haven't been there for one reason or another."

"I know, it's just that that's our time and I hate to miss it."

"Can't be helped. Have you gotten any more packages?"

And that was that as far as his father was concerned. Deal with stuff and move on. Wade grimaced and sighed. "Yes."

"What?"

"What does it matter?"

"Six weeks, son. This has been going on for six weeks."

"I know, Dad. I'm aware."

"And who knows how long she was watching you before

then? Learning your habits and—" His father blew out a hard breath and dropped his head in his hands.

Wade winced. His dad was right. At first it was just small things like a teddy bear with some of his favorite chocolate candies. He'd mistakenly thought Amy had gotten them for him for his birthday and had them delivered. But she'd claimed no knowledge. Neither had his sister-in-law. Or his father.

Next it had been a box of his favorite soap and aftershave, followed by two tickets to the concert he'd mentioned wanting to see. All things he'd talked about on his radio show.

Innocent gifts. Thoughtful gifts. Or they would be if they were from someone he knew. Coming from a stranger who obviously wanted to stay anonymous was a bit creepy. Okay, a lot creepy.

He looked into his father's frowning eyes. "This past Monday I got home from the office to find expensive matching baseball jerseys for me and Amy."

"Jerseys?"

"Atlanta Braves jerseys."

"Your favorite baseball team." His dad shook his head. "This is getting too bizarre."

"No kidding. One of my callers was worried about her marriage. I suggested doing something her husband enjoyed. She said he liked baseball so I talked a little about the Braves and how Amy and I enjoy going to the games every so often. I told her we got a lot of talking in during the drive there and even during the lulls in the game and that it was a good bonding experience. She seemed to like the idea."

"And someone sent you jerseys." His father seemed to have trouble wrapping his mind around it.

"Yes, but that's not the scary part."

"What is?"

"The size was perfect. Not just mine, but Amy's too."

[6]

Olivia paced outside Wade's room. She wanted to help in the search for Maddy, but knew the people involved were more than capable. Her job was to protect her client. Her phone rang and she slammed it to her ear after a glance at the screen. "Did you find her?"

"Yes."

A bolt of fear shot through Olivia at Haley's curt response. "Tell me."

"She's on her way to the hospital. We found her about thirty minutes ago." Haley's usually mild Irish accent had thickened. Her grim tone sent dread racing through Olivia's blood. "She was in the trunk of her car. The passenger window was blown out." A pause. "Liv, it's obvious that someone ambushed her." Haley's voice wavered. "I don't know if she's going to make it or not."

"That bad?"

"Her throat was cut."

Olivia gasped and stumbled against the wall. A nurse lifted her head and frowned. Olivia ignored her and tried get a handle

26

on her shock. Her usually unflappable emotions had just taken a hit.

"Sarah and her team are here working the scene." Sarah Baldwin, lead CSI for the crime scene unit. Knowing she was there brought a small measure of comfort. "But that's not all," Haley said. "Whoever did this left a note."

"What does it say?"

"It's three words written as two sentences. 'Apologize. He's mine.'"

Olivia stayed silent for a moment as she processed the message. "The second part indicates jealousy on the part of a woman."

"Oh definitely. We already knew that. It's the reason his father hired us."

"I know, I know. I'm just thinking out loud. Who's supposed to apologize?"

"Wade?"

"Maybe. If so, what does she want him to apologize for?"

"Some perceived wrong obviously."

"Yes, of course, but what?" Olivia forced her legs to work and paced to the nurse's station and back, her eyes probing faces, ID cards, body language. "Was the note handwritten or typed?"

"Neither."

She paused mid-stride. "Excuse me?"

"I'm sending you a picture. It looks like it's made up of words cut from a newspaper."

"Well, that's original." Not. "Also indicates forethought. She took the time to put the note together before the attack." Her phone pinged. "Hold on a second and let me look." She brought up the picture and studied it for several seconds before putting the phone back to her ear. "The lab will let us know what they find about that." She paused for a moment as she put it all together again in her mind. "So she attacked Wade in the parking lot, but didn't kill him," she muttered. "She's mad at him, but giving him a chance to redeem himself by apologizing for whatever wrong he's done to her."

"And she wants him to know she can get to him and no one is going to get in her way. 'He's mine,' she said."

"She wasn't writing the second part of the note to Wade," Olivia murmured. "She was writing it to whoever found Maddy."

"And what if the first part wasn't written to him. What if she was demanding an apology from whoever found Maddy?"

"That doesn't really make sense, but who knows how this person's mind works?" She took a breath and forced her thoughts into organization. "All right. Wade's stalker was watching him. Let's assume she was in a place to notice Maddy's attention focused on Wade."

"Maddy was being subtle and staying off Wade's radar. She was looking for someone to be watching and following Wade, not someone taking notice of her," Haley said.

A headache started at the base of her skull and Olivia pulled in a deep breath. "But did the person who attacked Maddy realize that she was his bodyguard, or did she maybe think Maddy was someone else who was interested in Wade?"

"Good question. The note says, 'He's mine.' Like he's her possession or something. To me that indicates she thinks Maddy was interested in Wade."

"Therefore Maddy was a threat. She was competition for Wade's affection. Attacking Maddy could also be a warning for other women to stay away from him—or for him to stay away from other women unless he wants them to wind up like Maddy," Olivia said

"But Maddy and Wade never met," Haley said. "They never spoke. He didn't even know about her. And if the stalker was watching him, interacting with him, she would know that. So why consider Maddy a romantic interest and therefore a threat?"

"I know. It doesn't make sense, but it's the only explanation I can think of at the moment."

"And if she wants an apology from Wade, why hurt him?"

"Obviously she was making a point," Olivia said.

"Yeah. That she could get to him."

"Who knows what was going through her mind? Warped brains don't make sense to those of us who have all our marbles— or at least the majority of them." She thought and paced a few more steps. "Anyway, she said he needed to apologize, so instead of killing him for whatever perceived wrong he's done, she gives him a second chance."

"Maybe."

Olivia glanced at the door to Wade's room. "I'm going to ask him a few questions. Stay tuned and keep me updated on Maddy's condition, please."

"Will do."

"Thanks." Olivia hung up and let the anger burn. Being a bodyguard meant accepting that the job came with risks. They watched over their clients while knowing the unthinkable could happen, but hoped it wouldn't. Maddy understood that. They all did. Still . . . it didn't lessen the punch of the blow one bit.

She saw the doctor Bruce had pointed out to her as Wade's— and a lifelong friend of the family. He'd been sleeping soundly when Bruce had called him about Wade, but hadn't hesitated to roll out of bed and immediately come to the hospital to take care of his friend's son. He looked to be in his midfifties and was dressed in black slacks and a blue short-sleeved polo shirt. She approached him and he looked up from the chart he was studying. "Dr. Worthington?"

"Yes?"

"I'm Olivia Edwards, Wade Savage's bodyguard."

He shook her hand. "Bruce told me about you."

"I'm not looking for you to violate any HIPAA regs, but could you just tell me the drug he was injected with?"

"You can tell her," Bruce said. Wade's father stood at the door to Wade's room, looking as though he'd planned on leaving for a brief moment.

Dr. Worthington nodded. "Did you need something, Bruce?"

"Just another cup of coffee."

"I'll bring it to you," Olivia said.

Bruce gave her a nod of thanks, then stepped back inside and shut the door again.

"Propofol," the doctor said.

Olivia nodded. "Thanks." She headed for the coffeepot, her mind spinning. She texted Angela Malone, the agency's administrative assistant.

> Pull up info on a drug propofol and send to me
> ASAP, pls.

Angela probably wasn't at the office yet, but she'd get the text soon enough. Olivia figured she could just ask the doctor, but didn't want to bother him. She had her resources and would use them. Coffee cup in hand, she turned to head back toward Wade's room.

". . . looking for Wade Savage's room?"

Olivia's head turned toward the man asking about her client. A tall man in his midfifties stood at the nurse's station. She moved forward before the nurse could speak. "May I help you?"

The man turned. His hazel eyes smiled before his lips. "Only if you know where I can find Wade Savage."

"Do you mind if I ask who you are?" He looked familiar,

but she couldn't place him. Maddy would have known him instantly.

He held out a hand, his gaze wary, but curious too. "I'm Cameron Short. I work with Breaking Free."

"The charity Wade set up." She'd read Maddy's notes on it. And on Cameron Short.

"Yes, yes. He's the executive director. I'm on the board. He and I pretty much run things." He paused. "And you are?"

"Olivia Edwards." This time she hesitated. "I'm working for Mr. Savage on some security issues."

"Security?" He frowned, then sighed, his expression worried. "Look, Bruce sent me a text telling me Wade wouldn't be able to meet this morning. He just said something about him being attacked in the station parking lot and being in the hospital. Of course, I had to come see for myself that he's all right."

"I'm getting ready to step inside and see that for myself. Why don't you wait here and I'll let Bruce know you'd like to speak with him."

"That would be wonderful. Thank you."

"Of course."

Olivia knocked on the door to Wade's room. "Come in." She recognized Bruce's voice. She stepped into the room and moved so she could see Wade sitting up in the bed. "You're looking better."

Confusion knit his brows together. "Thanks." Then his forehead smoothed. "You were here earlier."

She glanced at his father. Bruce looked resigned. She handed him his coffee and lifted a brow. He nodded.

"What is it? You two know each other?" Wade had caught the silent exchange.

"I'm Olivia Edwards. I'm part owner of the Elite Guardians Bodyguard Agency." She held out a hand and he shook it. She met his gaze, and his eyes, his very green eyes, didn't look away or blink. He simply stared. As did she. She waited, wondering what he was thinking. He finally let go of her hand and her fingers slid across his palm. His lips quirked in a small smile. Olivia cleared her throat and took a step back.

His frown returned as her words registered. "Bodyguard agency?"

"I hired them," Bruce said from his position in the chair. His jaw jutted and his eyes narrowed. "You've been getting weird gifts in the mail, hang-up phone calls, presents left on the front porch." He waved a hand. "You have a stalker. When you rejected my offer to hire a bodyguard, I simply did it anyway."

Wade's nostrils flared. "Of course you did."

"Son—"

Wade held up a hand. "I can't believe—"

"Maddy's throat was slit," Olivia said, raising her voice only slightly. Might as well nip the argument in the bud.

The room fell silent. Wade looked at her. "What did you say?"

"One of my employees, Madelyn McKay, was your bodyguard. She was following you, keeping you in her sight at all times, and was there in case someone attacked you. Instead, she's the one who was attacked and is now here at the hospital. Whoever drugged you got Maddy first. The attacker slit her throat."

"Slit her—oh my . . . I can't believe this." Bruce's voice was suddenly hoarse, shock paling his tan face.

"The attacker also left a note that said, 'Apologize. He's mine.'"

"You think the attacker's female?"

"Probably."

Wade's face paled even further, although Olivia wouldn't have thought it possible. "And you think she was referring to me?"

"We do."

"Why?"

She lifted a brow. "I think that's rather obvious, but before we get into it—" she turned to Bruce—"there's a man outside waiting to speak with you. Cameron Short?"

"Cameron?" Wade asked. "What's he doing here?"

"You had a meeting with him this morning," Bruce said. "I texted him and told him you'd be unable to attend. I gave him the really short version of what happened and I guess he decided to see for himself." He waved a hand toward the door. "He can wait a few minutes. Go on, please," he told Olivia.

She nodded. "Before last night, this person, and we're assuming it's the same person for now, was sending you harmless gifts. Then for some reason, she felt compelled to come to the radio station, attempt to kill your bodyguard, drug you, and leave a note staking her claim. What changed?"

Wade shook his head as though to clear it and his father looked ill. "Wait a minute," Wade said. "How is Madelyn?"

"She goes by Maddy. And I don't know. I'm still waiting to hear." *Dear God, please let her pull through.* The prayer slipped from her before she could stop it. She pulled her phone from her pocket one more time and sent a text to Katie.

Ask them to check Maddy for the drug propofol.

"Okay, let me make sure I've got this right." His gaze swung to his father. "You hired a bodyguard agency."

"Yes."

"When?"

"Two weeks ago. Right after you found the tickets for the concert in your mailbox." Bruce ran a hand over his face and Olivia thought she saw a few new stress lines that hadn't been there when he'd walked into her office two weeks ago.

"And this woman, Maddy," Wade said. "She was protecting me and got hurt because of it." He seemed to feel the need to say the words aloud in order to process the facts.

"Yes." Olivia nodded. "And that's why after last night's incident, we need your help. From this moment on, we're going to need your thoughts and input. The gifts she's sent you up to now haven't been threatening in any way. However, it's never a good thing to assume that just because the gifts are harmless, the sender doesn't have some kind of ulterior motive, some expectations." She tapped her lips. "And when you don't meet those expectations, bad things will start happening."

"Like earlier."

She nodded. "Like earlier."

He sighed, then gave a low, humorless chuckle. "The thing is, I know this stuff. You're not telling me anything new. I'm a clinical psychiatrist. I've worked with people who've had stalkers and I've worked with stalkers themselves. I've just never experienced it on quite this level of up close and personal." He shook his head. "This is so twisted."

"Agreed, but in her mind, she's showing you how much she cares. Your father was right to be concerned."

"So you hired someone behind my back?" Olivia heard the undercurrent of steely anger.

"Your mother had a stalker."

Those five words from his father silenced him. Olivia looked up to see Bruce staring at the floor. His pale face and still stature captured her attention.

"What?"

Bruce looked up at his son's quiet question and gave a small shrug. "She had a stalker. Right before she was killed."

"Who?"

"The cops were never able to prove it, but I suspect it was

the woman who sent her letters for over a year, calling your mother all kinds of horrible names, accusing her of stealing her husband's love and warning her to back off and disappear. Your mother was concerned, of course, but was convinced it would all blow over. I was scared to death."

"With good reason, it sounds like," Olivia murmured.

"Yes. And so when I saw the gifts and Wade finally told me about the calls he's been getting at the station, I didn't want to waste any time making sure someone was watching his back."

"When was your wife killed?"

"May 2, 1985."

Her gaze flew to Wade. "You couldn't have been more than a toddler."

"I was two."

"I'm so sorry."

"Regardless," Bruce said, "I could see history repeating itself, and as long as there's breath in me to do something to prevent it, I'll do it."

Wade studied his father, and Olivia could see the muscle jumping in Wade's jaw. Understanding mixed with anger roiled in his eyes.

"For some reason she's been content to admire from a distance, send harmless gifts, be anonymous," Olivia said.

"But all that changed this morning," Wade murmured.

"Exactly. But what triggered that?"

Wade sank back onto the bed. "I did."

"How?"

His gaze bounced between her and his father. "On the show. I mentioned the gifts. I said I appreciated them, but they really needed to stop, that I wasn't interested in an anonymous admirer. I said I had thrown away all of the gifts and would do so with any future gifts, so she might as well stop."

Olivia closed her eyes and let out a pained groan. "Oh no."

"Son . . . ," his father breathed.

Wade set his jaw. "Look, like I said, I've worked with these people. Sometimes when they're confronted and told to back off, they do. Sometimes they don't and they escalate." He scratched his chin. "This person involved Amy. She sent her a jersey. The cops won't do anything because there's been no overt threat. They agreed I needed to be cautious and take steps to protect myself and Amy, but their hands were tied." He held his hands up, then dropped them, resignation and defeat flashing for a brief moment on his face. "I couldn't just sit around and do nothing, so I decided to take a gamble."

"Not only did you lose that gamble," Olivia said, "I think you've stuck a stick in a hornet's nest."

[7]

Just before Wade was released, Cameron entered the room for a short visit. He shook Wade's hand and clasped his shoulder. "I'm so glad you're all right. When you're feeling better, call me and we'll get together to discuss business."

"Will do."

Cameron left, and while Wade appreciated his concern, he was glad the man hadn't dragged out the visit. He still felt physically weak and exhausted. He just wanted to go home and go to bed.

One piece of good news that had brightened Olivia's tense features had come as Wade was signing his release papers. Maddy had come through surgery and was still clinging to life. Barely.

He'd met Katie Singleton, who'd arrived with Haley Callaghan, and learned they were two more partners in the agency. Katie had scouted the area and deemed it safe to walk the four steps from the hospital exit to the passenger seat of Olivia's vehicle. Wade left the hospital with Olivia and his father at his side. Wade's father had his own car and would meet them at the house. Wade slid into the passenger seat of Olivia's SUV and buckled his seat belt. "How many employees are with Elite Guardians?"

She backed out of the parking spot. "In the beginning there were three of us. Katie, Haley, and I all met at the bodyguard school in Athens, Greece. We graduated and formed our own company. We've all been involved in one form of law enforcement at some point in our lives, so we put together a proposal and presented it to the mayor. She liked it."

"So you work for the mayor?" he asked as she pulled out of the hospital parking lot.

"Yes and no. We do contract work for her and the local police department when they have a need." She tapped her fingers on the wheel as she drove. "For example, if there's a big celebrity or politician in town or something and they need additional security, they call on us. One reason is that states vary in their laws for concealed weapons. Some bodyguards may not be able to carry their weapons in South Carolina. We can. So whoever is in need of extra security contacts local law enforcement, and local LEO gives them our agency recommendation. In addition, if there have been threats or angry letters, we're brought in to do a threat assessment, review the security plan, and make recommendations to the chief of police. Usually, they just hire us for the gig if they think they need specialized protection." She shrugged. "That's about it in a nutshell."

"But isn't that what the local force is for?"

"Of course. Like I said, we just work with them when they need some extra manpower or the person in charge of the security detail feels like his client would be better off with a personal protection specialist."

"And when you're not working with them, you're bodyguard-ing?"

"No. The bodyguard service comes first. When we get a call from a private client, we would take that job over one from the mayor if we have to make that choice. Most of the time we can handle both."

"I've never heard of anything like that."

She smiled. "That's because it's an experiment." She shrugged. "Normally, the clients pay for the protection. But in this case, as we were trying to build our business, we had the idea that we presented to the mayor. When she learned that the funding came from a private grant and that there wasn't any strain on the taxpayers' pocket, she was eager to see how we could all work together. And law enforcement welcomed the help. The mayor had nothing to lose and everything to gain."

"Sounds ideal."

"It really is. The good thing is, we've all been in law enforcement and we know what we're doing. And because we're employed on a contract basis via the mayor, we carry law enforcement powers. We can make an arrest, investigate a crime, do lots of the things a police officer can do."

"So the agency was started with you, Katie, and Haley."

"Yes." She made a left, then a quick right. "As the business grew, we added Maddy and may need to add another in the next month or so. I do have some contract people I work with on occasion should I need the manpower. And with Maddy out of commission for a bit . . ."

"Yeah."

She drove with confidence, her movements sure and steady even while she kept an eye on the rear and side mirrors. Wade let himself study the woman who'd probably saved his life last night. Straight blonde hair with some darker highlights and blue eyes that reminded him of the Caribbean waters on a clear summer day. She was physically beautiful, clearly competent, and intrigued him like no other woman had in a long time. Not since—

"You're staring," she said.

"You're interesting." He pushed that last thought aside. He didn't want to think about Justine.

She blinked. And laughed.

"What's so funny about that?" he asked.

She shrugged. "That's not usually what I hear from a man."

"Sorry."

"I'm not. It's refreshing."

He studied her to see if she was flirting. She wasn't. Again, his interest in her grew to another level. Again, he frantically pushed it away. "To have someone look beneath the first layer?"

A flush darkened her cheeks and she didn't look at him. "Something like that."

"So what's your story?"

She looked at him this time. "My story?"

"Yes."

"Let's put it this way. It's short and it's boring."

"Boring?" He let out a chuckle. "Right. I don't believe that for a minute, but I'll let you off the hook if you promise to tell me at some point."

She made a sound in her throat that could have been an agreement—or not. She pulled to a stop at the light and her phone buzzed. She glanced down. "That's Angela Malone, our agency's administrative assistant. She keeps us all in line and organized. She sent me some information on the drug you were injected with."

"Shot with, you mean."

Her gaze sharpened on him. "What do you mean?"

"It was a dart. I remember pulling it out, then dropping it as my legs gave out."

"Nothing like that was found near you." She narrowed her eyes and Wade thought he could see her brain spinning. "That's why she was stooped down beside you," Olivia murmured. "She was cleaning up after herself. She—or he—took the dart with her. I'm still not sure if it was a woman or a man." Olivia pulled over into a restaurant parking lot and put the car in park although she left it running. She picked her phone up. "'Propofol is the generic name for Diprivan, an anesthetic that causes unconsciousness.'" She shot him a look. "Guess we knew that. 'It's mostly used in surgeries and administered by IV. It's fast acting, but short-lived. Meaning in order for the patient to stay unconscious, it has to be monitored and a steady dosage maintained in the bloodstream.'"

Wade nodded. "The doctor seemed to think the side effects would wear off in a few hours. He said to give it twenty-four hours from the time of the injection for it to be totally out of my system." He shook his head. "Who would have access to that kind of thing? I wouldn't think it would be that easy to get ahold of that kind of drug. It would have to be obtained by someone in the medical field, right?"

"That would be my first thought."

She pulled back out and merged with the traffic. Five minutes later, she pulled into his drive. "You have a nice place."

"You mean you haven't been out here watching?" He couldn't help the edge of sarcasm.

"Yes, I've been here." Either she didn't notice the sarcasm or she didn't let it bother her. He had a feeling it was the latter. "Maddy, Haley, and Katie are the ones who've been doing most of the watching."

"Why not you?" He tempered his tone. No need to take his frustration out on her.

She shot him a grim smile. "I also have other duties that

demand my time, but now that Maddy's fighting for her life, I'll be taking a much more active role in guarding you, while we work to figure out who attacked you."

She pulled around to the back, past the wrought iron gate he'd left open, and up under the covered area. To the left was the main house. To the right, the three-car garage complete with guest home on the second floor. In front, a second wrought iron gate stood open, allowing him to drive through and around to the front of his home without having to back the car out of the driveway.

She'd definitely been here before. How had he not known? How had they watched him and he'd never known it?

And yet he'd known someone was watching him last night. He remembered the sense of evil and felt chills pebble his skin. He reached for the door handle as his father pulled in beside him.

"We'll probably need to keep these gates closed. It would be hard work to get into your house that way. Keeping this entrance sealed means lessening the risk of someone entering."

"I usually just leave them open all the time. But we can keep them closed now." He started to open the door.

"Will you please stay in the car?"

He hesitated. "Why?"

"Katie's going to check the area." She spoke into her phone and motioned for his father to stay in his vehicle as well. His father nodded.

Then she simply waited.

Wade released the handle. He thought it all ridiculous and yet he couldn't deny what had happened in the wee hours of the morning. He also couldn't deny the gifts he'd been getting. So he stayed silent.

She left the car running and the air conditioner blasting.

Late August in the South meant hot muggy days. He tried to see his place through her eyes and felt a sense of satisfaction dart through him. A little bit of pride, but mostly gratefulness. He didn't want to take his good fortune for granted.

Thanks to his mother's lucrative career as an actress in the late 1970s to early '80s, he lived comfortably. His father had set him up with a trust fund after her death. At the age of twenty-one, he received access to the money and had built this house on the small private lake just outside the city limits. He'd always found it a refuge. Peaceful and quiet. He had neighbors, but they were spread out, separated by strategically placed greenery.

He grimaced. At least it used to seem peaceful. Now his home just looked like an easy target.

"Do you have any clients today?" Olivia asked.

"Not today. I work Monday through Thursday in my office and do the radio show Thursday through Sunday." He shot her a look. "I thought you would know that."

"I do, but you're not exactly the most predictable client we've ever had." He supposed that was true. He often got calls from clients asking for last-minute appointments or met some of his friends from the radio station for coffee if he received an impromptu text or phone call. "And honestly, that's one of the best things you can do," she said. "Don't be predictable. Predictable will get you killed." She glanced at the door as though impatient for Katie to hurry up.

"You tell it like it is, don't you? No dancing around the topic with you, huh?"

She shot him a surprised glance, then shrugged. "It depends on the person, the client's personality." She studied him for moment. "However, you're not a 'dancing' type of client. You shoot straight when you can and pull your punches when the person you're talking to needs it. You prefer to meet conflict head-on—especially when the conflict is personal. Like you, I adjust my way of talking to the personality of my clients."

He flexed his jaw. She was right. And it was just plain creepy. How had she read him so easily? Just exactly how much did she know about him anyway? Did she know about Justine? Of course she did. As soon as his father had hired her agency, his past was an open book. His jaw tightened at the invasion of his private life. "You sure know a lot about me."

Her gaze softened a fraction. "I'm sorry. It's what we do, Wade. The information we have is only used to keep you safe, nothing else."

"So tell me something about you."

She looked away and he wondered if she would answer. Finally she shrugged. "Like I said, my life was pretty boring. I was raised in a series of foster homes. I graduated high school at the top of my class and went to the University of South Carolina on a full-ride scholarship. Which was a good thing because I sure couldn't afford anything else. I majored in criminal justice, graduated, and went straight into the police academy at the ripe old age of twenty-one."

Wade blinked. "Foster homes. Wow."

"That's all you got from that paragraph?"

"How did you turn out so well?" He coughed. "Um . . . that didn't come out right."

She gave him a small smile. "I understand. A lot of foster kids don't turn out great, but I was fortunate. I had some good homes, some great foster parents. The last one was the best and I was there for six years."

"Six years?"

"When they took me in, I was treated as one of theirs. There was no bias between their biological children and their foster children."

"So they're your family?"

She hesitated, then nodded. "Yes."

"Where are your biological parents?"

Sadness flickered in her eyes, then was gone so fast he wondered if he'd imagined it. "They were killed in a small plane crash when I was ten. Both of them were only children of deceased parents, so there wasn't anyone who could—or would—take me in."

"Wow. I'm sorry."

"Me too."

"But your last foster parents didn't adopt you?"

Olivia shook her head. "No." A guarded tension came over her, and he bit his tongue on asking why, but she finally volunteered the answer. "They wanted to. They weren't the problem. I was."

He studied her. "You didn't want to be adopted?"

"No." She hesitated again. "I did, but I . . . didn't. I still had a strong connection to my parents." She took a deep breath. "I just couldn't accept that they were gone for good."

"Didn't you go to the funerals?"

"Yes, but . . ." She shrugged and looked away, then cleared her throat. "So Maddy's told me a little about your charity," she said. "I think it's a wonderful thing you're doing."

He nodded. Allowed the change of subject even while his mind processed what she'd revealed. "Thanks. After my late wife took off, I had a huge adjustment to single parenthood. Amy was just a baby at the time, but her mother's abandonment and eventual death still had an effect on her. On us."

"Of course it did."

"I wanted to help parents and kids who found themselves in that situation. Fortunately, I had a father and the funds to make things easier on me. The majority of single parents don't have that. This charity makes a difference for them."

ALWAYS WATCHING

"It's a much-needed organization. I applaud you for founding it." Her eyes never stopped moving. He knew she was listening to him, but her alert status never wavered. For some reason that comforted him. Made his respect for her slide up a notch.

She held up a finger when her phone rang.

"Put it on speaker, will you?" he said.

She lifted a brow but did so.

"I have something, Liv," Katie said, her voice strong and concerned. "Let me finish clearing the house."

"What is it?"

"Someone left a gift on the front steps."

Olivia glanced at him and Wade narrowed his eyes. "What kind of gift?" she asked.

"A package. Stay put until I know whether or not it's rigged to go boom."

[8]

Wade flinched. "Go boom?" He sat, tension threading through every muscle. He could feel his heart beating in his temples and had to remind himself to breathe.

It seemed like hours before Katie's voice came back on the line. "The house is clear, you might as well come around to the front porch and see it. One thing I do know: it's not going to go boom."

"Well, that's a comfort," Wade muttered. In the rearview mirror, he saw his sister-in-law pull in behind him with Amy and Amy's friend Stacy Abbott. He'd forgotten all about Stacy staying the weekend.

He climbed from the vehicle, anxious to see what his stalker had left. He was grateful Olivia didn't try to stop him from entering the house, she just followed him.

Into her phone, she spoke to someone else. "Keep everyone out of the house for the moment. Did you check the guest house where the sister-in-law lives?" She cut the speakerphone off and listened. Spoke again. "Good. I'll let you know when it's clear to allow them to come in."

At the door, Wade paused and glanced back at his daughter. The frown on her pretty young face said she wanted to know what was going on and would pit bull him until he told her. She might have anxiety issues, but she also had her fair share of his stubborn genes. He sighed. And maybe it was time to talk to her. This whole situation seemed to be snowballing at a rate that would bury them all under an avalanche of danger if he didn't do something to figure out who was stalking him and put a stop to it.

He stepped inside the short hallway. To his right was a room his sister-in-law often used for scrapbooking and other craftwork. To his left was his office. He bypassed that and his dining room and stepped into the foyer. He opened the front door and found the person Olivia had been talking to. Katie. She was bent over an object on his front porch.

His father had pulled around to the left side of the horseshoe-shaped drive while Wade had been distracted with Olivia and the call. The man now stood next to Katie, his eyes on whatever she was also looking at.

His father's pasty-white face sent dread skittering through Wade, but he didn't falter in his steps. He wanted to know. Had to know.

Katie sat on the top step, looking down into a box that probably measured three feet long by two feet wide. It wasn't the box itself that caused his breathing to quicken, but the shape.

He skidded to a stop. "Seriously? A coffin?" His heart thudded, beating a painful, heavy rhythm in his chest. "How do you know it's not going to 'go boom'?" He identified another emotion surging through him. Anger. Pure white-hot rage that someone would dare violate his home, his life and family.

"Katie's had extensive training in explosives. She's ex-ATF," Olivia said. "If she says it's not a bomb, it's not."

"Oh." Feeling slightly better, he glanced at the woman named Katie. Tall, maybe five feet ten, a hundred forty or so pounds, she had black hair pulled back into a severe ponytail, olive skin, black eyes. She wasn't beautiful like her partner, but she was pretty in an understated, non-flashy way. She wore no makeup that he could see, and her clothes suggested she dressed for comfort, not fashion. She had gloves on her hands. The kind of gloves cops wore. "Then what is it?"

"I've called the police. We have to report this, but in the meantime, you can have a look inside."

Wade hesitated for only a brief second before he moved so he could see. Olivia stayed with him and together they looked into the box. He sucked in a silent breath. Olivia went still. Frozen.

On top of plastic that had been stapled to the sides of the coffin, a teddy bear with dark black eyes stared up at him.

The head had been decapitated.

Red liquid filled the area under the body. The plastic kept the blood from soaking the cardboard coffin, and the odor emanating from the object made him sure the blood wasn't paint or theater makeup. He turned away, feeling sick. "Who would do this?"

"Whoever you ticked off when you announced you were throwing her gifts away," his father said.

Wade looked back, the image now ingrained in his memory. "Whose blood is that?"

"I'm hoping it's animal blood," Katie said. "But we'll have it tested to be sure."

Wade set his jaw and stared. Then narrowed his eyes as he took in the details of the mutilated stuffed animal. "Wait a minute."

"What?" Olivia asked.

"I need to check on something." He opened the front door

49

and moved into the house. He heard Olivia follow him, but his focus was on finding out if he was right or not. He headed toward the back hall that would take him toward Amy's room.

Olivia followed him up the stairs. "What is it, Wade?"

"Hold on a minute and we'll both know." He pushed open the door to his daughter's room and went to her bed. A plethora of stuffed animals lined the headboard and propped themselves on blue checkered pillows. "It's here, I know it is."

Olivia waited behind him, her impatience nearly tangible, but at least she didn't push him. He'd explain soon enough.

There. He grabbed the bear and turned, holding it in front of him. "This. Anything stand out to you about this?"

Olivia stepped farther into the bedroom and took the toy from him. "It's the same one."

"Identical."

She glanced up. "I thought you threw everything away."

"Everything but that. Amy loved it so I let her keep it."

"Katie's called the police. We'll file the report about this latest incident. What's your security system like here again? I know we went over everything with your father, but maybe it's better that we have your input."

"I have a security system that I turn on when I'm not here, and I make sure Amy arms it if she's alone—which is pretty much never and definitely not since all of this started. The windows are wired, the doors . . . motion detectors and lights on the perimeter of the house. I've been much more meticulous about arming it these days, trust me."

"Cameras?"

"No."

"We'll definitely need to add those and some floodlights around the boathouse."

As she talked, she became more animated, her passion and

dedication for her job coming through. It comforted him and attracted him all at the same time.

He nodded. "All right." He needed to stop noticing things about Olivia that he didn't have any business noticing. There had been a lot of gorgeous women in his life. Women he'd simply noticed were beautiful, but he'd felt no special tug of interest in. Except for Justine. Beautiful, sweet Justine. He looked away for a moment as her memory rushed over him. He cleared his throat. Just because he'd gone and felt that spark of interest in Olivia didn't mean he had to get all distracted by that.

At least not right now. Probably not ever.

"And another thing," she said, "there will be a police officer assigned to your home. He—or she—will be here at all times to watch the house. Fortunately, I have a lot of friends on the force who are willing to earn a few extra bucks by lending their skills when needed. The police force itself doesn't have the resources to be able to watch you like you need it." Her phone buzzed and she looked at it. "Good. Cameras will be installed first thing in the morning."

"You have a lot of resources at your fingertips, don't you?"

"It's taken time to build the relationships, but yes, I'm very fortunate in that respect. When we started the agency, each of us brought resources with us. We utilize them when we need to."

Wade walked to the window. He stared out across the expansive acreage and wondered if she was watching his house now. The anger still simmered.

"Do you mind not standing right in front of the window?"

He turned to see the frown on her face intense, hand outstretched like she was ready to snatch him from the very jaws of danger. He stepped back and to the side and her stance relaxed a fraction. "I guess I'm going to have to start thinking as though my life depends on how smart I am, aren't I?"

"Definitely. I'm really wanting cameras installed. This person is brazen enough to come onto your property. Maybe with a camera we'll be able to get a picture." She shot him a stern look. "Don't mention the security upgrade on your radio show."

He rolled his eyes. "As if," he muttered. "I'm only an idiot on early Friday morning. This time of day, I'm good."

He thought he might have caught a slight twitch of a smile on her lips, then decided it must have been a trick of the light. She kept the bear and headed back down to the porch.

Wade followed, his mind churning, wishing he could delete the image of the decapitated bear. "It's not like it was a real animal, get over it."

"What?" Olivia turned, brows raised.

"Nothing." They entered the den.

While he'd been scavenging for the bear in Amy's room, three police cruisers had arrived along with several plainclothes detectives.

"What's going on, Wade? Are you all right? Why won't they let us in?"

Wade looked up to find his sister-in-law, Martha, ignoring a female officer's upraised hand and heading for him. Amy was right behind her, along with her friend Stacy. The officer started to exert force to keep them back when Olivia gave the woman a discreet nod. The officer shrugged and let them through.

"Yeah, Dad, what's the deal with all the cops?" She chewed her lip, her eyes bouncing from one person to the next. Her anxiety level was probably rising by the second.

He stepped forward. No way he wanted her or Stacy to see what was in the coffin. He caught Martha by the arm. "I'll explain later. Would you please take the girls over to your place until I give you the all clear?"

"Certainly."

"No, Dad, I want to stay with you." Amy wrapped her arms around his waist and clung.

He placed a hand on her shoulder and met Martha's eye. "All right, look, how about you and Stacy and Aunt Martha go into the kitchen and make some cookies?"

Martha nodded. "That sounds fun." Martha's troubled expression said she didn't want to make cookies, she wanted to ask questions, but he was thankful that she simply turned to Amy and Stacy. "Come on, girls."

Wade gave the top of Amy's head a kiss and gently set her from him. "Go on. We'll talk in a little while, okay?"

She frowned and the anxiety in her eyes pinched his heart.

Then Martha placed a hand on Amy's shoulder. "Your dad needs to deal with this without us being in the way. Let's go have a snack and I'm sure he'll come explain when he can."

"But—"

"No buts." Their voices faded as Martha led Amy away.

He turned back to find himself nose to nose with a man about his age. "Excuse me?"

"Sorry." The man stepped back. Dark eyes rimmed with long lashes glinted questions and a tad of . . . suspicion? Nevertheless, he held out a hand. Wade shook it and simply waited for the man to speak. The intense assessment finally stopped. "I'm Detective Quinn Holcombe. I've been assigned as the lead on this case."

"Case?"

"Maddy McKay was your bodyguard. Her throat was slit because someone was trying to get at you. You were attacked outside the radio station. You're now officially a case."

[9]

Olivia clenched her jaw. Quinn's tension scraped along her nerves like a physical touch. An unwelcome one.

Quinn and Maddy had worked together on several occasions during Maddy's four years with the bureau and then again when Maddy wound up working security for someone Quinn happened to be connected with. Olivia had watched them grow close and become good friends, and she knew he was taking Maddy's attack and attempted murder personally.

CSU worked, gathering evidence, imprinting the porch railing and the surrounding area, bagging the small coffin and the two bears. Wade ignored Quinn and watched the activity, his face expressionless, even while she knew his mind had to be spinning, questioning. But his adrenaline was crashing, his shoulders drooping.

"As soon as everyone is out of here, I recommend you take a nap," she said.

He cast her a tight smile. "I just woke up from one."

True enough. "You know what I mean." Another car pulled

up and Wade turned to watch. Olivia recognized the vehicle.
"That's Bree Standish."

When the woman stepped out of the car, Olivia nodded
to her. The detective returned the greeting with a small wave
and headed their way. Quinn stayed silent while he waited for
Bree's arrival.

One of the advantages Olivia had was her background in law
enforcement. She'd risen through the ranks from rookie cop
to detective within the same police department as Quinn and
Bree, and that fact gave her a distinct advantage. She already
had their respect and they all knew she had nothing to prove.

"We need to talk a little about your schedule when Quinn
and Bree are finished," Olivia murmured to Wade.

"My schedule?"

"I'm your new bodyguard."

"Oh. Okay then." He shot her a sideways glance. "You're
fired."

"You didn't hire me, you can't fire me."

Her low tone never changed. In fact she almost sounded
amused. "Then I'm firing my father," he muttered.

Bree held out a hand to him. "Wade Savage?"

"Yes." He shook her hand.

"Detective Bree Standish."

Quinn gave Bree a short nod of welcome. "Who has access
to your house?" he asked Wade.

Wade waited a moment, then he shifted his gaze and met
Quinn's head-on. Olivia's respect for Wade shot up a few
notches. He wouldn't be bullied. By a stalker or by a police
detective. Good for him. "Anyone who wants to drive up," Wade
said. "No one could actually get in the house without setting the
alarm off, but there's nothing stopping someone from driving
onto the property and walking up to the front door."

"You have any enemies?"

"At least one who likes to use drugs to incapacitate her prey," Olivia snapped.

Quinn shot Olivia an impatient look, but kept his questions directed toward Wade. "What about your clients? Anyone not happy with the way their treatment is going?"

Wade's lips tightened. "Not that I know of. You'd have to ask them."

"Excuse us a moment," Olivia said to Wade and Bree. She grasped Quinn's arm and pulled him to the side. "What's your problem, Quinn? Wade's not on trial and this isn't his fault. Quit questioning him like he's a suspect."

Quinn's dark eyes flashed. "My questions are standard. Maddy's lying in a hospital clinging to life because of this guy. I want to know everything he knows and I'll do whatever it takes to get it."

"Tone it down," she hissed. "The questions are fine, it's the attitude that's coming through with them that's detrimental. Maddy's not in the hospital because of Wade. She's hurt because there's a crazy person out there who's made him a target and Maddy took a hit doing her job. You know that as well as I do. Get ahold of your emotions." She was preaching to the choir, but wouldn't let Quinn know that.

"I don't need you telling me—"

"No, what you *need* is to do your job." She kept her voice low, controlled and cold. From the corner of her eye, she could see Wade's speculative glances even as Bree talked to him, her attitude more laid back and respectful.

Quinn paused and closed his eyes for a brief moment. "You're right. I don't know what my problem is. I just want to get back to the hospital and check on Maddy."

"Then let's get this done. I'm sure Wade's ready for you all to get out of here and let him rest and his family have some peace."

Quinn gave a short nod and walked back to Wade. Olivia followed at a close distance, ready to intervene again if she had to. Wade was now her client. She'd protect him physically and emotionally. But she couldn't deny she wanted answers too.

She ticked off the boxes of how she figured the investigation would go.

Check to see if there were any witnesses who could give an account of what had happened in the parking lot of the station.

Check any security cameras in and around the area to see if the attacks were recorded.

CSU would look for any trace evidence that didn't belong to Wade.

And more.

Maddy wasn't just her handpicked employee, she was also a friend and one of the few people in the world whom Olivia trusted without question. Haley had handled contacting Maddy's family, who were on their way, and Olivia wanted to be instrumental in tracking down her attacker. Which meant encouraging Wade to answer Quinn's questions without losing his cool.

Quinn's attitude had noticeably lightened and Wade's shoulders had relaxed a fraction. He rubbed his eyes. "I have a caller. She calls me during every show, sometimes several more times over the course of the three hours. She calls herself Valerie. I don't know her last name. I suppose it's possible my stalker could be her. I don't get those vibes from her. She seems like a nice person, just lonely and hurting."

"Lonely and hurting people have been known to seek comfort from those they admire, look up to, or fancy themselves in love with," Quinn said quietly.

Olivia nodded. "And when the feelings aren't reciprocated, they strike out."

Amy thought she might be dying. Her lungs felt too small to pull in any air, her chest had a giant rubber band around it, and someone was twisting the end, making it tighter and tighter. Her head throbbed and she just wanted to make it all stop. But she had no power to do anything about it. Powerless pretty much defined her.

The panic attacks controlled her. Her father dictated her every move, her aunt hardly let her out of her sight. And now the cops were combing through her home, her only safe place. Her escape.

At least Stacy hadn't noticed the attack yet.

She tried another breath. And another. Her hands tingled and her face felt weird. "Just a panic attack," she whispered. "You won't die. You'll feel like it, but you won't." Powerless. Out of control. She dragged in another breath.

"You okay, Amy?" Stacy asked.

"Fine," she whispered.

"Do we need to go to our place?"

"No, no, I'll be all right. I want to know what's going on." Their place was where they let their imaginations soar. They often met there during the week, but mostly on the weekends. Stacy lived in the neighborhood across the street. It wasn't as affluent as Amy's, but neither girl cared. All that was important was that they were within walking distance of each other and "the place." A little clearing, surrounded by big trees and bushes that made it an almost-perfect circle. When Amy was in there, she felt safe. Protected. Her dad had even let them camp out there one night, rigging the tent with electricity and a small refrigerator. She shivered and almost bolted for the door to seek out the comfort of the place. Or she could go to her room. It was closer. Her two favorite places in the world. Her room and the clearing. One inside and one out.

"Amy? Honey?"

Aunt Martha.

Amy turned, trying to keep her symptoms hidden. Aunt Martha might drive her nuts sometimes, but she loved her aunt and her aunt loved her. Doted on her—okay, more like smothered her—but at least she was there. Unlike her mother who'd run off and abandoned her and her father when Amy was a year old—then died in a car wreck a year later. "When are they leaving?" she asked.

"When they're done." Her aunt went to the cabinet beneath the sink and grabbed a sponge and cleaner and went to work scrubbing the already clean stainless steel. "And we don't need to make a fresh batch of cookies if you'd rather not. There are some in the jar from yesterday."

Amy rolled her eyes at Stacy, swallowed, and snagged a cookie from the jar. Stacy did the same but chewed on her bottom lip instead of the treat. Amy's aunt continued to scrub, her movements harsh and jerky. She was worried too. Stacy reached over and clasped Amy's fingers in a tight grip.

While taking comfort from her friend's quiet support, Amy watched the back-and-forth movements for another few seconds and miraculously felt her attack ease. The band around her chest released and she drew in a deep breath. Sweet relief filled her. After another minute of watching her aunt, she decided that if she wanted to know what was going on, she was going to have to put forth the effort to find out.

She tugged on Stacy's hand and motioned for her to follow. They slipped from the kitchen into the hallway that led to the den where the officers were still talking with Amy's father.

". . . my stalker could be her."

She froze. Wait a minute. Her dad had a stalker?

Her father said something else, but those were the words that registered. She shot a glance at Stacy, whose eyes were wide.

"Stalker?" she mouthed the word to Stacy.

Stacy shrugged and nodded.

Was that why he'd been so suffocating lately?

Amy felt the press of the attack start to rise again. She did her best to ignore it. Sometimes when she could focus on something else, the attack would ease—like back in the kitchen. And she had to hear this. She moved closer.

"Do you have her number?" the cop asked.

"It comes up anonymous on the screen."

"But you take the call anyway."

Her father shrugged. "She seems harmless enough and she's hurting. Like a lot of the people who listen to the show and call in. Some people have unlisted numbers and I'm okay with that. Some numbers I recognize, and others, I never know who's going to be on the other end of the line. That's just part of doing a live call-in show."

"And her name is Valerie?"

"Yes."

"You have her number?"

"Not memorized, but it would be in the log."

The detective called someone and told the person to find the number. When he hung up, he started questioning her father again.

The woman paced to the foot of the stairs and Amy pulled back a fraction. She wasn't quick enough. The woman's eyes caught hers. And softened. She came closer. "Hi."

"Hi." Amy brushed her hair back and tucked a few strands

behind her left ear. The woman had very pretty eyes. Stacy pressed up against her and Amy took comfort in her presence.

"I guess you want to know what's going on, huh?" the woman asked, her gaze bouncing from Amy to Stacy, then back to Amy.

"Yeah." She shifted from one foot to the other, wondering if she was going to be in trouble.

"I'm Olivia."

First names? Cool. "This is Stacy and I'm Amy. We're twelve, but I'm going to be thirteen next Saturday. I'm planning to have a really cool party. My dad's letting me invite ten people to spend the day on the boat and the lake, then me and Stacy are going to spend the night in our special place."

Olivia nodded. "I've heard a lot about you, Amy. It's nice to finally talk to you a bit. And your party sounds absolutely perfect. I think you'll have a wonderful time." She smiled and Amy thought she saw a dimple in her left cheek. It made her seem more approachable and nice.

"It's very nice to meet you," Stacy said.

"You too, Stacy."

Amy glanced over Olivia's shoulder to see her father shooting her a frown even while he was still talking to the other man. A police detective, if the badge and gun on his belt told her anything. He wasn't dressed in a uniform, but had on black pants and a gray button-down polo shirt. He was good-looking in spite of being old like her father. She looked back at Olivia. "Interesting. Because I haven't heard a thing about you. Who are you?"

"She works for me." Amy turned to see her grandfather standing behind her. His deep scowl pulled his salt-and-pepper eyebrows low so they practically met at the bridge of his nose.

"Doing what, Pops?" Amy crossed her arms and met him glare for stare. Her grandfather might scare some people to death with his intimidating laser-beam look, but she knew she had him wrapped. He was the one person who could make the panic attacks go away with a simple touch or a hug.

"Making sure your dad stays safe."

"And why didn't I know he *wasn't* safe?"

"It wasn't something you needed to worry about."

Amy's shoulders slumped. Everyone was always concerned about her anxiety issues. She was so tired of being afraid and anxious, but was even more tired of everyone's need to protect her from *everything*. She straightened her shoulders and planted her hands on her hips. "You could have told me."

"Would it help anything to know?"

"Maybe."

The cute detective came over before Pops could answer. Which was probably a good thing. "Dr. Savage has given us permission to speak to his daughter."

"About what?" Her grandfather stood straight and threw his shoulders back, turning his glare from Amy to the officer. Pops was only fifty-four years old and most people thought he had military training. He didn't, but his father had been in the navy, and Pops had grown up to adopt his military bearing and attitude.

"About whether she's seen or noticed anyone—women in particular—watching her father when they've been together." He turned his gaze on her and Amy blinked at the dark blue of his eyes. They reminded her of the deep-blue sapphire stones in the necklace that used to belong to her grandmother. The one she'd worn to the Academy Awards back in the late seventies when she'd been a famous actress.

She rolled her eyes at the detective. "Women look at my dad all the time. And watch him too. Frankly, I think it's super ridiculous."

"Amy—?" Her father cocked his head, surprise raising his brows. Then he narrowed his eyes and studied her as though wondering who she was and what had happened to his real daughter. She shrugged.

Then he did that thing with his eyes that meant he really didn't want to be pushed.

And she didn't want to lose her cell phone—or have Stacy taken home. She sighed. "But if you mean someone looking like a stalker, then no. I don't think so. Then again I haven't exactly been *looking* for that either, since no one thought it important enough to tell me about." Her throat tightened. She swallowed. Her father's raised eyebrows made her snap her lips together. She couldn't believe the words coming from her mouth. She never said stuff like that. But this was her *dad*. And he might be in *danger*.

She took a deep breath and noticed the tightness in her chest had eased. It was actually almost gone. Her grandfather had a glint in his eyes. Almost as though he was proud of her? She shrugged, enjoying the moment. Then looked back at her father and the officers. She ducked her head, the anxiety returning full force. "Can we go to my room?"

The detective laid a hand on her shoulder and she looked up. His eyes didn't look so hard now. "Sure, go ahead. But we could use your help if you're up to it."

Up to it? "My help?"

"Keep your eyes open and watch your father's back when you can, okay?" He handed her a card. "And if you see anything or anyone you don't like, call me."

Amy caught her jaw before it dropped. He actually thought she could be helpful? She gave a slow nod. "Okay. I can do that."

He winked at her and nodded. "I thought you could."

With Stacy on her heels, she bolted for the stairs and took

them two at a time. She needed her safe place. A place where the attacks would fade and she could think. Try to wrap her mind around the fact that her father had a stalker.

Her thoughts raced and plans formed. Maybe she could find a way to spy on her dad, definitely watch his back, but see if someone else was watching it too. The very idea of her father having a stalker terrified her. She'd already lost her mother. And while she didn't remember her, she'd felt the hole her absence had left her entire life.

Amy sank onto her bed and buried her eyes against her knees.

"You all right?" Stacy asked. Her friend laid a hand on her back.

Amy looked up. "What would happen to me if something happened to my dad?"

"Nothing's going to happen to him. And besides, you'd be fine. You have your aunt and your grandfather."

Amy sighed. "You're missing the point. I don't want anything to happen to my dad. They were hiding something from me. They didn't want me to see what they were looking at on the porch."

"So? Maybe it's better not to know."

"Better for you maybe. But I want to know."

[10]

The house echoed around him, the silence deafening after the chaos of the police in every nook and cranny of his home.

He walked to the couch and sank onto the leather cushions. He leaned his head back and closed his eyes. Fatigue washed over him. What was he going to do about this stalker? A stalker who knew he had a daughter and what size jersey she would wear.

Someone who wanted an apology from him. Would he do it? Actually go on the air and issue an apology? He considered his options. Apologizing to her would mean giving her power. Reinforcing her actions. Not apologizing meant antagonizing her, pushing buttons he might not want to push. *God, tell me what to do, please.*

Footsteps pulled his gaze to the den's entrance. Amy's slender form came toward him and he held out an arm. She slipped under it and leaned her head against him.

"Are you going to be all right?" she asked.

"I am. And so are you."

"Are you sure?"

"Absolutely positive."

She pulled back and looked him in the eye. "You can't be absolutely positive."

"Why not?"

"Because Pops says only God knows the future."

"Well, I guess I can't argue with Pops on that. How about 99 percent sure?"

"Where do you get your statistics from? Last year my math teacher said you better not throw out statistics unless you have the data to back it up."

He groaned. "Look, Amy, I don't know what the future holds. I don't know what the next thirty minutes might bring, but I'm not going to let it get the best of me."

Tears welled in her eyes. "How do you do that?" she whispered. "It always gets the best of me."

"What about using your coping skills?"

"Sometimes they don't work."

He kissed the top of her head and breathed in the scent of her strawberry shampoo. "Do you want to say it together?"

She nodded against his shoulder. "'Do not be anxious about anything, but in every situation, by prayer and petition, with thanksgiving, present your requests to God.'" Their voices echoed in the room. He tilted her chin up and looked her in the eye. "Keep saying it, honey—and keep believing it. God's watching over you."

"And you."

He hugged her. "That's right. And me."

They sat there a few minutes before Amy squirmed against him. "I'm in that play Sunday. You're going to come watch me, right?"

"Wouldn't miss it."

She paused and fidgeted some more, looked up at him, then away.

"What is it?" he asked.

She bit her lip, then pushed it out. Finally, she sighed. "I'm scared about getting up in front of everyone. Practicing with my friends is a lot different than having a bunch of parents watching."

"Well, I can see how that might make you a little nervous, but you've done great during practice. You've worked really hard and are about to see the results of that."

"I know, but it's still scary. I don't think I want to do it. It's a small part anyway. No one would even notice if I didn't do it."

Wade struggled to find the right words. The wrong ones could send her into a panic attack. He wouldn't insist she do the play, but he could encourage her to. "I think that if you don't do it, you'll regret it."

"Why?"

"Because you've worked really hard. If you quit now, you'll be mad at yourself for not finishing something you started."

"You think so?"

"Yes."

"Have you ever quit something?"

"Yes."

"Like what?"

He blew out a breath, then kissed the top of her head. "Like, I wanted to play for the high school baseball team and I worked really hard, practicing, hitting balls, playing catch with my dad and anyone who'd throw me a ball. I did that right up until the day of the tryouts." He paused and Amy leaned forward, intently listening. "The time to try out came and I was watching the other boys practice out on the field. They all seemed so good. I didn't think I was good enough to play, so I didn't try out. I went home instead."

"And you regret it?"

"Very much so, because now I'll never know if I could have

made the team or not. I had a lot of friends on the team and missed out on being a part of it." He hugged her. "I just don't want you to miss out or feel that way."

Amy fell silent, staring over his shoulder at nothing, but he could see her processing his words. "You never told me that," she finally said.

"I know. It's not something I like to think about very often."

She nodded, then cut her eyes at him. "So this is, like, a teachable moment, huh?"

He gave a short laugh. "I guess you could call it that."

Her lips twitched and he wondered at the sly look in her eyes. "So maybe I should just not do the play, then I'll have a teachable moment for my kid one day."

Wade blinked, then laughed. Out loud. "Amy Rene Savage, you crack me up. No, you should not be thinking of using this as a teachable moment for your kid. Trust me, you'll have plenty by the time you have children."

She grinned at him, then tilted her head. "I'll think about doing the play. One more question."

"What?"

All levity faded. "Do you ever think about her?" she asked.

Justine. He knew who Amy meant. The only woman since his wife's death who had captured his interest if not necessarily his heart. And then she'd died too, and his world had been shattered once again. Wade's throat tightened. "Yes."

"I do too. I miss her."

"I know you do."

"Do you still love her?"

Oh boy. How did he answer that question? Lie? No. Definitely not. "Justine was a good friend, Amy. She understood me—actually we understood each other—and she was crazy about you."

68

"But you were going to marry her so you must have loved her."

He frowned at her. "What?"

"I heard you talking about it a couple months before she died. She mentioned you two getting married. You said you thought it might be a good idea. Justine left and you looked confused, so I didn't say anything about it. So? Would you have married her if she hadn't died?"

"Maybe." He cleared the lump from his throat. "I was thinking about it."

"Even though you didn't love her?"

He gave a silent groan. "I did love her in a way. I loved her as a friend, someone I enjoyed being with, spending time with. I thought that might be enough." He'd married for love once upon a time and that had turned into a disaster. He'd figured why set himself up for more of the same? He decided to keep those thoughts to himself, but he knew that he'd been protecting his heart against the possibility of Justine leaving him like his first wife had. At least that was the conclusion he'd come to during many sleepless nights after her death. Now he was just filled with regrets. Justine had deserved better than that. Heck, he and Amy deserved better.

"Why did you think that would be enough?" she pressed.

He sighed. He had no idea how to explain his relationship to Justine to his closest male friend, much less his almost teenage daughter. "I just did."

"You're weird, Dad."

"Yeah. I know."

"I want to marry someone I'm madly and passionately in love with." She clasped her hands to her chest, gave a dramatic sigh, and closed her eyes.

He lifted a brow. "What do you know about being in love?" He left madly and passionately out of it. Her definition of those two words in the same sentence probably varied greatly from his. *Please, God.* Nope, he wasn't touching that one. Yet. Maybe ever. A pang hit him. These kinds of conversations made him long for a woman who could talk to Amy. Martha loved her niece, spent a lot of time with her, but he knew it wasn't the same as having a mother. Someone her dad was married to.

Amy opened her eyes and shrugged. "Nothing much, Dad. I'm only twelve, almost thirteen. I just know I'm going to marry someone who doesn't mind holding my hand when I have a panic attack."

"Maybe you won't have them by then."

"Maybe."

He heard more footsteps and drew in a slow breath of relief at the distraction. Stacy entered the room and paused, her gaze jumping between him and Amy. He could read her easily. She desperately wanted to join them, but didn't want to intrude.

Wade patted the sofa beside him and she grinned and raced across the room to settle herself next to him. She leaned her head against his arm. "I wish you were my dad, Mr. Wade."

His heart constricted. "I wish I was too, Stacy. You're a great kid. Any man would be lucky to be your dad."

"Ha. Too bad my real dad didn't think so." Stacy's father had left her and her mother three years ago and had dropped out of sight. Wade knew Stacy wanted a father but figured she was better off without that particular man around.

"Yeah, that's tough and it stinks. Your mother is a great lady," he said. "Maybe she'll find someone you wouldn't mind calling 'Dad.'"

Stacy shrugged her thin shoulder. "I don't know." She cut her eyes at him. "She says she'll only get married again if she can find someone like you."

LYNETTE EASON

Wade felt his ears start to burn but gave a low chuckle. "Well, I'll take that as a compliment."

"You should. She listens to your show every weekend and she said every woman should listen and take your advice."

"That's very kind of her."

"I guess. You should call her and ask her out."

Amy shot into a sitting position. "Yeah, Dad, you should, then me and Stacy would be sisters if you married her mom."

"Stacy and I," he corrected. "And you two quit trying to marry me off. I'm perfectly capable of finding a wife should I decide I want one." He gave each girl a rib tickle and delighted in their screeches of laughter. "Get out of here. I'll come up and tell you good night in a few minutes."

Stacy giggled and stood. "I'm going upstairs to watch TV. You ready, Amy?"

Amy nodded. "I'm ready. Forget TV. Let's go figure out how to get our parents together."

Wade rolled his eyes and decided he'd better prepare himself for some adolescent matchmaking attempts. The thought made him shudder. And saddened him. He'd hoped having Martha around would dull the ache that an absent mother had caused his daughter.

Six years ago, he'd mentioned to Amy he was going to start interviewing women for a nanny position. An hour later, Martha had come to him and stated no strange woman was going to raise her niece as long as there was breath in her body. He'd agreed and they'd worked up a nice arrangement that benefited them both. She'd been miserable in her job as head of public relations for the local hospital and had wanted a way out. He gave it to her.

The fatigue hit him again and he closed his eyes, his mind spinning. He had the radio show, then tomorrow—

71

A hand on his shoulder jerked him awake. He opened his eyes and stared into his sister-in-law's frowning face. "Are you all right, Wade?"

He sniffed and scrubbed a hand down his cheek. "Yeah. I guess I dozed off. What time is it?"

"About eleven fifteen."

He jumped to his feet and headed in the direction of his bedroom. "I've got to get going. I need to be on the air in forty-five minutes."

"You think it's safe?"

He stopped at the door and turned. "I don't know, Martha. I have a bodyguard so maybe—" He shrugged. "I'm not going to cower or hide or run."

"What about Amy?"

He sighed and dropped his chin to his chest, taking a moment to think. When he raised his head, he studied his sister-in-law. "You know I'll do whatever I have to do to keep Amy safe. Even if that means sending her away somewhere. But I won't let this person dictate my life."

Martha nodded. "I understand. Even admire that. I don't think you should run away, but I do think you need to be smart."

"And I will be."

"Amy would be devastated if something happened to you," she said softly. "And I would too. You and Amy have been my family for a long time now."

He sighed. She was right, of course. "I know. I can't tell you how much I appreciate everything you've done for us. Thank you for being here."

Martha shrugged. "Of course. Like I said, you're family." She shook her head. "I adore Amy, you know that."

Remorse filled him. "I fell asleep and didn't tell her good night."

"I think she'll understand. When I last checked on them, she and Stacy were upstairs plotting your marriage to Stacy's mother." He groaned. Martha laughed. "Apparently the woman is quite . . . um . . . *taken* with you."

"Oh stop."

She snickered again, then turned serious. "Do you think you'll ever be ready to marry again?"

He shrugged. "I doubt it. After Justine . . ." He blew out a breath and raked a hand through his hair. He absently noted he needed a haircut. "I have no plans to do so."

She lifted a brow and gave him a sad look. "That's a shame. Then again, plans can change when the right person comes along." He stayed quiet and she grimaced. "Sorry, it's none of my business."

"Hey, if it's anyone's business, it's yours." He crossed the room and hugged her. "You've been a rock for me and I appreciate it, but let's leave my love life out of things."

"Or the lack thereof?"

"Exactly."

"Works for me."

"Good." He gave her a half grin. "So how's your love life?"

She lifted her nose and gave him a haughty stare. "None of your business."

He glanced at his watch. "I need to get to the station. Where's Olivia?"

"In the kitchen on the phone with someone. Thought I heard her ask about someone named Maddy."

Wade explained what had happened to the former body-guard and Martha paled. He hadn't wanted to tell the details, but had decided that wasn't fair to her. She lived here and needed to know what was going on. He squeezed her hand and left her standing in the den, still processing everything, while he went to find the woman he was supposed to trust with his life.

He wasn't questioning her abilities. Bruce Savage would have only hired the best of the best. He just wondered if she was entirely necessary now that he knew he needed to be on his guard and watching his back. Time would tell.

He found her exactly where Martha said she'd be. She stared out the kitchen window above the sink, tapping her chin with her phone and looking deep in thought. She must have sensed his presence, because she turned fast and light on her feet, alert and ready. She relaxed a fraction when she saw him.

"How is Maddy doing?" he asked.

"She survived surgery and is in ICU with a guard on her door."

"Do you think she could identify who attacked her?"

"Possibly. That's why we're going to take all precautions and make sure the person who tried to kill her doesn't come back to finish the job when he—or she—hears that she's still alive."

He nodded and shoved his hands into his pockets. "I need to get to the station. Do you plan to go with me?"

"Of course. Do you feel like going? Because frankly you don't look all that hot."

Wade let a low chuckle slip past his lips. "I'm disappointed you don't think I'm hot."

Olivia's brow rose and her cheeks turned a light pink, but her blue eyes stayed cool. "You know what I meant."

"I do. And you would be correct. I don't feel all that hot. I'm slightly dizzy and a little lightheaded, but I figure the residual effects of the drug will wear off eventually."

"Don't want to let the fans down, huh?"

"No. I don't."

He didn't move yet. Olivia tilted her head. "What is it?" she asked.

"Is my family going to be safe while we're gone?"

She gave him a tight smile. "Good question. But yes. I've asked a few friends to stay close by and keep an eye on your place while I'm with you."

He blew out a slow breath of relief. "Good. Then I'm ready when you are."

She pulled her keys from her pocket. "Since you're still feeling a bit woozy, I'll drive."

[11]

One hour into the show, Olivia checked the doors one more time, then the windows. All were locked up tight and secure. Still, she paced from one end of the building to the other. Wade's voice came through the speakers in the ceiling low and soothing as he answered questions and fielded calls. Because he was the only person at the station at night, his callers seemed to understand that if the line was busy, they'd simply have to call back.

Or send an email. After every third or fourth call, Wade would answer an email question, then return to the phone lines.

Olivia heard him speaking again. "I know how it feels to lose someone close to you, but drinking your sorrows away is not the answer. Do you have a close friend that you can talk to? Someone you trust?"

Olivia tuned out the show and glanced out the window toward the highway beyond the station. Two police cruisers pulled into the parking lot, stopped next to the officer parked in plain sight, then circled the building and left again within five minutes. She continued her inspection of the building's security, finally satisfied for the moment that all was as it should be.

She moved back into the lobby area, staying away from the windows, but close to Wade, who was just behind the sound-proof glass.

She heard him cut to a commercial and peered into the booth. "Everything going all right?"

"So far."

She stepped inside and went to the pictures pinned behind the microphone. "You have that one on your mantel at home."

He released the one she'd pointed to and held it out to her. "Yes. That's my mom and dad and me on Dad's boat when I was about eighteen months old. It's a favorite. Mom looks completely happy and relaxed."

"Where was it taken?"

"At the old boathouse Dad used to have. It's about a mile east of where I live now, but still connected to the same lake."

"Ahh. Is that why you built so close to where you grew up? To have something from your childhood close by?"

He shrugged. "I don't know. Maybe." He met her gaze. "Probably." He glanced at the clock on the wall. "Time to get back to work."

Olivia stepped out and moved to sit in the chair in the lobby where she could keep an eye on the entry door in front of her and Wade behind her.

"And who do we have on the phone?" Wade's voice came through the speaker just above her head.

"Wade, darling," the voice whispered. "You've been a very naughty boy."

Olivia came to her feet. Wade's eyes met hers through the glass even as the rest of him went completely still. "Who is this?"

"You haven't figured that out yet?"

"Obviously not."

"That's because I'm not ready to reveal myself to you yet, but I will when it's time."

Olivia dialed Angela, who answered on the second ring. "Hello?"

"I need you to go downstairs and trace a call." Maddy already had the station line programmed in the tracing system. Now Olivia needed someone to activate it. Since Angela lived in the small apartment above the office, she was the one who could get the trace going the fastest.

"I'm on the way downstairs. Hold on."

A lifetime passed before her voice came back on the line. "Tracing the call he's on now."

"Good." She listened.

The caller was still talking. ". . . my apology? I've been listening and haven't heard it yet."

"Why should I give you an apology?" Wade asked, his tone mild, nonthreatening. Simply . . . curious.

"You said you were going to throw away my gifts. I spent a lot of time and trouble picking those out for you."

Wade fell silent and Olivia shot him a sharp look.

"Well?" the caller demanded.

"I'm thinking," Wade said.

"About what?"

"About the fact that you might be right."

This seemed to shock the person on the other end of the line. "Oh."

"Yes. I shouldn't have announced that I'd be throwing the gifts away on the show. That probably seemed coldhearted and uncaring. I didn't mean it that way, but I had no other way to get in touch with you or to tell you that the stalking needs to stop."

"I'm not on the air anymore. What happened? Why did you turn it off? Why is there a commercial playing?"

Olivia stood just outside the studio room and waved to Wade, motioning for him to keep going. "Ang? What do you have?"

"It's bouncing off a tower near the station, but the phone itself isn't traceable. It's coming up as an unknown number."

"A throwaway."

"Yes."

Olivia turned her attention back to Wade, who'd stood and was pacing in front of the console. ". . . a private conversation. No need to let everyone out there in on our business."

"Our business. It's our business now, is it?"

"What do you want from me?" Wade asked, his voice low.

"All I've ever wanted was for you to just *see* me. Maybe even love me."

"How can I do that when I don't even know who you are?"
Click.

Olivia waited. "There's nothing I can do from this end. I'm sorry," Angela said.

"I know. Thanks for trying." She hung up and shook her head at Wade.

He pulled his headset off and threw it on the desk. She walked around to the door leading into the studio. "She used a prepaid cell. Angela was able to get a signal that bounced off a tower near here, but wasn't able to pinpoint her location."

He sighed and pinched the bridge of his nose. "It's all right. She's not going to call if there's any chance of her getting caught."

"I wrote down her exact words. 'All I've ever wanted was for you to just *see* me. Maybe even love me.' That makes me think you know her, that you've been around her and made her feel . . . 'invisible' might be the right word."

He lifted his hands, indicating his helplessness. "I don't know who it could be. Seriously." He glanced at the clock. "I need to get back on the air in about ten seconds."

"I'm going to call this in to Bree and Quinn."

He pulled his headphones back on and waited for the commercial to end. Then he picked up on the show as though nothing had happened, keeping his voice smooth and calm.

At least until the power went out.

She froze and blinked in the sudden darkness. Her eyes started to adjust and she waited for the station's powerful generator to kick in. When it didn't, a slow chill snaked up her spine. She tried to think of a reason the lights would go out and could come up with a couple. She tried to think of a reason for the generator not to come on. And could come up with only one.

Thanks to a full moon shining through the blinds, she saw Wade rising from behind the microphone. She moved toward him and could see his frown through the soundproof glass. He lifted a brow in her direction. She held up a hand and motioned him toward her, then stepped over to the side of the window to see the officer still in the car. She could make out his faint outline behind the steering wheel. Hadn't he noticed the lights go out? She looked across the street. All the other buildings still had power.

She punched in Bree's number and put the Bluetooth earbud in her ear. The phone rang. And rang. Bree didn't answer so Olivia hung up. "Stay with me," she told Wade, who'd come up beside her.

"Why didn't the generator kick in?" Wade asked.

"I don't know, but I don't like it."

"Dale will be over here soon."

"Dale Price," she said. "The station manager."

"And a good friend. He'll be alerted to the power failure."

He rubbed his hands together, then blew out a breath. "I should call him and let him know what's going on, though."

"Let's make sure your stalker friend isn't here first and then we can worry about calling him. Where's the generator?"

"Outside. I could go check it, but I have a feeling that might not be a good idea."

"No, not a good idea. We know we're safe in here. Outside is another story." She moved to the next window and saw nothing alarming. Yet.

"You really think it's her?"

"I'm not dismissing the possibility." A thud sounded from above and Olivia pulled her weapon from her shoulder holster. Okay, so maybe she'd spoken too soon. Maybe outside would be more safe. "Is there an attic?"

Wade's gaze followed hers. "Yes. We use it for storage just like in a house."

"Is there a way to get up there from the outside?"

"I . . . don't think so. I don't know, I've never thought about it."

Olivia moved back to the window and peered out. The officer still sat in his car, oblivious. She dialed his number and he never moved. A bad feeling swept over her. She dialed Quinn's number this time.

"You know what time it is?" he grumbled, sounding sleepy.

"Get over to the radio station, will you?" she said. "The power just went out and the officer in the car outside isn't moving. Something's going on and I don't think it's good."

She heard a flurry of activity on the other end of the line. "Stay put, backup's on the way." The sleep was gone from his voice.

"Staying as put as we can." Another creak from above. As though someone was walking across the attic floor? "Can you hurry it up, Quinn?" She looked at Wade. "Let's head for the door."

They moved as one toward the front door. Wade started to push it open when Olivia grabbed his arm and jerked him back two steps. "Stop!"

"Why?"

She moved forward. She'd been checking that door for the last hour and a half. "That wire wasn't there before." She looked down along the doorframe, then backed away.

"What does that mean?"

Olivia spun. "It could be a bomb. There's a chunk of material strapped to the door. The wire leading out of it is what caught my attention. It could be part of a blasting cap. Something."

"A bomb?" Quinn questioned, his low voice rumbling in her ear.

Olivia jerked. She'd almost forgotten he was on the line. "Yes."

"So we need a bomb squad?"

"Looks like that's a possibility."

"Glad your phone didn't set it off. Hold on."

She heard a click, then silence, and knew he was making another call. She directed Wade to the back entrance. But stopped at the door. "I don't want to open it in case it's rigged too. I'd say let's go out a window, but they're all just the little push-out kind. No way we're fitting through one."

"What if she's planted bombs in the attic too?"

"Yeah. What if?" Her heart thumped, but she kept emotions out of it. Right now her main priority was getting her client out of danger—which meant getting him out of the building. "If she planted bombs in the attic, how does she plan to get out without blowing herself up?" she whispered as though to herself. "And how did she get in without us seeing her?"

Wade felt the darkness in the building pressing on him. The faint light from the moon didn't reach far. Fear thundered through him, making his heart beat fast and hard against his chest. He thought about the possibility that he might die tonight. That the building might blow up, leaving Amy an orphan. He swallowed against the idea. He knew his father and Martha would take care of her, but that didn't make the thought of dying any easier.

"What if we went through the attic to get out?" he asked.

"She's up there—or someone is," she murmured. She flicked him a glance and held up a finger. "Quinn's back on the line." She listened. "What is it? . . . Uh-huh . . . Okay."

Wade waited, impatient. Ready to get out of the building. "What did he say?"

"Bomb squad's on the way," she said.

"Should you be using your phone? I thought they could be used to set off bombs."

"They can. If the trigger is activated by radio waves, then yeah, the cell phone could set it off. But the phone and the bomb have to be on the same frequency."

"So you're saying it's not likely."

"No, it's not."

"But it's possible."

She sighed. "Yes. It's possible. If the trigger is programmed to scan for radio signals and it comes upon the one I'm on, then that would not be good for us." She glanced at his pocket. "You might want to turn yours off, though."

"Great." He did as suggested and powered down the device.

"I was already on the phone before I saw the bomb. Since we're still alive, I think it's a safe assumption that the bomb and my phone are on two separate signals."

"And if it has a scanner, it hasn't found yours yet."

"And that."

"So we can wait for help and possibly get blown up or we can try to get out, also with the possibility of getting blown up."

"That's a pretty accurate summary."

"I vote for taking my chances and trying to get out."

"I'm with you. Where's the attic access?"

Wade moved back down the hall and Olivia followed him. He stopped at a pull-down attic string just like the one in his house. He reached for it, then drew his hand back. "If someone is up there, she may have rigged this too."

"I was thinking the same thing."

He gave a low growl. "We have to get out of here."

"Yes, but we can't be stupid about it." She paced back to the window.

"I think it's pretty stupid to stay in a building with bombs strapped to it."

She shot him a dark look and he grimaced.

He was taking his fear and frustration out on her and she didn't deserve it. "So what do we do?"

She let out a low breath as she looked out the window again. "We don't have any choices. We don't know what's rigged and what's not. So . . . we wait."

Not the answer he wanted, but the red and blue lights of arriving emergency vehicles brought a small measure of relief. "How's the officer outside?" he asked in a low voice. He'd delayed asking. Not because he didn't care, but because he didn't want to hear the answer he was afraid was coming.

Olivia shook her head. "I don't know. Quinn, you here yet?" She disconnected the Bluetooth option and put it on speaker.

"Pulling in."

"Have someone check Officer Petite fast. He still hasn't moved and I'm afraid he's either unconscious or dead."

"On it. Bomb squad is approaching the building. Officers are holding back a man by the name of Dale Price. You know him?"

"He's the station manager," Wade answered. "He doesn't live too far from here. As soon as he heard there was dead air, he would have been frantic. He's probably tried to get ahold of me on my phone." Which was turned off. "When I didn't answer, he headed over to find out what was going on."

Wade looked out the window to see Dale pacing frantically. He would have already powered up the backup show from his home while he investigated the source of the dead air. And now he'd be worried about Wade.

"Officers are searching the area and the businesses attached to this one. The officer who was watching the building is alive, but drugged and out cold. Probably with the same drug she got Wade with last night."

Wade felt that bit of tension ease. He didn't know how he'd live with someone else hurt as critically as Maddy—or worse. He heard the commotion near the door. "Bomb squad is sending in the robot. Once we clear the door, we'll get you out and they can clear the rest of the building."

"Can you tell what will set it off? What kind of trigger it has?" Olivia asked.

Wade frowned at her.

"Going to have to wait on that one," Quinn said.

"What do you mean?" Wade asked her.

"I want to know if it's set off by us opening the door or . . . something else."

"Like a cell phone."

"Right."

"Or a remote control device where she can set it off whenever she wants?"

She shot him a concerned look and he knew he'd guessed it. She was worried whoever had planted the bombs was just waiting for whatever she considered to be the right moment to press a button and blow them all to bits.

[12]

Olivia didn't have time to offer much comfort to Wade, she was too busy watching the commotion outside. The small robot deployed by the bomb squad made its way slowly to the building. When it reached the steps, it rolled up to the door in front of them. The long steel arm lifted and the camera zoomed in on the device attached to the center of the two doors. After a few tense minutes and the viewing of different angles, the little robot backed away.

"What's going on, Quinn?" Olivia asked.

"They're going to disarm the bomb."

"So it's real."

"Did you doubt it?"

"Not really. Hoped it was a scare tactic, but . . ."

"Yeah." She heard someone say something but couldn't catch the words. "Hold on a sec," Quinn said.

An ambulance squealed off and out of the parking lot. Olivia guessed the unconscious police officer was the occupant. There were two other ambulances waiting at a safe distance. She hoped they weren't needed.

"There's a bomb rigged on the back door as well," Quinn said. "They're not remote detonated, they're set to go off if you push open the door." That was a relief. "However, there's also a timer on it. Looks like we have about six minutes to get you out or disarm it."

All relief fled.

"What about up in the attic area?" she asked.

"Still checking that out but got a bomb guy suiting up to disarm the one on the front door and get you two out. Now."

"What if it's a trick? You try to get in the front door and the back one blows?" Olivia asked.

"We've thought of that, but there's no evidence that's the case." He raked a hand through his hair. "And we're running out of time."

Olivia could see Quinn's grim voice didn't set well with Wade, but he had no choice but to put his life in the hands of people who knew more than he did. He didn't like it one bit. From the corner of her eyes, she saw his fingers curl into hard fists.

A figure who looked more like an extra in an alien invasion movie stepped up to the door and set a metal box on the ground next to him. His gaze met hers through the door and she breathed a sigh of relief. It was Katie's friend, Shaun Garrison. His eyes widened briefly when they met hers. She nodded and he did too. A silent promise not to let them blow up.

She believed him. Or rather, believed he would do his best to disarm the bomb. If he didn't, they'd find out on the other side of eternity. She gave a brief thought to the fact that she wasn't ready to die. Ready in the physical sense and the spiritual. "Shaun's got this," she told Wade.

He was watching the man outside the door with an intense expression. "You know him?"

"Yes. We're going to be just fine. He hasn't cut the wrong wire yet," she joked without humor.

"Why does that only make me feel marginally better?"

She gripped his fingers in a hard squeeze, forcing him to relax his fist. "Be ready to run."

"I've been ready."

Shaun bent down and went to work. "How much time do we have, Quinn?"

"Four minutes and counting."

Her stomach clenched. He bent his head as though listening. "What?" His voice thundered in her ears.

"What is it?" she demanded.

"The back door has two minutes and twenty seconds on it."

"She wanted everyone focused on the front," Olivia whispered.

"Surely she had to know we'd check the whole building," Quinn said. He listened again, then looked up, his eyes sharp. "The attic's clean now. Can you get up there?"

Now? "Yes."

Wade didn't waste a second. Still gripping her hand, he pulled her to the string hanging from the ceiling. With a hard jerk, he had the stairs down. She pushed him to go first. He hesitated, obviously wanting her to go first.

"Now's not the time for gentlemanly manners. Go."

He did.

"Give me the countdown, Quinn. Count it down in my ear," she said as she followed Wade up the stairs. She reconnected the Bluetooth option with one hand, never stopping her forward momentum.

"Fifty-nine seconds. Fifty-eight. Go, go. Fifty-six—"

Olivia registered the words. Once in the attic, she noticed Wade had his phone out and turned on. By the light of the white

ALWAYS WATCHING

booting-up-screen, she could make out the way they needed to go. But they didn't have to use it. One of the bomb squad members was already there, shining a bright light. "Come on, move it, people. I'm not ready to die."

Neither she nor Wade bothered answering, but she did notice he picked up his speed a bit. She kicked aside boxes, debris, and insulation, staying on the flat storage surface. "Forty-five, forty-four."

Guided by the squad member's light, Wade slipped through a hole in the wall that belonged to the business next door. Quinn's voice continued the countdown.

"Go, go, go!"

Wade slid down the stairs that were already down, thanks to the bomb squad. Olivia followed. The door was propped open by another member.

"Twelve, eleven, ten."

Olivia hit the door a fraction of a second after Wade. She heard the other two squad members running after them even as she counted down the remaining seconds in her head.

She saw Quinn grab Wade and shove him behind a barrier that had been erected. Next, hands were on her, pushing her. "Zero," Quinn breathed.

[13]

The explosion rocked the back of the building. Wade gave a grunt when Olivia's body slammed into his. She wrapped her arms around him and took him to the ground. He belatedly realized she was trying to protect him from any flying debris that might find its way around the barrier. Stunned, he lay still, ears ringing, adrenaline pumping.

When the decibel level of the chaos lessened slightly, Wade raised his head. Everyone else was also on the ground, but now stirring.

Quinn, who had landed beside Wade, pushed himself to his feet. "Anyone hurt?"

"Negative over here," someone called.

"Liv, you all right?" Quinn asked.

Wade untangled himself from her and she shoved her blonde hair back from her face. He honed in on the bruise on her cheek and lifted a hand as though to touch it, then stopped. "You're hurt."

She felt the cheek and shrugged. "It's just an asphalt scrape. It's fine."

"Wade? Wade! Are you all right?" Dale rushed toward him and Wade stood to clasp the man in a quick hug. Dale pulled back. "You scared me to death, man."

"I know. Scared myself there for a bit. Did you play the backup show?"

Dale gaped. "You almost just got blown to bits and you're worried about the show?"

Wade shrugged and tried for a cool façade, even though his insides still shook. "It's less stressful to think about the show than the fact that I was almost blown to bits."

Dale shook his head. "Yeah. I started it up as I left the house to come over here."

"Good. Good." Then he didn't know what else to say, because the reality of what had just almost happened hit him.

He swayed and Olivia's arm immediately went around his waist. "Sit back down for a minute," she said.

He decided not to argue and slumped back onto the ground, his arms resting on his knees while he gathered his composure. He noticed the crowd along the street. Cars had pulled into the grocery store parking lot opposite the station and a line of people stood on the sidewalk.

The firefighters were on the scene and Wade thought he'd spotted a news van or two. The sight spurred him back to his feet. "I need to get home and let Amy know I'm all right."

"It's the middle of the night, Wade," Olivia said. "She's not going to see anything about this until tomorrow when you're home safe and sound and there to reassure her."

Dale stared at the building.

"I'll rebuild the station for you, Dale," Wade promised.

His friend shot him a tight smile. "That's what we have insurance for."

"Yeah, but—"

"No buts. This isn't your fault. I'm just glad you're okay and hope they catch the lunatic responsible."

Wade was moved to speechlessness. Dale had invested his life savings in the station and now it lay in ruins. And the man didn't blame Wade for the destruction. Of course he'd make sure Dale came out on top of the whole situation, no matter the man's protests.

Wade stayed by Dale's side while Olivia stayed by his. The firefighters controlled the blaze and soon started packing their equipment back into the trucks.

"The bomb on the front door never went off," he said.

Olivia turned to him. "No, Shaun managed to disconnect the right wire again."

He gave a faint smile, remembering her reassurances that they'd be fine because Shaun hadn't missed one yet.

A bomb squad member walked up to Quinn and showed him something. He looked at it and shook his head. Olivia approached him. Wade followed.

"What is it?" she asked.

"Grant found it right before y'all put in an appearance in the attic." He nodded to it. "C4 and some wires. Rigged to blow when the attic door opened. Grant disconnected it in time."

Olivia breathed out a slow breath. "Thank you, Grant."

"My pleasure." Grant walked off to take care of the bomb and Wade felt his knees go weak again. He watched the officers work a little longer. When the sun started to climb in the eastern sky, he decided it was time to go home.

Olivia must have been watching him closely. "Let me know when you're ready and I'll take you home," she said.

He nodded. "I'm ready."

She led the way, but he couldn't help one last glance over his shoulder at the chaos left behind. Fury began a slow burn in his gut, along with a steely determination not to be a victim. He wouldn't let this person take over and control his life, his actions, his day-to-day living.

He refused. And yet he couldn't help wonder if he'd survive the next attack.

Exhaustion dogged her heels as she stepped into Wade's house. Katie and Haley had shown up at the station—probably notified of the events by Angela—and insisted on being a part of the escort back to Wade's home. Quinn had also followed. Upon arriving home, Wade showed them all into the den area. "I'll fill Martha in and check on the girls in a minute. First, I need to call Stacy's mother and let her know what's going on. Erin's out of town with her job, some kind of nursing conference." He moved a stuffed bunny from the end of the sofa and set it on the mantel. "Stacy was going to stay here all weekend, but now I don't know if that's the best thing. Who knows when this maniac will strike again?"

Olivia wanted him to get some rest while she had one last consultation with Quinn, Haley, and Katie, but it didn't look like that was going to happen. "One of us can take her to wherever her mother wants her dropped off if she doesn't want her to stay here any longer."

Wade pulled out his phone and dialed the number. Then waited. "Hi, Erin, it's Wade. Give me a call when you get a chance. Stacy's fine, but I just want to run something by you. Thanks." He hung up. "I'll go check on the girls."

"Good. I'll be talking to the team."

In the den, she didn't bother to take a seat. Instead, she paced to the mantel, then turned to face the others. "First, how is the officer who was outside? Officer Petite is his name. Does anyone know if he's all right?"

"I talked to the sheriff on the way over here," Quinn said. "Officer Petite was drugged with propofol. I believe you're familiar with that one."

Olivia nodded. "The same drug that was used on Wade."

"So whoever attacked Wade was the same person who put the bombs at the radio station," Katie said.

"Most likely. He—or she—caught Officer Petite by surprise and got him with a hypodermic needle in the side of the neck."

Olivia winced. "He had his window down?"

"Yes, both the passenger's side and the driver's side. His car was turned off, so he was probably hot and letting the air circulate. But he'll be all right," Quinn said. "At least that was the report I got."

"Good. That's good."

Wade stepped back into the room and Olivia didn't bother scolding him. He was a big boy. If he wanted to spend his time listening and contributing to his case, she wasn't going to protest that he would be better off sleeping.

Quinn looked at Wade. "I'm glad you came back. Let's talk about tonight. Tell us in detail about when your stalker called the show."

"That was about an hour into it," Wade said as he took a seat in the wingback chair next to the fireplace.

"Which would be around 1:00 a.m., right?"

"Correct. I talked to her briefly, then switched to a commercial while she was still on the phone because I didn't feel like the listeners needed to hear the conversation."

"Smart move," Quinn said. "Then when you hung up, it wasn't long before the lights went out."

"Right. And the generator didn't come on. Did you figure that one out yet?"

"It was sabotaged."

"Sabotaged? Of course it was." He sighed. "How?"

"Whoever it was simply cut the lock off the gate that surrounded the generator and pulled out the battery. It was sitting on the ground."

Wade shook his head. "This is all crazy."

"And the bombs?" Olivia asked.

"She had help. According to the time stamp on the phone records, while you were talking to her, someone else was taking out the officer and rigging the doors with those bombs."

"But how did he get them on the front door? I would have seen him."

Quinn shook his head. "It was really simple. Everything about the bomb was already put together. All the person had to do was wait until your back was turned, then walk past the door and push the pieces with the adhesive onto the metal frame of the door. Probably took about three seconds total. Unless you just happened to be watching, you never would have known he or she was there."

Olivia looked at Quinn. "Any video footage?"

"Some. We're still going through it. But from what I was told, the person was in disguise with a hoodie and dark glasses, gloves, and black clothes. I don't think the footage is going to be that helpful."

"Of course not," Olivia murmured, then sighed. "Okay, so the plan is to increase security. I'm going to need more manpower. From now on, you have two bodyguards instead of one."

Katie nodded. "Absolutely. I'll work on a schedule."

"And I'll work on getting more manpower." She looked at Haley. "Actually, can you call Lizzie Tremaine and Charlie Lee? I want to know if they're available for some contract work."

"Of course." Haley clicked a few buttons on her phone, then looked up. "I've sent them a text asking for a good time to talk."

She slid her phone into her back pocket. "I've also sent you the three résumés you requested."

"That was fast."

Katie pursed her lips. "I had them ready to send to you the moment you asked. This case is a bit different than any other we've handled. We definitely need more help."

"I agree."

"All right," Quinn said, "I'm going to head back to the station. I'll fill Bree in on the events of the night and we'll be in touch if we have any other questions."

Olivia escorted the man to the door and stood quietly, watching out the window while he drove away. Her mind went to their wild escape from the building and she shuddered. She guessed that one would show up in her nightmares sometime in the near future.

"Haley and I can stay if you need to go home and get a few hours of rest," Katie said from behind her.

"Or you can just stay in one of the guest rooms," Wade said, walking up to her.

"Thought you were going to get some sleep."

"Not while my adrenaline is still racing."

She gave a knowing nod. Unfortunately her adrenaline was crashing.

He placed a hand on her shoulder. "Seriously, there's a room all made up and ready. I don't mind if you use it."

Olivia wavered. Part of her wanted to go home and clean up. Another part of her didn't want to bother with the drive. And she always kept a change of clothes and a toothbrush in her car. "All right." She looked at Katie. "Wake me in a few hours."

Katie nodded and Olivia motioned for Wade to lead the way. He did and she followed him up the front staircase. They passed

Amy's bedroom, coming from the opposite direction they'd taken earlier. He stopped two doors down. "Here you go."

"It's very nice, Wade, thanks."

"Of course."

"Promise me you'll try to get some sleep. I know your adrenaline is still racing pretty hard, but you have to find a way to relax and rest or you won't be good for much of anything."

"Hmm. True."

"Katie and Haley have this. Katie won't let Amy and Stacy out of her sight and Haley will have the house, along with a couple of off-duty officers."

"Good." He nodded. "Let me know if there's anything else you might need."

"I will."

He hesitated and she looked at him. He cleared his throat. "Thanks for getting us out of the radio station alive."

She scowled. "I didn't do much."

"Yes. You did. If I'd been there by myself, I never would have noticed the bomb strapped to the door. If you hadn't been there, I would be dead."

She nodded. "I'm grateful it ended the way it did." Because she'd learned the hard way that not all endings were happy ones.

"Me too." He studied her. "What are you thinking about?"

"Nothing."

"Liar." He said the word softly.

<hr />

She took a deep breath, but before she could say a word, he took her hand. "If you won't tell me about the thoughts that caused the look of agony that just crossed your face, will you tell me why you chose this profession?"

She stiffened and he thought he caught another expression.

A flash of grief. A momentary blip that marred the smoothness of her features before she arranged them back into that unflappable expression she'd worn most of the night. "It doesn't matter, does it?"

"I know I'm just your client and you don't have to tell me anything about your personal life, but . . . tell me. Please."

She studied him and he saw indications of some internal struggle going on inside her. She finally gave a slow nod, pulled her hand from his, and shoved a strand of hair behind her ear. "A friend of mine was killed. She was a well-known country music singer. I was a cop, not a rookie. I was visiting her and word got out where she was in spite of her excellent disguise. We were mobbed. I tried to get her away, but the crowd got to her and grabbed her and hoisted her into the air." She blinked and shook her head. "It was surreal. I'd never seen people act like that. They just had no respect for . . . anything." She drew in a shuddering breath. "When they let go, she fell onto the wrought iron fence that was attached to the brick wall outside the restaurant. One of the spikes went right through her and . . ." She shook her head. "She didn't make it."

Wade's heart cramped in horror at the visual her words brought to mind. "I can't even . . . oh man . . . I don't know what to say." Such tragedy. Yet she recited the events like she was reading a newspaper account. Her clenched fists resting on her thighs said she wasn't as distant as she sounded. "Wait a minute." He straightened. "I remember that story. In Nashville, Tennessee, right? Shana Lee?"

She nodded. "I tried to help her, but it was too late. We walked out of the restaurant and it was like a swarm." Her eyes took on a haunted, distant look and Wade knew she was seeing the events unfold in her memory. "Or an uncontrollable tornado that ripped through to leave devastation in its wake." She shook her head. "It was senseless. A tragic, completely preventable incident. If she'd had a bodyguard—"

"Why didn't she?"

"She didn't want one. She loved her fans and never minded the constant interruptions. She said if she wanted to be alone, she simply stayed home. And going out in public became a game for her too. To see how well she could disguise herself. Sometimes it worked—" She spread her hands.

"And that day it didn't," he finished.

"Yeah." She blinked. "One of Shana's goals in life was to help as many people as she could. She did benefit concerts, visited sick fans in the hospital, raised money for missions, everything you could think of. She gave so much."

"She gave it all."

Olivia nodded. "She wrote something in her will that eventually changed my life."

"What?"

"She left me some money and said her wish was for me to help others. She'd written the will two weeks before she died. At the time, I was too mad to do anything more than throw myself into my job, figuring I was helping the people I was keeping safe by getting the bad guys off the street."

"But?"

"But after about a year, I decided to honor her wishes in a different way. I wanted to help people by keeping them safe, just not as an officer. You see, as a police officer, the job is more about reaction rather than prevention. I mean, there's some of that, but being a bodyguard allows me to ward off the threat of harm before it actually happens."

"It was what she wanted."

"Yes."

"How did you meet her?"

She paused. "She was the daughter of the last foster family I lived with."

"The one you were with for six years? So she was your sister."

"Yes." She swallowed hard. "Yes, she was."

"You were also a good friend to her."

She stood and ran a hand down her sleek, straight blonde hair. "Not good enough."

"Get some sleep." He backed out of the door and shut it behind him.

A wave of exhaustion pulled at Olivia. She glanced at the bed, the adjoining bathroom, and the door Wade had just shut behind him.

The bed beckoned. She'd get her bag later.

[14]

When she awoke, it was with a start, the nightmare still clinging to the edges of her consciousness. Only this time Shana hadn't been dropped onto the fence, she'd been blown up. But then it hadn't been Shana, it had been Wade and she'd been kneeling beside what remained of him, wailing. She shuddered. "For crying out loud." Olivia flopped over onto her side and rubbed her eyes. "Stupid nightmare."

She saw her bag on the chair near the bed and figured Katie or Haley had brought it in to her. She must have been sleeping soundly. She glanced at the clock, but didn't need to. Her stomach rumbled that it was time to eat. Way past time. She hadn't eaten breakfast and now it was one o'clock in the afternoon.

She checked her phone and saw nothing urgent in her messages that needed her attention. She lay still, staring at the ceiling, taking a few moments to gather her thoughts and let her pulse slow down.

She couldn't believe she'd told Wade as much as she had. She didn't spill her story to clients. She didn't get emotionally

LYNETTE EASON

involved with her clients. And yet she found herself doing exactly that with Wade and his family.

She cared.

And she didn't want to in spite of the fact that's exactly what her now dead friend, Shana, had requested—no, *expected*—from her. Shana had died almost ten years ago and still her memory continued to plague Olivia, her friend's last words echoing through her mind as she bled to death in Olivia's arms.

"Don't die, Shana, don't die," twenty-one-year-old Olivia had pleaded as she'd done her best to hold her friend still. She'd stared in horror at the spike from the fence protruding from Shana's chest. "Don't die."

Shana gasped and grasped her arm. "You were right. I should have listened to you." Blood dribbled from her mouth and Olivia wept and screamed for help. Sirens blared, help was on the way. "Shana—"

"Look for God, Liv. He's . . . there. He . . . loves you. Let him help you. Tell my family I love . . ." Another gasp, a wince. Shana's grip slackened, but she kept her eyes on Olivia's. "Carrie—"

"I'll take care of Carrie." Carrie Blaine. Another performer like Shana but one who'd been receiving threats. One who'd also refused a bodyguard.

Shouts reached Olivia's ears. Help had arrived.

But she knew. She knew and didn't want to know. She let the tears flow freely down her cheeks.

Olivia cried out and sat straight up, her heart pounding in her throat. The dream. Again. This time the way it had originally happened.

She must have dozed back off. She sat still, gasping for breath, and let the images fade. Only they didn't fade fast enough. She got up and padded barefoot into the bathroom, splashed water on her face, brushed her teeth, and turned on the shower.

Fifteen minutes later, she towel dried her hair and still couldn't shake the dream. It had been even more vivid than usual. She stared into the mirror, but all she saw were Shana's pretty features standing out in detail. Memories of that day surged to the forefront. Was it because she'd allowed herself to talk about Shana last night?

The screams of the crowd still echoed and she pressed her hands against her ears. Even ten years later, standing in the steamy bathroom, she could almost feel the press of the hot, sweaty bodies. Feel the ache in her lungs as the crowd crushed tighter, stealing her breath and keeping her helpless, unable to get to her friend—or her weapon. Other bystanders had been horrified and tried to help. To get the rabid ones to release Shana. Only it had backfired. They'd not released her, they'd dropped her. Right onto the fence. Shana's agonizing cry played over and over in her mind.

Olivia shuddered. "Stop," she whispered. "Stop, stop." She pushed away from the sink and blinked, trying to dispel the images, the memories.

The horror.

She quickly changed into the clean clothes from her bag and headed downstairs to find Wade and Amy in the den, playing a game of Jenga. Stacy sat in the recliner reading a book. Wade was intently placing his block on the top of the stack when he looked up to see her. The stack crashed to the coffee table and Amy jumped up with a shriek. "I won! I won!"

Wade shot Olivia a rueful look.

"Sorry," she murmured but couldn't hide the smile curling her lips.

He shrugged. "It's okay. I just have to make her bed for her for the next week."

Amy did a little dance and poked her finger at her dad while she mocked him. He grabbed her with a growl and tackled her to the floor, gently, taking care not to hurt her, then tickled her until she begged for mercy. He let her go and the preteen lay on the floor laughing in between her gasps.

Olivia watched their interaction and had a brief flash of her own father pushing her on a swing in a park on a clear summer day. She blinked. Where had that come from? She shut the memory down. Even now, all these years later, it hurt to think about what could have been, had her parents not been killed, how different her life would be. But what was the point in dwelling on it? It did no good and just brought up feelings better left unfelt.

"You hungry?" Wade asked Olivia.

"Starving." She looked around. "Where's Katie?"

"She's patrolling the grounds every so often. She left just a minute before you came down."

Olivia nodded. That was standard operating procedure. She watched the workers installing the alarm system. She'd gotten a list of names from the person she'd hired and had a background check done on each one. Nothing suspicious had popped up on the three men and one woman, and she felt confident the finished product would meet her specifications. She knew Wade resented the need for the improvements, but she appreciated him holding his tongue.

Wade clasped his hands in front of him. "Haley left and said she was going to the hospital to check on Maddy, get some rest, and would be back at midnight tonight."

Olivia nodded. "Good."

Wade stood. "Follow me and I'll feed you."

"Can me and Stacy have some ice cream?" Amy asked.

"May Stacy and I. And sure."

Amy and Stacy trailed them to the kitchen where Wade opened

the refrigerator and pulled out a plate of sub sandwiches. He handed them to Olivia. "Will this work?"

"Like a charm. Thanks."

"Martha made them before she left to run some errands. I usually hang out with Amy on Saturdays, and Martha does whatever she wants to do without worrying about us. Chips are next to the coffeemaker."

She set the tray on the counter and took one of the sandwiches, placed it on a paper plate, and grabbed a bag of Doritos. She seated herself at the table while Wade scooped a generous helping of ice cream for Amy and Stacy.

Olivia glanced at Wade. "Did you get some sleep?"

"A little. I don't seem to need much anyway."

Olivia nodded and watched the girls devouring their ice cream. "So what are your plans for the rest of the day?"

Wade shrugged. "Just hanging out here. Thought we'd take a swim in the pool."

Olivia tensed. Swimming was outside. But it was behind the house and surrounded by a fence. She nodded. "Sounds like a good plan. We can work with that."

"Would you like to join us?"

Olivia hoped she hid her shudder. "No thanks. I'll stick to watching the area, but you three have fun."

He studied her for a moment, then nodded. "All right then."

Amy finished the last bite of her ice cream and stood. "Come on, Stacy, let's go get our bathing suits on." The girls raced out of the kitchen and Olivia finished her sandwich while Wade sat silent.

"What are you thinking about?" she asked.

His eyes flicked up to hers. "Who this person is."

Of course. "I have a recommendation."

"What?"

"Enjoy the time with the girls, don't think about Thursday night or last night. Just leave the worrying to me and my team, and live your life."

He pursed his lips and gave a slow nod. "Easier said than done, I think." The girls bounded into the kitchen, dressed in swimsuits, towels slung around their necks. Wade smiled at their exuberance, then swung his gaze back to hers. "But I think it's good advice for now."

He rose. "Give me a few minutes to change. I'll be back in just a sec." He left and Olivia let a slow breath escape her lips even as her stomach churned. She'd rather face a ticking bomb than a swimming pool. "You guys better know how to swim really well," she muttered. Because there was no way she was jumping in the water.

[15]

SUNDAY MORNING

Olivia rolled over in the bed and stared at the clock. Everyone
had survived the swim in the pool, including a nervous Olivia.
The girls swam better than fish, and Olivia never had to con-
template whether she'd actually be able to jump in if someone required it. She'd walked the edges of the pool and the
perimeter of the grounds several times. Thank goodness, all
had been quiet.

Katie had taken over guard duty at midnight and Olivia
had come home to get some rest. Seven whole hours felt like a
vacation. There'd been no nightmares and no one had called
with any emergencies during the night. Maybe Wade's stalker
needed some sleep too, she thought with no little sarcasm.

Her phone rang and she rolled over to snag it from the bed-
side table. "Hello?"

"This is Quinn. Just wanted to let you know that we're still
trying to track down that particular caller who seems to like
the DJ so much."

"His name is Wade."

"Yeah. I know. Anyway, we finally managed to get her address from the trace on her number. Her name is Valerie Mathis. She's one of the few remaining people with a landline. She used that number to call Wade at the station numerous times. When we got to her house around 8:00 this morning, the place was empty."

"You went in?"

"Nope. No reason to. But her car was gone and the neighbors say they haven't seen her since early yesterday morning."

"Convenient."

"Seems like it, but apparently she was talking about visiting a sister out of town, so they think that's where she went. We'll check again later this afternoon. She works as a waitress at that little restaurant on Coffee Street downtown."

"Thanks for the update. I appreciate it."

"I know you do. That's why I don't begrudge sharing with you. I'll be in touch."

And then he hung up just as her phone beeped another incoming call. She tapped the screen. "Hi."

"Just checking in," Katie said.

"I'm getting ready to get up and get dressed. How did last night go?"

"Quiet. Eerily quiet."

Olivia nodded, even though her friend couldn't see her. "Good. Let's hope it stays that way."

"Hmm. We can hope."

"Right." She caught the nuance behind Katie's words and agreed. "The eye of the storm?"

"Oh yeah."

"All right. I'll be on my way shortly. What's on his agenda for today?"

"Church."

Was it Sunday already? *Ugh.* "Don't you want to cover this morning? Church is more your speed than mine."

The silence echoed back at her and Olivia closed her eyes. Where was her professionalism? Why had working with the Savage family sent her spiraling into emotions and uncharacteristic actions? She cleared her throat. "Sorry. I must not be fully awake yet. It's my shift. I'll be there shortly."

"Are you all right?"

The soft question vibrated within her. "Of course, I'm fine. I'll see you in about fifteen minutes."

"I'll do the church duty if you want, you know that."

"You need your rest too. Haley and I are up for this one."

"Oh, by the way, Charlie and Lizzie both answered the text Haley sent them. They're ready to work whenever you need them. Haley said she really stressed the urgency of the situation, and after today, their schedules are cleared for however long you need them."

"Great." Olivia breathed a sigh of relief. "I'll email them everything we have so they can play catch-up on the Savage family. I'll see you soon." Olivia hung up. She rolled out of bed, walked to the mirror, and stared at her reflection. "Get it together, girl. You have a job to do. Emotions don't get to have a place in it." She lifted her chin a notch, then turned and walked out of the bedroom door.

※※※※※※※※※※※※※※※※※

Wade straightened his shirt over the top band of his jeans and slipped on his brown loafers. Amy and Stacy were already in the kitchen devouring whatever had produced the mouthwatering smells that had him hurrying from his bedroom. He'd been unable to reach Stacy's mother last night, which had him concerned. He'd called three more times and left messages reassuring her that Stacy was fine, but he really needed to talk to her.

He glanced at his phone. She still hadn't returned his call.

He shoved his wallet in his back pocket and glanced at the clock. They needed to leave in about thirty minutes. The service started at ten sharp. He entered the kitchen.

Martha looked up from the stove. "Grab a plate. I've got pancakes and bacon and a side of eggs if you want it."

His stomach rumbled. "I want it all." He ruffled Amy's hair, then Stacy's, eliciting giggles and protests all at the same time.

Amy finally huffed. "Now I have to brush my hair again. You really have to stop doing that, Dad."

He gave her a mock frown. "I'm so sorry, I forget you're almost grown."

He saw Martha hide a grin while he loaded his plate. "What made you go all out like this?"

"The girls asked me yesterday." She shrugged. "And I know you like a big breakfast on Sunday morning."

Katie stepped into the room and her gaze landed on the two girls. "Good morning," she said.

"Morning." He nodded to the food. "There's plenty if you're hungry."

"I'm fine. I'll grab something on the way home. It looks delicious, but if I eat all that, I'll fall asleep at the wheel." She looked at her phone. "Olivia will be here any moment."

Wade's pulse accelerated at the mention of her name and he drew in a steadying breath. His reaction to the woman had taken him by surprise at their initial meeting. The fact that he was still reacting said it wasn't due to sleepless nights or someone trying to kill him. He wanted to get to know her. But why? Why her and why now? How could he even consider that while he was trying to evade a stalker? It didn't make sense, but berating himself for bad timing wasn't going to do any good.

Martha finished a quick clean-up and headed for the guest house to get ready for church. A few minutes later, a knock on the door sent the girls into a flurry of activity. Katie placed a hand over her weapon and moved to peer out the window. She relaxed and opened the door. Olivia stepped inside. Wade could see she'd rested after she left last night. While her eyes looked a bit shadowed, the fatigue had faded.

She nodded. "Good morning."

"Good morning."

Katie gave them all a short salute. "I'll see you all later."

Katie left and Wade gestured to the food. "Would you care for any?"

She hesitated a brief moment, then gave him a small smile. "I'd love some."

While she fixed herself a plate, he looked at the girls. "Go over and tell Aunt Martha we'll leave in about ten minutes, will you?" He stood at the window while the girls scampered out the kitchen door, across the connecting overhang, and into Martha's living area. He'd kept the two wrought iron gates shut last night, minimizing the access to the back of his house via the drive. It also ensured added protection for Martha. The girls could go back and forth between Martha's apartment and the main house without him worrying about someone snatching them. He shuddered at the thought and waited for Olivia to seat herself opposite him.

She wore dark blue jeans and a black T-shirt with a long-sleeved denim shirt over that. He figured the overshirt was to cover the shoulder holster. She looked professional and capable. And somehow vulnerable. She ate slowly. "This is good."

"You didn't eat breakfast?"

"I didn't have time."

"Slept in, huh?"

"Actually, yes. Figured I'd take advantage of the opportunity while I could." She rested her fork on her plate. "Tell me about this church."

"What do you need to know?"

"How big is it?"

"It's a big church. About eight thousand people."

Olivia winced. "Would you please consider staying home?"

"Amy's in a play this morning. She's been so excited about it, I can't take that away from her unless you can give me a very good reason." Amy might not care—in fact, she would probably be relieved—but after their last conversation about it, he didn't want to give her any excuses to back out.

"Someone trying to kill you twice isn't good enough?"

He sighed. "I hear what you're saying. I tossed and turned all night as I thought about what to do. I considered not going. But the more I thought about it, the madder I got." He met her gaze. "I won't become a hermit," he said softly. "I won't live in fear or let Amy see me hiding. I can't. There's no telling what that would do to her."

She stared at him like he had no common sense. "There are too many people, Wade. I won't be able to effectively protect you and Amy."

"No offense, but what's the point in having you around if that's the case?"

She sighed. "The point is, my presence lessens the odds of something happening. But in a crowd that big, it's easy for someone with evil intentions to hide—then strike when the opportunity presents itself. Anything could go wrong. I've got two more people to add to the team, but they can't start working until tomorrow. If you can just lay low until then."

He narrowed his eyes and gave it some thought. Then he echoed her sigh. "You have a valid argument, but this is what we do on Sunday morning." He held up a hand when she opened her mouth. "I know what you're going to say. It's too predictable. Maybe so, but with her anxiety issues, Amy needs consistency. She's been practicing for this play for weeks. If I tell her she can't do it, it may throw her into an anxiety attack that will last all day. She's looking forward to going and I have to take her."

"What about at a different time. A church that big has got to have more than one service."

"It has four, but this is the time we have to go so she can be there for the play. If we change on her, a panic attack will ensue and it won't be pretty. I can't do that to her."

"What happens if she's sick and can't go or something happens to throw her schedule off?"

He shook his head. "Like I said, it's not pretty. But usually when she's sick, it's not as bad because she's too sick to care."

The door to the kitchen opened and the girls rushed back in. "She's almost ready," Amy said and shut the door behind her. "Are we still taking the boat out today?"

"Of course."

Olivia blanched. "What are you talking about?"

He frowned at her reaction. "I promised to take Amy out on the boat and let her go swimming after—"

A knock on the front door brought Olivia to her feet, her hand on her weapon. Wade tensed when she moved on silent feet to look out the window. He noticed her movements mimicked Katie's from earlier. "It's a woman on your front porch," she said. "Come here and tell me if you recognize her."

Wade stood and made his way to stand beside Olivia. She parted the curtains and he looked out. And relaxed. "That's Joanna."

"Joanna Clement. I recognize the name."

"She's Martha's best friend and like another aunt to Amy." Joanna stood at a statuesque five foot ten inches. Just about three inches shorter than Wade. "You can open the door," he said. He liked Joanna, but even after all this time, her presence brought back memories of the past. He'd gotten used to them popping up in his mind whenever she was around and knew it was just because when Martha and Joanna were together, he kept expecting to see Pamela with them.

His dead wife, Pamela.

Joanna, Martha, and Pamela had been inseparable in high school. When he and Pamela had married the day after high school graduation, they'd been so young nothing much had changed for the three friends. He'd been happy to hang out with his guy friends while Pamela did the girl thing. And sometimes they gathered as couples. Always fun. Sometimes trouble. And then Amy had been born and Pamela had resented the intrusion of the baby. Taking care of an infant didn't figure into her life of parties and nonstop fun. He frowned, not wanting to go down that path of thought.

"I remember her name, she's on the list." Olivia's words shook him back to the present.

"The list?" he asked as she opened the door.

"Of people in your life who we did a background check on."

"Compliments of my father?"

"Indeed."

Joanna stepped inside, brows raised. "Hi?"

Wade gave her a brief hug. "Hi. What are you doing here?"

"Martha and I are going out after church, so she told me to bring my car over here and just ride with her." Her curious gaze landed on Olivia. "Are you the bodyguard I've heard about?"

"One of them," Olivia said and held out her hand.

Joanna shook it. "Nice to meet you."

"And you."

The kitchen door shut and footsteps sounded behind him. The girls hurried to him and Martha was right behind. She spotted Joanna. "Oh good, you're here. Is everyone ready?"

Wade looked at Olivia. "So how does this work?"

"We can take your car, but it would be better to let me drive."

"So you're a chauffer too?"

She shrugged. "Comes with the territory."

Wade considered telling her he would handle it from here on out, then looked at Amy. He gave Olivia a tight smile. "Then we're ready when you are."

[16]

Olivia pulled into the parking lot of the Celebration Community Church. Her stomach knotted at the thought of going inside. She always felt like such a hypocrite when she had to do "church duty" with a client. Shana had loved church, and for six years, Olivia had been a faithful attender with her foster family, had even gone some while she was in college. But once Shana died, she'd stopped going. The nagging knowledge that Shana would be disappointed often rose up to haunt her. Like now. She squared her shoulders and lifted her chin. This was her job and she'd do it.

Haley pulled in beside them and climbed out. Whenever there was an active threat, when her clients were in public, Olivia preferred to have another member of her team with her as backup. Preferably two. And since Maddy was still in the hospital fighting for her life, they were all putting in extra hours until Charlie and Lizzie could join them on the schedule.

She stood beside the Armada and waited for the girls and Wade to exit the vehicle. "You take the girls. I'll stick with Wade."

Haley nodded and shoved her earpiece in. She looked at Olivia, who'd already placed hers in her ear. "Can you hear me?"

"Crystal clear."

"Excellent." She turned to the wide-eyed preteens. "Why
don't you girls show me where you're supposed to go?"

Amy eyed her. "We go to the youth room." She glanced at
her dad, then at Olivia. "But I . . . I think I want to stay with
my dad."

"No you don't," Stacy said. "They're having donuts and
stuff, remember? And we've got one more rehearsal for the play
this morning, then all the parents are coming in." She looked
at Olivia. "It's so cool. We're up on the stage and they play
a movie behind us and we interact with the characters in the
movie and—anyway, it's cool." She turned her attention back
to Amy. "Let's go."

"We just ate. I'm not hungry and I don't want to be in the
play anymore. My part is so small, it won't matter if I'm in it
or not." Amy edged closer to her father.

Wade placed a hand under Amy's chin and tilted her face up
to his. "Hon, you were really looking forward to this. Do you
remember what we talked about?"

Amy shifted. "I remember." A shudder went through her,
followed by a look of rising panic.

"It's okay. Hold my hand and breathe. We'll go inside and
you can think about it."

"I don't need to think about it. I don't want to be in the play
now. I want to stay with you."

Stacy frowned. "Come on, Amy. I'll be with you. And the
youth room is right across the hall from the auditorium if you
want to leave and go sit with your dad."

Amy looked like she might change her mind and go with her
friend, then shook her head and leaned against Wade.

Stacy shrugged. "Okay, I guess I'll see you later then. If I wasn't in the play too, I'd stay with you."

"It's okay. I might come later." Amy watched her friend walk away and took two steps to go after her, then stopped and reached for her dad's hand. Stacy disappeared through the double glass entry doors just ahead. Wade looked pained but didn't say anything, just clasped his daughter's fingers and started for the same glass doors.

People streamed in from the parking lot, and Olivia kept her eyes on everyone who waved or spoke to Wade and his family. The news reports had downplayed the story, thanks to the intervention of the mayor. No one seemed intent on trouble or overly interested when expressing their concern. And that was the problem with some stalkers. Sometimes they just weren't obvious. She stepped up next to Wade. "Any word from Stacy's mother?"

"No. Not even a text. It's got me more than a little worried."

"I can ask Quinn to see if he can locate her."

"Let's see if she shows up for church. If she's not here like we'd planned, then I'll definitely be concerned."

She nodded. "When we get in there, could you please sit on the end of a row? I don't want you to have to step over people if we have a reason to exit quickly."

His jaw tightened and she thought he might say no as he opened the door for Amy, Martha, and Joanna. They stepped through and into the lobby area of the church, and he gave a short nod.

"Vicky!" Amy called as soon as she crossed the threshold. A young girl about Amy's age turned and the two girls hugged.

That middle spot between Olivia's shoulders tingled. She stayed alert. She wished she'd insisted Wade stay home this morning, but that was one of the whole points in hiring personal bodyguards. So one didn't have to stay behind closed doors, so one could carry on with life feeling confident that someone had his back.

Still. Someone *had* tried to blow them up yesterday.

Olivia kept her eyes on Wade and the people around him. Martha and her friend Joanna stood about a foot from Haley, speaking with two other ladies. Amy and the girl she'd called Vicky moved to a stand serving coffee and other treats.

"Apparently the donut lovers aren't limited to the youth," Olivia said.

Wade nodded. "We have about ten minutes before the service starts. It should start clearing out in here pretty quickly."

"I'd feel more comfortable if you would go find a seat. It's too hard to keep an eye on everyone with so many people around. Haley's going to be in the balcony watching the crowd throughout the service. I want a bird's-eye view of this place."

From the corner of her eye, she saw Martha disappear into the auditorium and Joanna keep walking until she disappeared into the room at the end. "Where's Joanna going?" Olivia asked.

"She volunteers to count money the first and third Sunday of the month."

Olivia nodded. "All right. She's taken care of then."

Others followed Martha into the auditorium, and to Olivia's relief, she saw Wade was right. The crowd thinned considerably.

"Wade?"

He turned at the voice. With a subtle step, Olivia placed herself in between Wade and the woman heading toward them. A quick glance behind her showed Amy still in the line. Her nerves twitched. She didn't like Amy and Wade being so far apart when she was the only one to watch both of them. She turned back to see the woman still coming. Olivia could see both hands, one at her side, the other clasping her purse. Olivia's gaze traveled upward. She made a mental note of the smile on the woman's ruby red–glossed lips. Five seven or eight, slightly overweight, but with a graceful stride and a mane of gorgeous red hair, she didn't slow her approach or seem to take note of Olivia's protective stance.

Wade reached out his hand to the woman and Olivia did her best to hover without being suffocating. The two clasped hands, and while the woman gave Olivia a dismissing glance, she kept her smile wide, revealing perfect white teeth—and her pleasure at seeing Wade.

"Erin," Wade said. "I'm so glad you're here. You really had me worried when you didn't answer your phone all weekend."

"I'm so sorry. I had turned my phone off for the conference and never turned it back on all weekend."

Olivia eyed her. What mother turned her phone off and didn't call her children for days? A slack one? One who was overworked and overtired? It rankled her, but she stayed silent. The woman had made sure Stacy would be taken care of during her absence. It was a lot more than some parents bothered with. "I was just leaving the hotel for the drive in this morning when I saw your calls," the woman said. "Is everything all right? Is Stacy really okay?" Her shadowed eyes conveyed her worry.

"Stacy's fine, it was just an exciting weekend, to say the least." He gave a brief explanation of what was going on with him, leaving Olivia's part in the incident out of the telling. Erin's eyes widened to about three times their normal size. The woman placed a hand over her chest. "Oh my goodness. That's awful." She hugged him, then stepped back. "I'm so glad you're all right!"

"I am too, thanks." Wade gestured toward Olivia. "This is my . . . um . . . friend, Olivia Edwards. Olivia, this is Erin Abbott, Stacy's mother. In case you hadn't figured that out yet."

"I did." Olivia nodded and Erin gave her a brief smile. Speculation sparkled in her suddenly narrowed eyes, along with a coldness that gave Olivia a slight shiver. Now the woman wasn't quite so dismissing. Olivia noted she was being sized up. Erin thought she was competition. "Nice to meet you."

"You too." She heard the insincerity in the greeting and couldn't stop the sudden surge of compassion for the woman. Wade would never be interested in her romantically. Which immediately put her on the suspected stalker list.

Erin then air-kissed the area around Wade's left cheek. "Again, thank you so much for keeping Stacy this weekend. And I apologize for not being more in touch. I've just been overwhelmed with work, not to mention having my hands full with the younger ones." Her lashes fluttered a bit in a flirtatious expression that made Olivia bite the inside of her cheek. Underneath the makeup and overbright expression, she could see faint shadows beneath the woman's eyes. She didn't have it quite as together as she wanted everyone to believe, with her well-packaged body and perfectly made-up face.

Wade smiled. "No problem. Stacy and Amy would be inseparable if we'd let them."

"I know." She pursed her lips and gave a mock pout. "I listened to your show Friday night. It sounded like you were live, then it went to a recorded one. Is that when everything started happening?"

"Yes."

"Well, I just hope they catch whoever is doing this. That's just wrong. And quite frankly, I don't know what I'd do without you on the weekends. Just listening to you talk and handle all those crazy callers makes me see that my life isn't nearly as wretched as others'. It gets me through my week, so you be careful, you hear?"

"I hear." Wade shifted, and Olivia caught the embarrassed hunch of his shoulders and the heightened color in his cheeks. Yet he stayed cool and kept the smile on his face. "And I'm glad you find value in the show."

"Oh I do. And I know I'm not the only one."

Olivia let her gaze roam, moving from person to person, watching facial expressions, body movements. She let her eyes land on the donut stand, searching for Amy.

Who wasn't there anymore.

Neither was Vicky.

"Stacy went to the youth room. She knows to meet you at your usual spot after church," she heard Wade say. Again, Olivia panned the area.

No Amy. Or Vicky.

Olivia frowned. Erin Abbott walked off with one last wave to Wade and a short nod for Olivia. Olivia touched Wade's arm. "Amy's wandered off. Where would she go?"

"What?" Wade turned.

"Amy, I don't see her. Where would she go?" There were simply too many people. She should have insisted they forgo church. But the client was the boss and she had to work within the limits of that fact.

Wade frowned and made a beeline for the donut stand. He started asking the people near him if they'd seen Amy and her friend Vicky. Olivia stayed near him and kept her gaze roaming in an arc. From the door to her right, to the area in front of her and around to the door to her left. No Amy.

"No one remembers seeing her," he said.

"Maybe she went inside the auditorium." Olivia pressed her earpiece in tighter. "Haley?"

"I'm here."

"Did Amy come inside the auditorium?"

"I didn't see her and I've been watching the doors. The lights are low, though, and people are still mingling." She paused and Olivia knew what was coming. "I've got my binoculars out and I'm sweeping the room, but there are just too many people."

"I should have told Katie to come."

"No, we should have convinced Wade to stay home." Haley paused. "We do need to bring someone else on board if he's going to insist on going out in public like this. I don't think Amy's in here, Liv," she said, her voice low but crystal clear. "Martha is here . . . Okay, it looks like people are settling down and it's getting ready to start. There aren't any teenagers in here that I can see."

"Because they're all in the youth room."

"You need to check there. Maybe she changed her mind."

Wade shoved his way to the auditorium doors and stepped inside. Olivia stayed right on his heels. Darkness swallowed them and she blinked to allow her eyes to adjust. It didn't take long. The lights from the stage soon pushed aside the dark. The music had already started.

She grabbed his arm. "She's not in here," she said into his ear.

"How do you know? She may have decided to come sit with Martha and Joanna. She's comfortable with them."

"Haley's in the balcony with binoculars and she hasn't seen her. Let's check the youth room."

She followed Wade out of the auditorium back into the lobby.

Three loud cracks rang out. She dove for Wade and took him to the floor.

[17]

Amy jumped at the loud booms and slapped her hands over her ears. To her left, Stacy let out a scream. To her right, Vicky squealed. The screams and roars from the others in the large room echoed around her.

Amy felt the panic rising, her throat closing, her lungs shrinking. She rose to her feet and ran from the room. She had to get away, get out. She couldn't have an attack in front of her friends. She ran down the hallway that was filling fast with people rushing from the auditorium. She made a left and raced to the bathroom in the children's wing. No one ever used it until after the service, and she'd found it the perfect place to catch her breath and find calm.

She pushed inside. Vacant, just like she wanted. Panting, gulping air, she went to the sink and turned on the faucet. She ducked her head to put her lips to the water, gulping it down her dry throat. She choked, coughed, and sputtered.

She turned the faucet off and grabbed a handful of paper towels and dried her face. She threw the paper in the trash, then went into one of the stalls. The small space would soothe her attack. She knew it was weird. Small places made some people crazy, but they made her feel protected. She'd felt an attack coming on once before in the youth room and had run to the bathroom before anyone could notice. Discovering the tight space made her feel better had been a huge relief. One of the reasons she liked coming to church so much. She felt safe there. Or at least she had. The attack started to ease. She pulled in a lungful of air and glanced up, wondering why she had to be different, why she had to be afflicted with the panic and anxiety. Sometimes she even wondered if God hated her. Her dad promised that wasn't the case, but privately Amy wasn't so sure.

She rubbed her eyes, not caring that she smeared the carefully applied mascara or eye shadow. She stared at the door and thought. Maybe she should ask her dad to have doors like the stall doors put on her classroom at school. She didn't know why, but she liked the bathroom stall doors.

They weren't regular metal stall doors. These were nice, with handles that locked. They reminded her of the blinds on the den at her house or the bathrooms in that fancy restaurant Aunt Martha liked to go to where all the ladies wore dresses and the men had to wear a coat and tie. The doors were brown and tight and no one could see in. She tested the handle.

Locked.

She was fine. She sat on the lid of the toilet and wrapped her arms around her stomach. Tears leaked down her cheeks and she wanted to wail. Why was this happening to her? *Why, God?* She breathed deep, felt it catch. Relief flowed through her. *When I am afraid I will trust—*

The room went dark.

Amy froze. The squeezing in her chest returned.

She heard the creak of the main door as it shut. She'd been

so lost in her own panic she hadn't heard the door open. Or had someone been in the bathroom and she hadn't noticed?

Soft footfalls reached her ears. No. Someone had come in and shut off the lights. Her heart thudded, her mouth went dry. She pulled her legs up and wrapped her arms around her shins. Her body shook and the panic wanted to overcome her. She squeezed her eyes tight, then opened them. Her chest hurt, but she ignored it.

Why would someone turn off the lights? Did they know she was there? Did the person think the bathroom was empty? But why turn off the lights and step *in*side? She hesitated, then opened her mouth to call out.

"Amy?" The raspy whisper froze her. Her stomach cramped and she thought she might be sick. A wave of dizziness hit her and she leaned her forehead on her knees, desperately trying to control her breathing. Conscious of every sound she made. *Be quiet, be quiet, be invisible.*

She thought of her father's stalker. His worry that something would happen to her. Was this the person?

Another footstep. A thin beam of light reached under her door and she bit back a gasp. The light moved across the floor to the next stall and on down. Amy lowered herself to the floor and peered under the partition. The light continued to move, but her eyes had adjusted to the dark enough that she could see dark shoes slowly moving with the light. "Amy? Where are you?"

Amy thought her thundering heart would alert the person as to her location. Fear kept her quiet. Did she recognize the voice? Something . . .

No. Not that soft creepy whisper. *Daddy! Where are you? Come get me! Jesus, Jesus, Jesus—*

Her dad wasn't coming. No one was coming. Jesus wasn't going to help her. She'd have to do this alone. The person moved farther away. "Amy? I need you to give your father a message for me."

Amy stayed frozen for a brief moment.

"I know you're in here. Tell your father Justine is waiting for him." The voice gave a low chuckle, the footsteps moved closer, and Amy's breath lodged in her throat.

Yes, she'd have to do this. And now. She moved as quickly and quietly as possible, crawling under the stall divider into the next space, then the next. The footsteps started back in her direction. She had one more stall and she'd be in the open.

But also right next to the door.

The steps continued. She glanced back. The light came faster.

Amy scrambled out from under the stall, bolted to her feet, and beelined it to the door. Her fingers fumbled for the handle, turned it.

A hand brushed her shoulder and she screamed.

Wade didn't know how long he and Olivia lay in a tangled heap behind the information desk along with others who had taken cover there, but it seemed like an eternity. In reality it was probably more like sixty seconds as they waited for more shots.

When that didn't happen, Olivia rose cautiously to her feet, staying in a crouch, her weapon in her hand. Wade mimicked her position and rubbed his elbow. His heart thundered in his ears as his terror level reached new heights. Had someone shot at them? He looked around and saw nothing amiss. No bullet holes, nothing that looked damaged. Just people on the floor, terrified expressions on their faces.

To his left Wade heard running footsteps. A young man wearing a staff T-shirt came into the lobby holding up his hands in a surrendering gesture. "It's okay, everyone. That was a bit louder than we'd planned. It wasn't gunshots, just a recording in the youth room turned up too loud. I mean those *were* gunshots, but they were recorded and the door was open and . . ." He eyed the weapon in Olivia's hands and swallowed hard. "Um, we didn't mean to scare anyone. Really." He backed up, eyes wide. He turned and found Haley behind him, weapon also drawn. "Whoa. What's going on?"

Olivia holstered her gun. "It's okay, Haley. False alarm. But we've still got to find Amy."

Stacy hurried into the lobby, her eyes searching, then looking relieved when they landed on Wade. "I can't find Amy. She came in the youth room with Vicky and said she decided to be in the play, but then there were these loud bangs and she ran out."

"Where would she go to feel safe, Stacy?"

Stacy's worried eyes lit up. "The bathroom in the children's wing. She goes there sometimes." She spun on her heel and raced back the way she'd come. Olivia and Wade followed her. Haley pulled up the rear. Wade noted they had the undivided attention of the people in the lobby, as well as two security guards who spoke into their radios as they hustled toward him. He ignored them. He had one goal, one purpose.

Find Amy.

He passed more parishioners coming out of the auditorium to investigate. Some looked scared, others more cautious and curious. He passed them without a glance, rounded the corner, and nearly wilted when he saw Amy racing toward him, her makeup streaked, her tearstained face bleached of all natural color.

"Dad?" She hurled herself into his arms.

He hugged her for a brief moment, then gripped her forearms and pushed her back to look at her. "Are you all right? Where did you go? You scared me to death when you disappeared." He could see the strain on her face, the panic in her eyes.

But she swallowed and gulped in a breath as her gaze darted between him, Stacy, Olivia, and the others. "Vicky wanted to go to the youth room so I decided to go with her. I told Miss Joanna where I was going."

Wade closed his eyes. He could feel his blood pressure still pounding way too high. "She didn't tell me."

"She said she would, I promise. I wouldn't have just left like that. But then the shots went off during the play and they scared me. I know it was only a recording, but it was so loud and I ran to the bathroom and got in the stall and I couldn't breathe and then someone came in and turned off the lights and she called my name and I—"

"Wait, wait, breathe," Wade soothed. "Slow down a minute." He could see Olivia standing next to him, listening to every word.

She stepped closer. "What do you mean someone came in and shut the lights off?"

Amy nodded and tears gathered. "She scared me."

"She?" Wade asked. A murderous rage built inside of him at the thought of his child being terrorized.

"I think so. I mean it was the ladies' room. But I pulled my feet up on the toilet and the light went past me so she didn't know I was in that stall, but she knew I was in the bathroom."

"Light?" Totally confused, Wade glanced at Olivia. "Let's get out of here so we can figure out what she's talking about."

Olivia nodded and spoke to Haley via her earpiece. "Check the ladies' room in the children's wing and see if anyone is in there. If so, question them, get their statements about where they were when the shots went off, then meet us at the front door."

"What about my sister-in-law and Joanna?" Wade asked.

"Haley," she said into the microphone. "Find Martha and Joanna and let them know what's going on. Martha was in the auditorium and Joanna is in the money counting room." She looked at Wade. "I want to talk to Amy first without an audience."

Wade looked up and noticed the crowd gathered around him, their interest focused on Olivia, him, and Amy. The two security guards finally caught up to them and the youth pastor launched into another explanation about the noise that set off the panic. Wade wasn't worried about that. Now that he knew there wasn't an actual shooter, he wanted to know who was in the ladies' room with his daughter and why.

Olivia pressed the button to speed-dial Katie while Wade and Amy stood to the side in a small alcove next to the front door. It was perfect. No windows, just two couches, a big-screen television mounted on the wall, and a coffee table with several church pamphlets sitting on it.

"Hello?"

"Sorry to interrupt your sleep—"

"I'm dressing now. Where do you need me?"

"You're about fifteen minutes away from the church. I need you to come do a sweep of the vehicle." She gave Katie the license plate and the location of the SUV.

"I'll be there in twelve. Wait for me to give you the all clear."

The phone clicked off and Olivia paced the opening of the alcove. She reached the end and turned to face-plant into Wade's chest. She gasped and stepped back, heat flushing up into her cheeks.

"A sweep?" Wade asked, grasping her upper arm in order to steady her.

"Sorry," she said.

He didn't seem to notice her momentary discomfiture. She cleared her throat and put a little more distance between them. Her brain seemed to work better that way.

"Your stalker was here," she said. "She knows where you live, where you go to church, and what vehicle you drive. And now you've made her mad at you. And even though we don't know the whole story yet about her being in the bathroom with Amy—or even if it *was* her—we do know that *someone* was there, and that person scared Amy."

"True."

"And since I don't know the motive behind that—other than to scare you—I'm going to assume the worst and take all precautions."

Wade glanced back at Amy. Olivia followed his gaze. Amy had her attention glued to the television screen. Closed captions ran across the bottom. Olivia didn't know if she was listening to the sermon or not, but at least she'd calmed down. "And by those precautions you mean a sweep of my vehicle for . . . ?"

"A bomb, Wade. I'm looking for a bomb."

He swallowed hard and blinked. Then his jaw tightened and he gave a short nod. "Right. A bomb. Because the first time didn't get the job done." He blew out a slow breath. "I'm going to talk to Amy and see if she can tell me anything more about the woman in the bathroom."

Olivia's earpiece buzzed. "Go."

"I'm heading your way," Haley said. "The service is winding down and the closing music's going to start any second."

"Katie should be here any minute."

"Sweeping the car?"

"Yes."

Martha entered the lobby, followed by Haley.

Martha rushed over to Wade, Haley right on her heels. "What's going on? What happened? We heard loud noises, but didn't think much of it since they kept going with the service, but Haley said it set off some panic."

Joanna appeared from the door she'd vanished behind earlier and bolted over to Martha and Wade. "What is it? I got your text. What's going on?"

Wade stepped forward, a ferocious frown on his face directed toward Joanna. "Why didn't you tell me Amy was going to the youth room?"

"What?" Joanna stepped back. "She said she was going and I told her she needed to tell you."

"She said you told her you would tell me."

"No. I specifically said, 'You need to tell your father where you are.'"

"I thought you said you would tell him," Amy said softly. "I thought you said, 'I'll tell your father where you are.'"

"No, I'm so sorry." Joanna held out a beseeching hand. "You must have misunderstood—"

Wade placed a hand on Amy's shoulder. "It doesn't matter now. Misunderstandings happen. Amy's fine and that's all that matters."

Joanna clamped her lips together and nodded. She held her arms out to Amy, who slid into them. The two hugged.

Olivia's phone rang and she snatched it to her ear while Wade went into soothing mode with his sister-in-law.

"Katie?"

"Yeah, I'm here," Katie said. "Going over the vehicle now. Stay on the line with me."

Olivia did. She could sense Wade listening in on her side of the conversation while Martha turned to Joanna and began discussing the incident in soft tones.

Haley walked up to Olivia. "Bathroom had three females in it," she said in a low voice. "No way to know if one of them was in there when Amy was. I asked and they all claimed to have come from the auditorium. Could be true, could be not."

"Any cameras in the hallway?"

"Yes. The whole building has security cameras."

"Check and see if Quinn can take a look and determine who went into the bathroom and scared Amy."

"Okay, the car is now clean," Katie said in her ear.

"*Now* clean?"

"No bomb, but it had a GPS tracker on it."

Olivia sucked in a breath. "All right. You removed it of course."

"And bagged it. We'll see if one of our contacts at the lab will do us a favor and see if it can be traced."

"Good deal. From now on, we do a complete sweep of the vehicle before Wade or anyone in his family gets near it." She hung up and motioned to Haley and Wade. "We're good to go."

Wade gripped Amy's hand.

"Well, what about us?" Martha asked. "Do you think we're in any danger if Joanna and I continue with our plans for the day?"

Olivia considered the question. "The stalker doesn't appear to be after you or consider you to be a threat. So far her targets have been Wade and Amy." She glanced at Haley, then back to the two women. "In other words, I can't make that call. That's up to you. If you're with us, you'll be under our protection. If you go off on your own, you won't be."

Joanna shook her head. "We'll be fine, Martha. The psycho is after Wade. In fact, if you think about it, we'll probably be safer away from him."

Martha frowned and Olivia could see her trying to decide. Olivia glanced at Wade and wondered if he'd taken that last comment personally. His expression didn't give her a clue.

"Frankly," Olivia said, "I would prefer you stay with us until we know for sure the person isn't going to go after anyone else."

"No," Martha said. "Joanna and I will go on with our plans for the day. It's ridiculous to let one individual have that much power over us." She lifted her chin. "Let's go, Joanna."

Joanna nodded. "Fine."

The two ladies left and Olivia nodded to Wade. He took Amy's hand and Olivia led the way to the parking lot. Haley brought up the rear, keeping an eye on their flank, her hand never far from her weapon. At the vehicle, Wade helped Amy into the back, then climbed into the passenger seat. Haley slid into the seat next to Amy. Olivia walked over to Katie, who now sat in the driver's seat of her own vehicle. "Will you follow us back to Wade's house? I want you to hear whatever Amy has to say."

"Of course. I'll clear the house before you go in."

"Thanks."

Olivia returned to Wade's SUV. She settled herself behind the wheel and cranked the engine while Wade buckled up. He blew out a slow breath. "I have a charity dinner Thursday night."

"I know."

"Should we call it off?"

"You're willing to do that?"

"I'm not worried about myself so much as I'm worried about"—he glanced in the rearview mirror—"others worrying about me."

She nodded, understanding his convoluted sentence. "That's four days away. Do you need to know right now?"

"Pretty soon."

"Give me all the information and I'll check on the security that'll be present. Depending on that, we can make the decision by tomorrow evening."

"That'll work."

She wove through the maze of the parking lot and finally made it to the street that would take her to the interstate.

"Where are we going?" Amy asked.

Olivia glanced at Wade, who also looked interested in the answer to the question. "I'm going to take you home and then I'm going to see about watching the security footage from the church." And calling in reinforcements. Amy needed someone with her 24/7. Whoever was after Wade had just proven she'd use Amy to get to him.

And that simply wasn't going to happen.

[18]

The drive to the house was uneventful, but frankly Olivia didn't anticipate any problems while she—or another bodyguard—was around. At least not yet. Not in an in-your-face kind of way. A sneak attack was going to be more her style.

Wade's stalker had already proven she was clever—and not afraid to kill. But she had only attacked individuals. She hadn't gone after Wade—or Amy—when they'd been with a group of people. Even at the church, with the big crowd, she'd still managed to get Amy alone.

And that was the key.

She pulled into the drive and put the car in park. Haley got out. "I'll do a perimeter search as well. I'll let Katie know." She was already on her phone as she slipped out of the vehicle.

Olivia turned to Wade. "She went after you when you were alone." She tapped the wheel as she thought. "And she went after Amy when *she* was alone. Granted, she orchestrated that, but she still wanted her—and you—alone."

"So as long as we travel in a group, we should be fine?"

"No, no, I'm not saying that, I'm saying *it appears like* she's not confident enough to take on more than one person at a time."

He snorted. "Well, that's a comfort."

"Sarcasm?"

"Sorry," he muttered. "But yeah."

"She's a behind-the-scenes kind of girl. A wallflower, but not necessarily physically unattractive."

"Always the bridesmaid, never the bride?" Wade murmured.

"Hmm. Yes. Something like that. Maybe by choice, maybe not. You probably intimidate her. Beneath it all, she doesn't think you would find her appealing, but she's decided not to let that stop her from having you. One way or another. She's slowly gaining confidence to make that happen. Or maybe that's been her goal for a while and she's just now figured out a way to get you to notice her."

"And she's progressed to the point that she's willing to use the dark of night to . . . uh . . . take out one of your employees." He was mindful of his daughter still in the backseat. "You're trying to analyze her."

She shrugged. "Profile her."

He nodded and went silent.

"What does 'profile her' mean?" Amy asked.

Olivia glanced in the rearview mirror. The girl hadn't said a word from the time they'd left the church to now. Her question had been subdued, but at least she was talking. "It means to try and understand how someone thinks or figure out why they behave the way they behave." There was more to it than that, but she figured a simple explanation would be best here.

Olivia's phone pinged and she looked at the text. Katie had already cleared the house. No decapitated gifts this time. No bombs adhered to the doors. That was a step in the right direction.

"Oh. Because once you understand how someone thinks, you can help that person, right?" Amy said.

Olivia smiled. Helping wasn't really on her priority list. Taking that person down and putting her behind bars was more in line with what she had in mind. "Yes. Something like that."

Amy nodded. "That's what my dad does. He figures out how people think, then helps them."

"I know. Your dad's a smart man."

"Not as smart as Pops." Amy opened her door and got out of the car.

Wade cleared his throat. "We'll debate that another time," he said to Amy's back. His daughter slipped inside the house.

"She seems okay," Olivia said in a low voice, "but I don't really know her well enough to tell."

"She's not okay. I can see the tremor in her hands and she hasn't looked me in the eye since we got in the car." Wade led the way into the house via the kitchen door. Katie had already entered the front. Amy grabbed a box of raisins from the counter, but didn't stop to speak or acknowledge Katie's presence. She darted past her and disappeared up the stairs.

Katie lifted a brow. Olivia looked at Wade. He sighed and ducked his head for a second, then looked up. "Okay, let's go."

"She went to her room, I assume?" Olivia asked.

He nodded. "It's her safe place."

"Is it all right if we invade it?"

"I think we need to. We need to get her to talk while her memory is fresh." His jaw tightened. "I want to know who was in the bathroom and get the full story. Come on."

"You go first and clear the way a bit. I want to talk to Katie for just a few minutes."

Wade nodded and headed up the stairs.

"What is it?" Katie asked from behind her.

"I just spoke with Haley. I told her we had this covered so she's heading home."

"That's fine."

"And Quinn's pulling security footage from the church. He said he'd come by and show it to Amy and Wade if there was anything worth looking at."

"Great."

Olivia drew in a deep breath. "Now, let's go see if Amy will fill us in on what happened at the church."

Wade sat beside Amy and wrapped an arm around her shoulders. She pulled away from him. "Go away."

Stunned, he simply stared at her for a brief moment. "What?"

"Go. Away."

"Amy—"

"I don't want to talk to you right now."

Disbelief and anger fired to life. "Now look here, young lady—" She crossed her arms and turned her head, refusing to look at him. He stopped. She didn't need a reprimand. She'd been terrified. "Amy," he whispered. Her jaw tightened. He touched her shoulder. "Honey, talk to me."

"Why should I?"

Wade was floored. His mind froze. With all of his expertise in counseling others in their relationships with family members, he couldn't figure out how to talk to his own daughter.

"Why are you mad at your dad?"

Wade turned to find Olivia in the doorway with Katie behind her.

Amy flinched and looked away.

Wade didn't know whether to be mad or glad at the interruption. He stayed silent since he wanted to know the answer himself. Olivia kept her gaze on Amy. Amy stared back for a few seconds, then dropped her eyes to the stuffed animal she held in her lap. "He didn't come get me," she said, her voice barely above a whisper. "He didn't come save me. No one did."

Wade's heart shattered. He'd failed his child. She'd expected him to come rescue her and he hadn't. He'd let her down. He fought the lump in his throat. "I didn't know where you were, sweetheart," he finally said.

"I know that now, but—"

"But what?"

"I still thought you'd come."

"I know. And I was looking for you." He lifted her chin and looked her in the eye. "You saved yourself, Amy. I know your panic attacks overwhelm you at times, but you proved something to yourself."

"What?" she whispered.

"That you're clever and smart and strong and that the panic attacks don't define you. You're an overcomer and you're going to be just fine."

She gave him a faint smile. "Like Mandisa's song?"

"Yeah, just like it."

She threw herself into his arms and clung. Wade hugged her and fought the tears that wanted to fall. "Joanna didn't tell me you were going to the youth room because of the misunderstanding, so I had no idea where you were. Which is why I was searching for you." She nodded against his chest. He pushed her back. "Can you tell us what happened in the bathroom?"

Olivia and Katie, who'd been standing quietly just inside the room, moved closer to the bed.

Amy shoved her hair back and looked at them. "I went to the youth room and they were doing the play. Everything was fine until the loud gunshots." She shrugged, but he saw the fine tremor that shook her. "I don't like loud noises."

Wade listened as his daughter recounted the incident, his muscles tightening with each word that rolled from her tongue.

"I prayed, but nothing happened. You didn't come and the lady didn't go away. So I crawled under the last stall and ran for the door. She grabbed my shoulder, but I turned and kicked her. She let go and I got through the door and then went to find you."

Wade hugged her again. "Good job, sweetie. You did great."

"I was really, *really* scared." She sniffed and wiped the tears from her cheeks.

"I know you were." His arms tightened. He couldn't believe she'd managed to control her panic and get away. "God was with you in that situation."

She stuck her lower lip out and shuddered. "Well, I sure didn't feel him."

"But he allowed you to think clearly and do what you had to do to get away, right? Just like what we talked about a minute ago."

She paused, then nodded. "Yes." Another pause. "But I was still scared." She pushed her hair back and shuddered, then froze. "I forgot," she whispered.

"Forgot what?"

"She said I was supposed to give you a message."

Wade stilled. "What message?"

"She said to tell you that Justine was waiting for you," she whispered.

Goosebumps pebbled on his skin. The room stayed silent.

"And then I ran," Amy said. "I thought she was going to kill me." Her voice wobbled.

Wade hugged her close and fought his roiling emotions. Rage at the unknown person had him trembling.

"We're going to make sure you don't have to feel that way again," Olivia said softly. "You're going to have your very own bodyguard. Actually, you'll have two who will take turns watching you."

Amy pulled away from him and looked at Olivia. "Who?"

"Me," Katie said.

"Cool. Who else?"

"A woman named Lizzie. She had to finish up a case she was working on before joining us, but she'll be here tomorrow."

"Is she nice?"

"Very nice. She's got a daughter about your age."

Amy thought about that, then rubbed her nose and looked at Katie. "Just one more question."

"What's that?" Katie moved closer.

"Do *you* like kids?"

"Love them. Especially twelve-year-old girls with beautiful dark hair and eyes."

That got a shaky smile. Amy nodded. "I think we'll get along just fine then."

[19]

Olivia slipped from the room and made her way down to the den. She needed to discuss Justine with Wade and knew that wasn't going to be a fun conversation. She'd wanted to leave that painful topic alone, but now his possible stalker had brought her into this situation.

She pulled her phone from her back pocket. It had buzzed twice while she'd been listening to Amy, but she hadn't wanted to interrupt the girl's story and distract her. She glanced at the screen. Quinn. She called him back. "What's up?" she asked.

"I got that security footage from the church. They have some sweet technology at that place."

"They have a lot of money at that place."

"Hmm. Well, anyway, the footage shows Amy running for the bathroom, her hands clasped over her ears."

"That fits."

"And a short minute later someone enters behind her. I think it's a woman, but it's hard to tell. She has one of those zip-up hoodies on and her hands shoved into her pockets."

"The person in the parking lot of the radio station had on a hoodie," Olivia said.

"This woman's also wearing jeans and tennis shoes and carrying a bag over her shoulder."

"What about the footage of people leaving the bathroom?"

"Got that. We even have a woman coming out with what looks like the same bag. We just need an ID on her."

Olivia frowned. "Okay. Let me know when you know something."

"Of course."

"How's Maddy?"

"The same."

She nodded. "That's better than worse."

"Yeah."

"Thanks, Quinn. Talk to you soon." She hung up and turned to find Wade behind her. "Quinn's got the video footage."

"I heard."

"They're trying to ID a woman who has a bag over her shoulder that looks like the one someone went in with shortly after Amy entered."

"Is she the one who did this?"

"Possibly. That's what they're trying to find out. How's Amy?"

"Still talking to Katie." His shoulders slumped. He moved to sit on the couch, hands clasped between his knees. His head drooped.

"You couldn't have known," she said.

"I should have been more alert." He looked up at her, eyes narrowed.

"No. I should have."

He sighed. "No. She *should* have been fine." He shrugged. "But she wasn't because of a stupid misunderstanding."

"We'll have to make sure misunderstandings don't happen again. Joanna may need to be reminded of the seriousness of the situation. If she's going to be around a lot, we'll have to explain it to her."

"She'll be around. She's a longtime friend. She and Martha are practically inseparable. Kind of like Amy and Stacy. And I think the scene today is reminder enough. She gets it now if she didn't before."

Olivia nodded. "Both Maddy and Haley noted her frequent presence in their notes. Where does she live? I'll request an officer to ride by her place every so often. Even though she hasn't been directly threatened, it might not be a bad idea."

"I'm not sure where she's living right now. She changes addresses about as often as I change my socks."

"Why?"

"She says she likes adventure. And she said it's cheaper to move where the deals are. You know, sign a twelve-month lease, get two months free. A room for rent comes open and she'll move into that for a few months. Then something else will come along and she'll move into that place. That sort of thing. I used to help her move, but finally told her I was done."

"Is that really cheaper?"

"Who knows? It seems to work for her."

"Is she that tight financially?"

He shrugged. "I don't think so. I think she gets bored and needs a change every once in a while. Moving is her way of adding a little excitement to her life, I guess."

"Any men in her life?"

"A new one every couple of months or so. She says she'll settle down when she finds the right guy."

"Interesting."

"Yes. But she's been a friend since high school. A good friend.

She'd do anything for me or Amy or Martha. She's become family."

Olivia nodded. "All right, let's keep going." She paused. "Amy said she doesn't like loud noises. Is that common knowledge?"

He rubbed his chin. "People who know her would know that." He sighed. "I've never tried to hide Amy's anxiety disorder. It's a part of who she is, but it doesn't define her. It's just something we deal with. I even talk about it in some of the speeches I make at different charity functions. I try to let people know that it doesn't matter where you come from or how much money you have in your bank account, we're all together in this thing called life and we need to help one another. It's no secret I'm well off financially, but by using personal stories of hardship and what I'm going through, I'm able to relate to almost anyone." He looked down. "Just because I have money in the bank doesn't make me somehow 'unaffected' or 'untouched' by life."

"I know," she said.

He looked up.

Olivia cleared her throat. "So how would someone change the volume on that movie to blast those gunshots?"

"I suppose someone would just have to get ahold of the remote and crank it up."

She nodded. "Of course. That makes sense. Someone who knew the loud shots would freak out Amy and send her running to the bathroom. Someone who was in the youth room at the time of the movie. Someone who belonged there."

Wade paled. "I'm not liking the direction of your thoughts."

"That whoever is doing this is someone close to you?"

"Yes."

"I don't know that it is, but we have to consider the possibility."

"But it could be someone who sat in on one of the charity dinners and listened to me talk about Amy."

"True." She leaned forward. "But the knowledge that she flees to that particular bathroom when she gets overwhelmed at church—" She pressed her lips together. "We'll investigate every angle and see what comes to light."

"*We'll* investigate?"

"I know I'm not a cop anymore, but I've got friends in high places."

"Right."

"So what's your schedule for the rest of the day?" she asked.

He blinked, not expecting that question. She hadn't brought up Justine yet, but he knew it was coming. Should he go ahead and say something or just wait on her? He'd wait, try to mentally prepare himself for that conversation.

He blew out a sigh. "I would still like to take Amy out on the boat. She loves it and I sort of promised her." He glanced at her. "How would that work security-wise?"

"Might be a nightmare."

"Might be?"

She pinched the bridge of her nose. "Well, on the water, you'd probably be safe. Unless there was a sniper on another boat or on the shore."

"A sniper." He swallowed hard.

"I'd have to get Katie or Haley to go with you."

"Why?"

She lasered him with a fierce look that held a bit of defiance. "I don't do boats or water."

"Really? You can't swim?"

"I can swim, it's not that. Water and I just don't . . . um . . . get along."

"Then I've got a patch you can use if you get sick on the water."

148

"Getting sick is the least of my worries," she muttered. Then sighed. "Let me think about how we can work it."

"Fine, but let's think about it over food. I'm starving." Or at least he was until she brought up the whole sniper thing. But they had to eat. He looked around, then back at her. "How are your culinary skills?"

"The fact that I have forty-two different restaurants listed in my contacts list is one of my crowning achievements."

"Impressive."

She held up her phone. "I think so." She gave him a slight smile. "So what are you in the mood for? Thai? Sushi? Italian? Mexican?"

He gave a low chuckle. "Surprise me. I like everything."

She tapped the screen with her thumb a few times, then lifted the device to her ear. "Chinese it is."

Wade shook his head and swallowed a grin that threatened in spite of everything he and Amy had been through today. The woman intrigued him, he couldn't deny it. He didn't have time for romance or relationship building right now. He had to focus on his family and keeping them safe.

But he was still intrigued.

When she hung up, she stuck the phone in her back pocket and placed her hands on her hips. "It should be ready in about twenty minutes. Katie will be here and I'll go pick it up."

"You could have told them to deliver it."

She lifted a brow. "Not hardly."

He paused and thought about it. "Yeah, I guess that would be a bad idea."

"We just can't take a chance on a call being intercepted and have a fake delivery person show up at your door."

"I get it."

"Good."

"But I'll go with you."

"What? That's not necessary and might even put you in more danger."

"I know."

She simply waited, her brow furrowed.

He sighed. "Look, I understand my father's reasoning in hiring you and your agency. I even appreciate it. But the truth of the matter is, if I stay holed up in this house with massive protection coverage, we're never going to catch the person responsible."

"So you're saying you want to set yourself up as bait and draw the stalker to you and anyone you happen to be with?"

He grimaced. "It sounds stupid when you say it like that." She lifted a brow. He pinched the bridge of his nose. "It *is* stupid, isn't it?" Again she didn't answer. "Of course I don't want to put myself in danger, much less anyone else, but I don't think this person is going away. I don't think I can just wait her out and she'll disappear once she realizes she can't get to me. I have a feeling she will outlast all of us."

"Now that, I'll agree with."

"Which means the only other option is catching her. And no one can do that unless we get her out in the open and are prepared for her."

Olivia gave a slow nod. "I see your point, even understand it."

"Good."

"But that doesn't mean we want to act in a rash manner or move too fast, without thinking through all of the ramifications of doing something like that."

"Okay, then let's work out a plan."

Her phone buzzed again. "Hold that thought." She looked at the screen. "It's Quinn."

"Again?"

"He must have some more information." She pressed the button to answer the call and then put it on speakerphone. "Hello?"

"I've got more on the footage from the church. I'm going to come out there so we can talk and I can show Savage some pictures."

She glanced up at him and he nodded. "Okay. We'll see you when you get here."

"Great."

She started to hang up, then had a flash of brilliance. "Wait!"

"What?"

"Which way are you coming?"

"Up I-85. Why?"

"Stop and get our dinner on your way over here, will you?" She gave him the address. "We'll be waiting for you. I'm anxious to see this footage."

"I'll be there as quick as I can."

"Just don't forget the food. And get extra, please, because I'm not sharing."

[20]

SUNDAY LATE LUNCH

Quinn arrived with brown paper bags filled with tantalizing smells. His partner, Bree, stepped inside with a gallon of tea and a six-pack of Cokes. Olivia gestured to the kitchen. "Thanks for picking it up."

"Not a problem. Do we eat first or watch the video first?" Quinn asked.

"Eat," Olivia said.

"Definitely eat," Wade echoed as he started pulling plates from the cabinet.

Quinn snorted. "I see you share her priorities."

"My stomach definitely does."

Katie stepped into the kitchen. "Should I fix a plate for Amy?"

"I'm already on it," Wade said. He and Quinn opened the boxes. Wade placed a small amount of food in the center of a blue dish. "Is she coming down?"

"I don't think so. She's seems to prefer her room." Katie moved down the line, adding her own food.

LYNETTE EASON

Wade sighed and nodded. "Fine. I'll let her get away with it today."

Katie took the filled plate from him. "I'll be back for drinks."

"I'll bring them up," Olivia offered.

Thirty minutes later, with the small talk finished and Olivia's nerves on edge from waiting, Quinn pulled a laptop from the black bag he'd brought inside. He pushed his plate aside, placed the laptop on the table, and lifted the lid.

Bree rose. "I'm going to do a perimeter search of the house. Any alarms I need to know about?"

Wade told her and she left. He then scooted his chair around beside Quinn. Olivia rose to stand behind the two men so she could see the screen.

Quinn already had the footage pulled up so all he had to do was press play.

The parking lot of the church came up. Quinn pointed. "There's the vehicle, right?"

"Yes." Wade leaned in.

"I've run it forward to this point. Wait until it gets to 10:41."

Olivia watched the clock count. When it reached the time Quinn specified, she narrowed her eyes. "There."

"I see it."

A figure walked past Wade's vehicle. Stopped, then walked back. "Of course she has a baseball hat on," Olivia muttered. Then sucked in a breath. "Wait a minute. That's a male."

Quinn shot her a smug look. "Exactly. You people keep saying 'she.'"

"The person in the parking lot of the radio station was a woman," Olivia said.

"Without a doubt?"

She paused. Thought back to the night she'd found Wade unconscious. Pictured the person dressed in black hovering over

153

him. "No, not without a doubt. I thought it was, just from the way the person moved, but she—he—whoever, had on a black hoodie, a ski mask, and black sweat pants. Nothing form fitting. So, no, I can't say for sure. The 911 operator asked me too, and I couldn't tell her."

"But the person in the bathroom with Amy was a female. We watched the video footage of that. No male person entered that bathroom," Wade said.

They watched more of the video. Quinn pointed again. "There. He's putting the tracking device Katie found on the car. Right under the license plate."

Olivia watched the man slip the GPS device under the plate, stand, pull his baseball cap lower, then shove his hands into his pockets. He strode toward woods just beyond the parking lot and disappeared into the trees.

Olivia blew out a breath. "What color was his hair? Could you tell?"

"Not with this black-and-white footage. It looked dark, but . . ." Quinn shrugged. "He kept his face from the cameras, did you notice that?"

"Yes, I did," Olivia said. "So the hit at the church was planned."

"Looks like it," Quinn agreed. "And whoever planned it knew the schedule. Knew the play that was going on, knew how to get to the remote and crank up the volume, knew that Amy would head to that particular restroom."

Olivia shook her head. "I *really* don't like this."

"And I *really* don't blame you." Quinn clicked a few keys on the computer. "But the good news is, we found the woman carrying the bag from the bathroom. She claims she found it in one of the stalls and took it to the lost and found."

"You believe her?"

"Yes, we checked her out and she's clean. She keeps the nursery and was in there the whole time except for the bathroom break after the service, according to the other two ladies working with her. We went to get the bag, but it had been claimed."

"By whom?"

"We don't know. And yes, we asked about cameras on that hall, but the one covering the lost and found wasn't working."

"Wasn't working or was sabotaged?" Wade muttered.

"Wasn't working. We asked. Apparently it's been down for about two weeks and just hasn't been fixed yet."

"She knew that too," Olivia murmured. "She set up her entire plan around that broken lost-and-found camera."

Quinn nodded. "It's possible. Take a look at this." The video played. "There's Amy running down the hall."

Olivia heard Wade's indrawn breath and felt the renewed tension in his body. She knew he was feeling the anguish of his inability to help his daughter. Behind the others' backs, she gave his shoulder a slight squeeze, then let go, immediately appalled at her less than professional behavior. Yet, curious too. She wanted to comfort him.

"There." Quinn pointed. "That's the woman following behind Amy."

"I guess it's a woman," Wade said. "Medium height; short, shaggy hair; hoodie. She . . . he . . . is thin and wearing loose clothing." He let out a disgusted grunt. "I can't tell."

Olivia leaned closer. "Whoever it is, the person dressed to be on camera."

"Amy thought it was a woman because everything happened in the women's bathroom," Wade said. "But what if it was a man?"

"Compare the time stamp of the person in the bathroom to the person putting the GPS tracker on Wade's vehicle," Olivia said.

Quinn did. "Well, look at that. Everything's going down at the same time."

"You know what this means, don't you?" Olivia said.

"No. What?" Wade asked, turning to look at her.

"It's possible you don't have *a* stalker."

"I don't?" Wade frowned, confused.

"No. You might have a *team*."

Wade flinched. "What are you talking about?"

"I think the woman in the video—and I think it is a woman in spite of her efforts to disguise herself—is the one who's stalking you." Olivia rushed to say, "But it looks like she's enlisted help. I don't see how it could be just a simple coincidence that someone goes after Amy in the bathroom while someone else goes after Wade's vehicle in the parking lot. They've got to be working together."

"I definitely don't think it's a coincidence, therefore I have to wonder," Quinn said.

"Wonder what?" Wade sighed.

Quinn's eyes met Olivia's before he answered Wade. "That maybe this is more than just a simple stalker situation. Isn't that what you're thinking, Liv?"

"Yes." She looked at Wade. "Any ideas?"

Wade pinched the bridge of his nose. "No. I mean, what more could it be?" He sighed. "I don't know anything anymore. I just want it to stop."

Olivia pursed her lips. "I know."

Quinn took a call and exited as Bree slipped into the room and took her seat at the table. "All looks quiet out there. The officer on duty said he hasn't seen anyone or anything to set off his alarm bells."

"Good," Wade said. He tapped his fingers together and sighed. "Should I cancel my appointments for tomorrow?"

Olivia glanced at Bree, who nodded.

Wade pulled his phone from his pocket. "I'll call Linda."

"Your administrative assistant," Olivia said. "Maddy mentioned her too."

"She's great. The office would fall apart without her." He dialed the number he kept on speed dial.

"Hello?"

"Hi, Linda." Linda Birch had worked with him since he and his partner had opened the practice.

"Wade, how are you? I talked to Cameron and he told me what happened. I wanted to call, but didn't want to interrupt anything."

"Everything is pretty calm for now." He paused. "You know all of my clients."

"Yes."

"Can you think of any one that stands out as particularly . . . um . . . stalker-ish?"

"Stalker-ish?"

He could feel Bree and Olivia's attention centered on him. "Yes."

Linda hesitated. "No, not offhand. I mean, you've worked with some pretty *intense* people, but I can't think of anyone that's shown undue interest in you. Not like you would think a stalker would." She cleared her throat. "Except for those gifts that were left here. And then it was only the two."

"Right. Well, if you think of anyone, will you let me know?"

"Of course."

"And cancel my appointments tomorrow. I think my first one was at nine."

"I'll take care of it."

"Thanks." He hung up and found Bree and Olivia watching him. He shrugged. "Linda couldn't think of anyone." He stood. "I'm going to check on Amy." He wasn't worried about her physical state, but he was very concerned about her emotional one.

A knock on the front door startled him. He moved to answer it, only to find Olivia had moved faster. She pushed aside the sheer curtain, her hand on her weapon. Then he saw her relax. "It's your father."

She opened the door and his dad stepped inside. "Just thought I'd stop by and see what kind of progress is being made."

Bruce didn't know about the incident at the church yet and Wade wasn't in the mood to rehash it. "I was just going upstairs to check on Amy. You want to go with me?"

"Sure." He frowned. "Is she all right?"

Wade gave a quiet sigh. So, rehashing it was on the agenda. "Not really. Come on, I'll give you the abridged version." They climbed the stairs together. He felt Olivia's eyes on his back. If they were lasers, he'd be see-through. He knew she was concerned, but he needed a break. From everything. And everyone except his family.

She didn't stop his ascent and he figured she might understand a bit of what he was going through.

The rage at the person terrorizing his family hadn't diminished one bit. And while he kept it under control, he could feel it simmering, boiling, growing.

Ready to be unleashed as soon as he had a target.

Olivia watched the two men disappear around the corner at the top of the stairs. She could hear Wade telling his father about the incident at the church. She had to admit she and her agency were looking incompetent. If she were Bruce, she'd fire them all and hire someone else.

The whole situation made her frown.

"What is it?" Katie asked from the top of the stairs.

"Just thinking."

"About?"

"About the fact that if I were Bruce Savage, I'd fire us."

Katie lifted a brow. "Yeah." She started down the stairs. Voices from the kitchen floated to Olivia even as her brain struggled to figure out this complex problem of keeping the Savage family safe from an invisible enemy.

"Wade has a charity event Thursday night," Olivia said.

"Another dinner." Katie reached the bottom and stopped in front of Olivia.

"Yes. Just the very idea of it makes me want to break out in hives."

"There's no way he'll give up going," Katie said.

"I know." She pursed her lips. "I'm missing something," she said softly.

"What?"

"I don't know. If I knew, I wouldn't be missing it."

Katie rolled her eyes. "So what's the plan for now?"

"We've already established that this person—or persons—who are after Wade know him well."

"Yes. She . . . he . . . whoever . . . knew he'd most likely be at church this morning."

"And planned ahead of time. She moved easily within the church. No one thought it strange that she—or the guy helping her—was in the youth room. They didn't stand out and that worries me." She rubbed her nose. "I want background checks done again on all of his family. The people at the radio station. Even the church members."

Katie bit her lip. "Do you know how long that will take?"

"Yes. But I'm willing to bet that whoever is stalking him is a member of that church. She knew the camera on the lost-and-found hallway wasn't working. She also knew if she left a bag in the bathroom, someone would turn it in. She was probably hanging out watching the whole time. As soon as the bag was turned in, she simply picked it up and slipped out."

Katie nodded. "That makes sense. But even if we come up with someone who might be after Wade, it'll take effort to prove it."

"I know. Start with the staff and volunteers first." Olivia narrowed her eyes. "Have Angela talk to some of the people in the youth room. See if she can get a list of names of all the people around the video equipment. We'll check them all out and see if we pull out any skeletons."

"Okay."

"Also, there was a woman this morning who was very flirtatious with Wade. Erin Abbott. I'd be interested to know more about her."

"I'll put her on the list. What about the sister-in-law, Martha?" Katie asked with a lowered voice and a glance toward the empty doorway.

Olivia nodded. "I've wondered about her, but her background is clean, and this morning she was in the service when the craziness went down."

"Plus, she's lived with him all this time, why start stalking him now?"

Olivia shrugged. "You never know about someone. We'll keep an eye on her and keep looking."

"Although if the stalker isn't Martha, why doesn't his stalker consider her a threat? Seems to me she'd be the first one to get rid of."

"That's a good point," Olivia said, "but there have been no threats against her."

"Then the stalker *knows* she's not a threat and isn't worried about her *being* one?"

"Could be."

"And the friend? Joanna?"

"Same story."

"So it's someone who knows Wade well enough to also know that she doesn't have to worry about Martha and Joanna being competition for his affection."

"That's the way it appears."

Katie snorted. "We all know appearances can be deceiving." She pulled in a deep breath and blew it out slowly. "Anything on the caller Quinn and Bree were trying to track down?"

"No. Nothing yet."

"So, who are we looking at as a primary suspect?"

Olivia almost smiled. You could take the girl out of the job, but once a cop, always a cop. "*We* aren't looking at anyone. Quinn and Bree are going to go after the caller who calls two or three times during Wade's show."

"When are they going to talk to her?"

"As soon as she gets back into town."

"And until then?"

"We keep our eyes and ears open and Wade and his family safe."

"How do you propose to do that?" Wade asked from the doorway.

"A number of different ways. But first I need knowledge. Knowledge is power and I think some things have been left . . . unsaid."

He shot her a wary glance. "What things?"

"The elephant in the room."

"Which is?"

"Justine."

[21]

Wade flinched. "What about her?"

Katie nodded to the stairs. "I'm going to check on Amy."

She left and Olivia sighed. "I read the notes, the background that was done on you when we took this assignment from your father. I know she's a painful subject for you."

"Yes. She is."

"But whoever was in that bathroom with Amy wanted *you* to know that *she* knew about Justine."

He nodded. "It's not a secret. Her death was in the paper, the gossip column—along with pictures of us taken at various charity events." Tension threaded through him, tightening the already tight muscles at the base of his neck. "The media hounded me for weeks until something new came along to snag their interest."

"When you're a high-profile personality trying to fly under the radar—" Grief flashed in her eyes and Wade knew she was thinking about her friend, Shana. "I remember seeing the news reports," she said, "but didn't pay a whole lot of attention to it."

"Justine committed suicide six months into our relationship."

Saying the words brought a fresh wave of grief. And guilt. How had he missed the signs?

"Do you know why?"

He shook his head. "No. That one little word 'why' haunts me, but I'm having to take to heart the advice I give to people. To those who've had a loved one commit suicide."

"What's that?"

"Don't ask why. Unless they've left a detailed note, the only person who knows why is gone. Instead, live your life doing your best to make a difference, to share that there is hope and suicide isn't the answer. Clinging to God when life crashes around you is what you do, no matter how bad you want out."

Olivia blinked and her throat tightened. His words were affecting her, making her want to know more about the faith that he clearly had. "Is that what you're doing? Clinging to God?"

"Yes. And, of course, doing my best to utilize the resources he's provided."

"Such as?"

He gave her a faint smile. "You and your agency for one."

"Ah." He had a good point. One she'd have to think about. She moved on. "Justine didn't leave a note?"

"She did. Or rather, I got a text." He closed his eyes for a moment. When he opened them, he stared at his hands clasped in his lap. "'I'm sorry, Wade,'" he quoted, "'but life is just too much. I can't keep going on like this. Tell Amy I'm sorry too. I love you both and will miss you.'"

"That's it?"

"That's it."

"As soon as I read it, I raced over there and . . . found her. She'd shot herself."

Olivia frowned. "I didn't realize you were the one who found her. I'm so sorry."

"I am too."

They stayed silent for a short minute, then Olivia tilted her head and looked at him. "That text doesn't say much."

"Says a lot, as far as I'm concerned. It says I didn't know her at all." He pulled out his phone and tapped a few buttons. He passed the device over to her and she read the text. He'd quoted it verbatim.

"You kept the text."

"I can't bring myself to delete it." He took the phone back and stared at it. "I guess I think if I look at it enough times, at some point it will say something different." He gave a self-deprecating smile and shook his head. "I don't know. I think it just still shocks me that I can't text her back. Deleting the text is like saying goodbye for good."

"I understand. You'll delete it when you're ready."

"And maybe there's some guilt involved too." He snorted. "Not maybe. There *is* guilt."

"Guilt?"

He nodded. "I never saw it. Never picked up on one sign that she was depressed or suicidal. Sure, she was tired some days and other days she cried over what she had to deal with at work." He cleared his throat. "But she'd found her stress relievers and I thought they worked for her."

"I'll come back to the stressors in her job in a moment. Let me clarify a few things. You dated her for six months."

He nodded, then shrugged. "Well, we started out as friends. We actually only dated for about four months." He cleared his throat. "We talked about getting married only because it would benefit us both, not because we were in love."

Olivia lifted a brow. "Okay. How would the marriage have benefited you?"

Heat rose in his neck. "That didn't come out right. It wasn't as coldhearted as I've made it sound." How did he explain without sounding . . . arrogant?

"That question makes you uncomfortable."

He rubbed his eyes. "I don't know how to word the explanation."

"Just do your best, I won't judge."

Her blue eyes held sympathy. And curiosity. He sighed. "Do you read magazines? Like entertainment ones?"

"Sometimes."

"I was on the cover of one not too long ago." He named the popular magazine title and she nodded. "I was in Los Angeles promoting the charity. There were some pretty big names in attendance, celebrities who knew my mother, politicians," he waved a hand as though dismissing their perceived importance, "but for some reason, the reporter focused in on me. Got a picture and slapped it on the cover of the magazine. There was also a shot of my mother holding me when I was about six months old. The article talked about Lucy Savage's son hitting it big or something like that. It also talked about my practice, the radio show, the fact that my father had moved us across the country, and how we'd dropped off the Hollywood radar, but wondered if Wade Savage would follow in his mother's footsteps." He shrugged. "It was a mess for a while. I had reporters camped out on my lawn. Then it all died down when my life stayed pretty boring."

"But?"

Again he felt the heat in his neck. "But I had women coming from everywhere, introducing themselves in the grocery store, following me home from work, camping out at the radio station." He rolled his eyes. "It was ridiculous. But once I met Justine and people put us together as a couple, most of that faded. But neither Justine or I were interested in marriage. She'd come out of an abusive one and planned to stay single the rest of her life. I have a daughter to raise and—" He looked away, gathering his thoughts. "But . . . Justine wanted to get into politics and she needed that picture-perfect family to woo voters. Being a part of my family would carry some weight."

"So you decided to marry, but you didn't love her." Her soft statement pierced him and he couldn't respond for a moment.

"No, I didn't love her," he finally said, "not the way a wife deserves to be loved. I was attracted to her. She was a beautiful woman inside and out, but—" he shrugged—"I think we'd both been too wounded by past relationships to let ourselves love fully and deeply." He shook his head. "I regret that, although, who knows? In time, we may have learned to do that. Unfortunately, she chose to cut her time short." A muscle jumped in his jaw and he did his best to relax. "Amy loved her and Justine loved Amy." He rubbed his hands on his thighs. "Our relationship wasn't built on romantic love, but we respected one another and thought we could make the marriage work for the benefit of all of us."

"How did you meet?"

"She came to one of my charity functions. She was a child psychiatrist, specializing in pediatric trauma cases. She worked a lot with the police and the children in foster care."

Olivia blew out a low breath. "Okay, now I understand what you meant by she'd be upset about what she had to deal with. I'm sure that was very hard on her emotionally."

"Very." His brows dipped. "But like I said, she seemed to handle it well. She knew she had to do something to process everything she saw on a daily basis. She was very athletic, worked out, jogged, did some kickboxing—and taught Sunday school to children who weren't traumatized by life. I could hardly keep up with her. She said all the activity was her stress reliever."

Olivia nodded. "I do the same thing. It does help for sure."

"So when she shot herself—" His throat tightened around the words. He cleared it. "When she shot herself, it was a huge shock. To everyone who knew her."

"She was shot with her own gun?"

"Yes, it came back registered to her." He shook his head. "I didn't know she even owned a gun."

"When was it purchased?"

"The week before she died." He laced his fingers together and studied them. "The police said she must have been planning it for a while."

Olivia frowned. "And the autopsy supported the suicide report." It wasn't a question. Just more of a statement as she thought through what he was telling her.

His frown deepened. "Of course. Why?"

Olivia stood and paced in front of the mantel. "Why would your stalker bring up Justine? To Amy especially?"

"She said it was a message, remember?"

"Exactly. But what kind of message?"

He blinked. "I don't know. I haven't had a chance to process it, but maybe she's trying to play with my mind? Get to me on a psychological level?"

"Maybe."

"But?"

"What if Justine's suicide . . . wasn't?"

"Wasn't—" He stared at her. "But if it wasn't suicide, you're talking . . ."

"Murder."

[22]

Olivia could tell the idea that someone murdered Justine was almost too much for him to take in. But she knew that, in a strange way, he found it more palatable than the fact that she would have chosen to take her own life.

Wade kept his head down as he worked on the boat inside the boathouse. Olivia stood well away from the edge of the water, watching him. She knew he was thinking. Analyzing her theory about Justine. Every once in a while she'd walk to the door and step outside. She noticed he never looked up when she came back in. "Wade, you really need to be more aware."

"Of what?"

"Of someone coming up behind you. I've left and come back twice and you never even looked up."

"That's because I knew it was you."

"How?"

"By the way you walk. You have a very distinct soft-sounding step."

"No I don't," she scoffed. At his raised brow, she paused, curious. "I do? Really?"

"Really." He grinned—not a big grin and not one filled with joy, but at least it was better than the grim face he'd been wearing. Though she could hardly blame him for it.

"Will you tell me about your wife?" The grin faded and she almost regretted the question.

He stopped what he was doing and stared at her. "What do you want to know?"

"What was she like?"

He shrugged. "We met in high school. She was popular, always the life of the party." He looked up and she saw his mind go back in time. "She was pretty." He glanced at her. "And she knew it."

"Ah. One of those."

"Yeah. But I was a jock and arrogant. We were made for each other. Together we were such a cliché."

"Clichés happen for a reason."

"True." He shook his head. "High school was a blast. We did the whole partying, drinking thing. Some recreational drugs and never got caught, never suffered any consequences. No one died, nothing bad happened. Pamela and I got a marriage license the day after graduation and had a local pastor marry us. Pamela's parents freaked. I thought my dad would write me out of the will, but we both started college in the fall and I think our parents were actually shocked. Then Pamela got pregnant." He dropped his head and closed his eyes for a brief moment. "She was furious. Wanted to have an abortion. I told her if she did, we were done." He cleared his throat. "You have to understand, after she got pregnant, she let me know quite plainly that she didn't marry me because she loved me, she loved my money and my ability to show her a good time and she relished the status of being a Savage."

"Oh Wade, I'm so sorry."

"It hurt. I won't try to shrug it off and say it was okay. It wasn't. I was . . . crushed. But I wanted our baby. I convinced her that she'd wind up with nothing if she had an abortion."

"So she had the baby."

"Yes." His hands clenched into fists. "And it wasn't long after that she was back to partying, drinking—gone all the time. She failed her second semester of college. I rarely saw her. But Amy's birth changed me. She was just . . . perfect in every way. I loved her from the moment I saw her, and I vowed to be the best dad I could be so she would have an amazing life."

Olivia's heart flipped, her attraction for the man growing with the visual he created. "How did you manage?"

"Dad helped a lot. He was determined I was going to finish college and he hired a sitter for Amy since Pamela couldn't be counted on to actually take care of her child. It wasn't too long after Amy's first birthday that Pamela disappeared completely. Dad tracked her down and found her living with another guy, hooked on drugs. He got her out and got her in a rehab center."

"Where were her parents during all of this?"

"They'd written her off and moved to Europe to be near their son who's in the military."

"What happened when she got out of rehab?"

"She went to see Joanna. The two got drunk. Pamela stole Joanna's car and drove it off a cliff."

Olivia let out a slow breath. She'd read his wife had died in a car wreck that had been ruled an accident while driving under the influence. "How awful."

"Yes, it was a dark time. If I hadn't had Amy and my dad, I probably wouldn't have made it. After that, I turned back to my faith, finished my degree, and went on to medical school." He sighed and rubbed a hand through his hair. "Okay, enough of that. Let's get this boat on the water."

Haley was up at the house with Amy, and Olivia knew the girl was eager to get on the boat. However, Olivia couldn't stop the niggling concern inside her. Wade grabbed a case of bottled waters and one of soda and headed down below deck. When he came back up the stairs, Olivia paced to the windows, looked out to see nothing alarming, then back to Wade. "How often do you take the boat out?"

"Just about every weekend when it's warm enough. Why?"

"You sure like that boat, don't you?" she asked him.

"Of course. Why the questions?"

"And the water."

"Yep," he said, sounding a bit exasperated. He stepped onto the dock and studied her. "Why?"

"Would you change your plans if I asked you to?" she asked.

He paused and planted his hands on his hips. "Maybe. Change them in what way?"

"I want you to do something different. You did the radio show and almost got blown up. You went to church this morning and look what happened."

He rubbed his chin. "You think something will happen if I take the boat out this afternoon?"

"I have no way of knowing. I know you promised Amy you'd go and she's expecting it, but what if you told her she could skip school tomorrow and you would take her out on the lake instead? Do you think the change would cause a panic attack?"

"If it's a change she likes, then no, it wouldn't cause an attack." He let out a low laugh. "Yeah, she'd probably go for that. Missing school is pretty high on her list of favorite things to do." He shrugged. "All right. Missing one day won't hurt her. Sure, I'll tell her." She blinked at his easy acceptance of the idea and he laughed, then sobered. "I haven't made being my bodyguard an easy task, have I?"

"No."

"I'm sorry."

She gave a faint smile. "It's all part of the job."

He wiped his hands on a towel hanging from a nail in the wall. "All right, let's go tell my daughter I'm allowing her to play hooky."

Amy took the news well. In fact, she went straight to her phone to text Stacy and let her know she wouldn't be in school on Monday. Wade motioned for Olivia to join him in the den. When they were both seated, he leaned forward. "Tell me more about yourself."

She lifted a brow. "I've already told you I grew up in foster homes. What more do you want to know?"

"Where did you grow up?"

"Here in Greenville."

"Did you always want to be a bodyguard?"

"No." She stood. "Look, this is pointless. You're a client. I'll lay down my life to keep you safe, but my personal life is off-limits."

Wade stiffened. "I see. Very well." He stood. "I guess I'll just go get some work done. Let me know if there's any sign of trouble."

Immediate remorse filled Olivia. "Wade, I'm—"

He held up a hand. "I get it, Olivia. I'm a client." He turned on his heel and left the room.

Frustration pinched her hard and she was appalled at herself. He'd just spilled his guts to her about his wife and she'd just snipped the bond that had been growing between them. All because he'd gotten too close before she'd realized it. But he hadn't wanted to hear her apology and she didn't really blame him. Her phone buzzed, interrupting her self-chastisement. It was a text from Katie:

Katie
Checking in.

Olivia
All is quiet for now. See you at midnight.

Her phone rang. Haley. "Hey."

"Can you talk?"

"Sure." Going after Wade to apologize probably wasn't a good idea. "What do you have?"

"Erin Abbott. I gave her name to Angela, who worked her magic. Mrs. Abbott is clean as far as any criminal past. She works as a nurse at the hospital, single mom of three whose husband ran out on her a couple years ago. Kids are four, nine, and twelve. Dates occasionally, but nothing serious according to a co-worker. She's good at her job, but has seemed kind of out of it lately."

"Out of it?"

"Tired, forgetful, scattered. She hasn't messed up at work, but the co-worker described her as stressed."

"Okay, well, she's a full-time single mom with three young kids, full-time demanding job, no support from her ex . . . yeah, I can see how trying to juggle it all would be stressful. I sure couldn't do it. I'd be forgetful and scattered, not to mention probably ready for a straitjacket."

"For sure. But here's another thing. She wasn't at any conference this weekend."

Olivia stopped mid-pace. "She wasn't? Where was she?"

"Her credit card said she was staying at the Marriott downtown."

"Well, now," Olivia said softly. "That puts a different spin on things, doesn't it?"

"A bit."

"Was she with anyone?"

"Not anyone that's listed as being in the room with her."

"But anyone could have come and stayed and no one at the hotel would know anything about it."

"Of course. But she was a busy little thing. She had a massage, ate at the hotel restaurant on Friday night, ordered room service for Saturday breakfast and dinner, used the manicure services, and had the Do Not Disturb sign on her door the entire time."

"Did she eat with anyone at the hotel?"

"No one seems to remember. I did check her phone records. She had no phone calls going out from her cell phone the entire weekend."

Olivia thought about everything Haley had just told her. "She took the weekend off."

"What?"

"She checked out of her life and into the hotel. She had her phone off and spent the entire weekend pampering herself."

"So you don't think she was with anyone?"

Did she? "I don't know. It sounds to me that she needed a break and arranged one."

"Possibly. Or she was setting everything up to give herself an alibi when she went after Wade."

"True. And she could have used a throwaway cell phone for the weekend. A burner phone or something."

"Possibly. I also checked the station's calls received against her numbers since we had permission to get the phone logs. For the past couple months, Erin's landline number showed up every weekend with three or four calls each night Wade was doing the show. Her cell phone number just a few times. But not this past weekend."

"My, my, now that is interesting. Okay. She was at church

this morning. Why don't we pass this information on to Quinn and see what he can come up with."

"I'll do that."

"Thanks for the update."

"Of course. Talk soon."

Olivia disconnected the call and let her mind sort through the information. So Erin Abbott had lied about attending a conference. Why? So she could stay home and stalk Wade? A sense of satisfaction filled Olivia. Finally, they might be on to something. Wade deserved to be free of this nightmare.

She thought about all he'd been through, his love for his daughter, his generosity with his sister-in-law, and his respect for his father. Most of all she thought about the way his eyes gentled when they landed on her or the spark that flared between them whenever they came in contact.

Lashing out had been mean, but it had also been an act of self-preservation. Getting involved with a client had never been an issue with her, so her attraction to Wade had completely thrown her. She wasn't used to that and didn't know how to handle it. Obviously.

With Wade, she knew it was going to be hard to resist temptation if he was interested in starting . . . something. And from the looks he was sending her, he was interested.

In the kitchen, Olivia checked the door once again.

"Everything all right in here?" Martha asked from the doorway.

Olivia nodded. "Just fine."

"I'm going to say good night to Wade, then head up to my apartment. You need anything?"

"No. Thanks."

Martha nodded.

"Before you leave, do you mind if I ask you a question?"

"No, I don't mind."

"You've known Wade a long time."

"I have." She looked wary. "Why?"

"Can you think of anyone who might be causing him all of these problems? Anyone from his past? A girl he dumped, someone at church? Anyone at all?"

Martha tucked a strand of stray hair behind her ear and the wariness morphed into thoughtfulness. "I truly can't," she said softly. "Wade is like his dad in a lot of ways. He's kind, will talk to anyone, generous to a fault." She shook her head. "You know Cameron Short?"

"Yes. The director of the charity."

Martha nodded. "His wife was sick a few years ago with cancer. Brain cancer." She clucked her tongue. "Nasty stuff. It was hard on Cameron. He loved her so much. You can imagine, the bills were astronomical. Wade and his father paid them off. Every last one of them."

"You're right," Olivia murmured. "That's incredibly generous."

"That's just one example of the good this family does. So, yes, I think women would be drawn to that. Could be obsessed with it, even. But I can't for the life of me think of someone who would do this." She shook her head.

Olivia smiled. "Thank you for telling me."

Martha shrugged. "It's not like it's a secret."

A noise caught Olivia's attention. She walked over to the window, stood to the side, and flipped the plantation shutter blinds open a fraction. When her gaze met equally surprised dark eyes, she bit back a yelp.

She heard Martha's startled exclamation as Olivia bolted for the door.

[23]

Wade stepped into the den and stopped. Turned and found Martha coming from the kitchen.

He glanced behind her. "Where did Olivia go?" Immediately her pretty face came to mind, the way she'd worked to find a way out of the radio station, her determination to save them. Her expression as she put him firmly in his place.

Martha's frown deepened. "She's outside." She glanced at the clock on the mantel. "Has been for the past fifteen minutes or so."

He stiffened. "What? Why?"

"She thought she heard or saw something at the window and went to look."

"Fifteen minutes ago? Saw something at the window? Why didn't you come get me?"

"I didn't want you to worry. You've had to deal with so much . . . I was just trying to protect you. And besides, I was standing right there and didn't see anything but a shadow. It could have been anything and is probably nothing."

"I don't need that kind of protecting." He changed direction and headed for the front door.

"Wait a minute, Wade. You can't go out there. What if it's your stalker?"

He paused. "What if it is and she's found a way to slit Olivia's throat too, Martha? I can't hide out in here when Olivia might need help." He opened the door and stepped onto the front porch.

Olivia could hear Katie through the Bluetooth device inserted into her ear. She stood at the edge of the trees that had been strategically planted to offer a semblance of privacy in the backyard. The black fence that she knew was on the other side of the trees blended with the night.

Automatic lights had come on when she'd walked in front of the sensors, which made her believe no one was in the back. And yet she'd seen someone staring at her through the kitchen window. Or had she just imagined it? Granted it had been a blink-of-an-eye moment, but she had to check it out.

"Katie? Where are you?" she asked, her voice low, almost nonexistent.

"Pulling up to the front," Katie said. "So far all is clear from where I am."

"All clear in the back as well. The officer watching the front didn't see anything either. He's looking too."

Olivia moved along the edge of the perimeter. She was now out of range of the sensor for the floodlights and they'd clicked off. She paused and turned her back to the side of the house, backing up until she felt the brick. She paused and considered the lights again while she waited for her eyes to adjust to the sudden darkness.

Had the lights clicked on when she was in the house and she hadn't noticed? Had the person at the kitchen window just done what she had? Waited for the lights to go off, then moved to the window?

With her back against the side of the house, the area in front of her was bathed in darkness.

She stayed still, ears tuned to the area.

"Liv?"

"Just a second," she whispered.

"Wade's coming down the front porch."

"What?" Olivia froze.

"He just disappeared around the north side of the house, probably coming your way. I've parked and am going to follow him."

"What is he thinking?" she hissed. She moved quickly yet silently, hoping to intercept him before whatever possible danger that was outside got him.

She heard footsteps coming her way. She pulled her weapon as a precaution. It could be Wade. It could be Katie. It could be someone else. She took a deep breath. "I've called for backup!"

She moved fast, away from her current location, expecting to hear the blast of a gun and feel the air broken by the whine of a bullet. She heard nothing except retreating footsteps. Her statement about backup seemed to send the person running. She kept her Bluetooth on. "Katie?" she whispered. "Location?"

"Eyes on the client."

"Stay with him. Call for backup, I'm going after her."

"He's headed your way. I am too."

Olivia bit her tongue on a few choice words that wanted to escape. She held them back with surprising effort. Ever since her foster mother had gently told her real ladies didn't cuss, she'd done her best to make the woman happy. Wade was the first client who tempted her to renege on her promise to keep her language clean.

The figure slipped down the sloping hill toward the lake. She was in the open for a brief minute and then disappeared behind the boathouse. Olivia kept going, not liking the exposure at all, but she wasn't sure the person knew she was following her. And she wasn't sure where the person thought she was going. The boathouse ended at the water. Olivia used the concrete walkway instead of the grass.

She picked up the pace and came to where the intruder disappeared. She kept her weapon ready, aimed toward the sky, as she moved to the edge of the building. She peeked around the corner and could see pretty much nothing, even though she could hear the water lapping against the sides of the structure. No lights came on. Her nerves danced. Had someone disabled the sensors she'd just had installed on the boathouse? Her heart pounded in her throat, but the calm, clearheaded coolness she always felt on the job was there.

Olivia made her way down the wooden dock attached to the boathouse. Mentally, she pictured the layout. At the end of the dock was the water. The rest of the structure housed three boat slots. There was nowhere to go at the end of the dock. If she turned right, there was a bit more dock, then the power doors that would open for the boats to glide in. But there was no way to cross to the other side of the dock without getting in the water.

Which she had no intention of doing. She shuddered and focused on developing a plan. So unless the person took a swim, Olivia should have her trapped just ahead and hiding around the corner of the building with the water in front of her, the water to the right and left of her. Cornered.

Or was she? There was no way to know if someone waited in

the darkness beyond. The moon tossed shadows in a haphazard manner. She took a deep breath and planted her back against the building. She listened and could hear faint commotion up near the house.

But no more sounds from the person she'd been chasing. Olivia had no choice. She moved on silent feet to the end of the dock, brought her weapon down to eye level, and rounded the corner.

Only to find it empty. Her breath whooshed out. The woman had gone into the water.

But had she attempted to swim cross the lake? Or had she ducked under the boathouse door and come up on the other side? Was she now inside the boathouse?

Olivia swallowed hard. Only one way to find out. She retraced her steps back down the dock to the grassy area and slipped across to the front door. She placed her hand on the knob. It was wet.

Movement to her left. She ducked.

A quiet *swish* near her ear and then a heavy *thunk* next to her. She swiveled in time to see the person disappear into the treeline at the edge of the property.

She gripped her weapon, but didn't fire it. She had no identifiable target and she wanted to know without a doubt who or what she would hit when she pulled the trigger.

"Katie?" Olivia whispered.

"I'm here. Told Wade to get back inside but he ignored me. He's coming down the hill now. Stay alert and don't shoot him. I'm near the trees on the west side of the property. I think I saw some movement."

"You did. She's closer to you now. See if you can grab her. I'll take care of Wade."

"Copy that."

She stopped talking and just listened while she tried to look for any movement, any shadow that shouldn't be a shadow.

A noise beside her made her spin and drop to the ground even as she lifted her weapon.

"Olivia? Are you all right?"

Wade stood next to the corner of the boathouse. He raised his hands, the flashlight he gripped now pointed toward the sky. She lowered the muzzle of the gun at the ground. Fury rose hot and swift, churning the acid in her stomach. She swallowed once. Twice. Filtered her words as she rose to her feet. "Are you *trying* to get yourself killed?"

"No. Are you?"

"What?"

He nodded to the ground and aimed the flashlight on the object at their feet. "Someone just threw a knife at you."

[24]

Olivia released a breath and let some of her anger go with it. "Katie?" she spoke into her Bluetooth. "Did you find her in the trees?"

"No. He . . . she . . . whoever . . . was just gone. It was a little freaky actually."

Freaky? "Gone? How?"

"I had her in my sights, she vanished into a cluster of trees, and then she wasn't there. I searched, but came up with nothing."

Olivia's blood chilled. "We need to do a sweep of the houses nearby."

"There are no houses nearby."

True. The houses were spread out, each piece of property ranging in size from eight to ten acres. "Nevertheless, we need to alert the neighbors. She could be making her way to one, and if she finds a house unlocked and enters . . ."

"Yes. Or she could have gone into the water."

Olivia grimaced. "Keep searching, I'm calling Quinn." She hung up and dialed Quinn, who answered on the first ring. "I need you here." She paused. "And a crime scene tech. She threw her knife at me, maybe we'll get a print. She also touched the doorknob to the boathouse, but so did I, so I probably smeared any prints there."

"Everyone all right?" Quinn asked.

"Fine for now."

"You plan to go back to boring anytime in the near future?"

"ASAP. See you soon." She hung up and assessed the situation.

The intruder had run to the end of the dock, slipped into the water, up under the electric door, and out the other side of the boathouse. She had taken a chance on throwing the knife at Olivia and leaving evidence behind. What had she hoped to gain? Time? A chance to escape? Probably. And she'd gotten what she wanted.

Olivia held on to the anger that burned a path from her stomach to her throat, and looked at a still silent Wade. "Go back in the house. I don't want you out here where you're a target." She looked back at the fence, her tension an almost tangible thing.

He shook his head. "I was worried about you. Martha said you'd been out here for almost fifteen minutes and that you thought you saw someone in the window." He ran a hand over his face. "I kept thinking about Maddy and—" He broke off and looked away.

Olivia felt her anger dissipating and found herself strangely touched at his concern. She frowned and instead of snapping at him again, made sure to keep her tone even. "This is what I'm trained for, Wade, I don't think you've allowed yourself to accept that. But you need to let me do my job. Now go in the house. Check on Martha and the girls. I don't want to leave this evidence and I can watch you enter the back door from here."

He shook his head. "I'll wait here with you."

Olivia pulled in a deep breath and stopped her prayerful plea for patience before it slipped out. "Wade—"

"She's gone."

"She could come back. She could have a rifle with a scope and a bead on your head at this very moment." Olivia didn't bother to keep the resurrected anger from her voice. She blinked. What was wrong with her? She didn't act this way. She was a professional and stayed cool no matter what. Yet Wade's stubbornness raked over her nerves like fingernails on a chalkboard.

He studied her, then looked back at the knife. "I wasn't the one she threw the knife at."

Olivia paused. Looked down at the weapon. He had a point. Sirens in the distance caught her attention. Finally. "She only threw it at me because I was the one after her. She didn't know you were being stubborn and refusing to stay inside where it was safe. Otherwise I feel sure her aim would have taken a different direction."

He tilted his head. "Okay. If you say so."

Katie's voice came through her earpiece. "It's all clear in the front. The officers are arriving. Quinn's here too, as well as Haley. I explained to Quinn about the need for a house-to-house search. I think it's a long shot, but he's putting together the manpower to do it." Olivia glanced out over the water as Katie talked. "Officers are also going to search the other side of the lake as well, just in case she decided she could swim across."

"Good," Olivia said. She looked at Wade. "Please. I really need you to go inside. Law enforcement is going to be all over this place and we need you to be out of the way." She turned to see Quinn headed her way down the hill, then spun back to Wade. "And when the crime scene folks get here, they'll probably need impressions of your shoes."

He nodded. "Process of elimination?"

"Exactly."

"Dad?"

Wade flinched and turned. Amy was bolting toward him with Katie on her heels and Martha not far behind.

Amy launched herself at her father and wrapped her arms around his waste. "What's happening? What's going on?"

Olivia figured his daughter would be the catalyst to get him inside the house. She caught Katie's eye with a raised brow.

"She slipped out," Katie said. "By the time I realized what she was doing, she was already coming down the hill."

"Get her back inside."

Katie nodded and touched Amy on the shoulder.

Amy shrugged her off, still looking up at Wade. "The lights woke me up."

Wade hugged her, then guided her toward Katie. "Go with her to the house. Someone was snooping around outside, but it's safe now."

"Who was it?"

"I don't know. Could have been a nosey neighbor. When I find out, I'll tell you."

Amy narrowed her eyes and crossed her arms. "No you won't."

Wade took a deep breath and looked his daughter in the eye. "I will. I promise."

Amy's defiance faded and she dropped her arms. "Really?"

"Really. Go with Aunt Martha and Katie and I'll be there in a few minutes."

"Okay." She took three steps backward, as though still judging Wade's sincerity about telling her anything, then turned and started back up the hill next to Martha. Katie followed behind.

"What's your favorite movie?" Olivia heard Katie ask.

Their voices faded and Olivia turned to Quinn, who'd just signed in with one of the first officers who'd arrived on the scene.

Wade's house—and now boathouse—was a crime scene once again. She wanted it treated that way so as not to compromise any evidence that might lead back to his stalker. Once they caught the person, Olivia didn't want her getting off on a technicality. "We've got to stop meeting this way," she said to Quinn.

"I'm all for that."

"Do you have an update on Maddy?"

"Still critical, but seems to be slightly better. What do you have?"

She nodded to the knife. "Someone was looking in the window. I came outside to investigate, followed her down to the boathouse, and she tossed that at me."

"She?"

Olivia shrugged. "If it's Wade's stalker, it was probably a she."

"You're assuming again."

She nodded. "I am, yes. Might not be the smartest thing to do, but until proven otherwise, I'm going with that deduction."

"CSU is on the way."

"They keep having to make the trip out here, they might as well just set up camp."

Quinn blew out a breath and knelt to get a good look at the knife. He aimed his maglight at the weapon. "Looks sharp. That would have hurt a bit. Glad it didn't hit you."

She shot him a sour look. "Yeah, me too. Thanks."

He pulled gloves from his back pocket and snapped them on. Next he snagged a digital camera from the other pocket and took several dozen shots of the weapon and the area around it. Quinn would want his own pictures if at all possible. The crime scene photographer would take some, of course, but Quinn was a lone ranger. He did things his way while staying just on the inside of the law.

"You going to bag it too?"

Olivia turned to find Sarah Baldwin watching them. Quinn gave the petite woman a wry smile. "Naw, why would I do that? That's your job."

Sarah stood five feet two, if that. A little on the heavy side, she carried herself like a queen. One didn't notice her height or her size. Her eyes were magnets. Once they landed on you, they drew you in and you immediately felt like you were her best friend. "Yeah? So when has that made a difference?"

Quinn gave her a rueful smile. "Can't argue with that."

"About the only thing you don't argue about."

"Come on, guys," Olivia said, amused and annoyed at the same time. "Can we get this done and end this night?"

Sarah and Quinn were like brother and sister. Always snipping and sniping at each other, but if push came to shove, they would have each other's back. And Sarah knew that if Quinn collected the evidence, it would be done right. Sarah sobered. "How's Maddy?"

Quinn's lighter countenance darkened. "Critical." The same answer Olivia had gotten. "But still alive. That's the good news."

A black crime scene van pulled to a stop under the covered area where Olivia had parked earlier. Haley pulled up next to the van.

Olivia waited for her to join her. "I have an idea."

"What's that?" Haley asked.

"Let's find Wade and I'll run it by you at the same time."

They found him in the den staring at the pictures on the mantel. "Do you have a minute?" Olivia asked.

He turned, eyes shadowed, expression tight. "Of course." He gestured for her and Haley to have a seat. "Katie's upstairs with Amy, Martha's in the kitchen, and I'm at a loss as to how to keep them safe."

"Maybe my idea will help with that," Olivia said.

Wade wasn't sure he liked the look on her face. "What's that?"

Olivia tapped her lips with her forefinger as she stared at him. "I think it's time to take this whole protection detail in a different direction."

Haley lifted a brow and Wade shot Olivia a wary look. "What direction would that be?" he asked.

"I think you guys are overdue for a vacation."

"Vacation?" He gave a short laugh, but there wasn't any humor in it. "What kind of vacation?"

"We take you to a place where nobody can find you and no one can track you. A place where no one comes in or goes out without proper identification."

Wade's frown grew. "I can't just leave, I have responsibilities. I have a charity dinner and the radio show and Amy has school." He paced to one side of the den, then back, his face flushed, breath quickening as his temper shortened. "Look, I agreed to this bodyguard business because I was under the impression that you could keep us safe without massively disrupting our lives." He ran a hand through his hair and turned his back on the two ladies as he thought. Then he spun and pointed a finger at Olivia. "There's no doubt that the threat is real and danger is present and that I need help because this stalker stuff is way over my head. But I will not give this person the satisfaction of making me run."

"What if running is the only thing that keeps you alive?" Olivia asked.

Wade stared at her, her words resonating within him. The anger drained. What if she was right? He closed his eyes and asked for divine guidance. A minute ticked by. He finally looked at her. She'd simply waited him out. Because she knew he'd come to the same conclusion she had? "Okay. Say we go somewhere for a week or even two. When we come back, she'll still be waiting."

"Or she'll be in custody."

"How?"

"They're still testing the gift from the porch," Haley said, "trying to track down the store that sold the teddy bears, analyzing the GPS tracker found on your vehicle. All of those are things that could lead us to the person—or persons—responsible."

Olivia was nodding.

Wade sighed. "I don't know. I don't want to cancel the Thursday night charity event." He ran a hand over his head. "I've got parents and kids counting on me. The money the charity brings in funds some of their daycares and after-school programs. If I start canceling, then the kids lose out. And I lose credibility."

Olivia straightened. "Not if you use this to your advantage."

Wade tilted his head. "What do you mean?"

"I mean you tell everyone exactly why you're canceling the event and ask them to give anyway."

He was already shaking his head. "They'll think it's some gimmick. My reputation is spotless. I had all kinds of sympathizers when Justine died. The money poured in." He looked away, feeling the sting that always came with memories of Justine. He cleared his throat. "But if I do this, there will be questions, speculation, the money will fall off, and families will suffer. I just can't take that chance."

Olivia pursed her lips and paced the den, her actions mimicking his from only moments ago. She came back to him. "You're right, of course. It could backfire." She rubbed her chin and nodded. "All right, we'll do it your way for now. Charlie and

Lizzie have the time to help. We'll put them on the schedule and double your coverage."

He rubbed his forehead. "If you still think we need to go someplace else after the dinner Thursday night, I'll . . . consider it."

Olivia nodded. "I think that's wise. Not as wise as leaving now, but I'll take what I can get." Because she had a feeling Wade's stalker had more sinister plans for him and she was going to do whatever it took to keep him out of this madwoman's hands. She just hoped his sense of responsibility toward his charity didn't get him killed.

[25]

Wade backed out of Amy's room and shut the door. She was snuggled into her bed, the blankets pulled to her chin.

He leaned his forehead against the shut door and drew in a calming breath. What was happening? *Why* was this happening? *God, I don't understand. Give me strength, please.*

Footsteps fell softly on the carpet runner behind him. He recognized Martha's tread and turned. She looked shaken. Worried.

"Are you all right?" he asked.

"I think that should be my question for you."

"I'm fine. Amy is asleep and whoever did this is long gone."

"For now."

"Yes. For now."

"Olivia is downstairs looking for you."

"Thanks."

"I think I'm going to bed, if that's all right," she said.

"Go on. If they need you for any reason, I'll come get you."

He watched the red and blue lights from the law enforcement vehicles bounce off the walls in his hallway. He pulled his phone from his pocket and dialed the station manager while Martha stood at the window and watched the action.

After making arrangements for the show, he hung up, relieved Dale could play the recording from his home. He and Dale really needed to sit down and figure out how to keep the show going until the building was repaired. If that's what the man wanted.

"You should build a soundproof room that would allow you to do the show from home," Martha said.

He'd thought about it but hadn't wanted to shell out the expense. Not that he couldn't afford it. And it *would* be convenient. And safe. But it galled him. He shouldn't have to wonder if he was going to be attacked in the parking lot of the station or if someone was going to strap bombs to the doors. "I'll give it some more consideration."

"Good." She turned to go, then spun back. "And remember, Joanna and I are spending the day together again tomorrow. Since Amy's staying home with you, I told Joanna we could do some therapy shopping and see a movie. She needs more girl time since she broke it off with her latest."

"Joanna and her men. You think she'll ever settle down?"

Martha shrugged. "She and I are kind of two peas in a pod. We just can't seem to find what we're looking for."

"It'll happen."

She smiled. "I'm not terribly worried about it. You and Amy are all the family I need for now. One day that might change. If the right man were to come along, but for now . . . I'm content."

He hugged her. "I don't know what I'd do without you."

She laughed. "You'd manage."

"Wade? Could I talk to you a moment?"

He turned. Olivia's silky smooth voice soothed his nerves and calmed his racing thoughts. "Of course."

Martha patted his arm. "I'll see you in the morning." She nodded to Olivia as she passed her and went to the stairs.

"Is Amy all right?" Olivia asked him.

"Yes. Thanks." He tilted his head. "Do you think I should see if Stacy can come over here after school tomorrow? If it was my kid, I'd want her so far away from this house . . ." He sighed.

Olivia paused, then shook her head. "You could call Stacy's mother and let her know what's happened. Then she can make the decision for herself."

He nodded. "I'll do that. After I speak to her, do you mind talking for a moment?"

"That would be great."

He led the way and soon found himself seated in his favorite recliner with her across from him on the love seat. He made the call to Stacy's mother, but she didn't pick up. He left her a voice mail to call him as soon as she got the message, then turned his attention to Olivia. She leaned forward and clasped her hands together. He couldn't help noticing the strong line of her jaw, the sleek muscles in her forearms, the way her eyes never missed a thing. She was cool, professional, beautiful. And she'd made it clear she was off-limits.

"The officers spoke with your neighbors and no one saw anything," she said.

"The houses are pretty spread out around here." He shrugged and tried not to let his wounded pride get in the way of just talking to her. "It's one of the perks of living on the lake. A lot of land and a lot of privacy." He paused. "Did they search the boathouses?"

"Yes and still nothing." She rubbed her eyes. "You're right about there being a lot of land. We're going to have to patrol it."

"Do you have the manpower to do that?"

She nodded. "We'll find it."

"Thank you," he said quietly. "For everything. For putting your life on the line and for making sure we stay alive in spite of my stubbornness."

She nodded. "Sure."

"I won't take the boat out tomorrow. Amy can still stay home, but we won't take the boat out."

Her expression softened. "I think we can make arrangements for y'all to enjoy the boat on the water tomorrow." Then her eyes sharpened. "After I have a conversation with Quinn."

[26]

"Murder? You have no proof," Quinn said. He leaned back in his chair and crossed his arms.

Olivia sat across from him, his wooden desk between them. She'd come to his office first thing this Monday morning while Haley and Katie took over bodyguard duties. After she went home and caught a few hours of sleep. Fatigue tugged at her, but she wouldn't give in until she got her way.

"Exactly. That's why I think you should exhume her body," Olivia argued. She let her gaze fall on the wall behind him. Pictures of his family adorned it. He said he put those there to remind him to be careful and not take unnecessary risks. A picture of Maddy sat at the corner. She picked it up and her heart hurt for her friend and the man who cared so much about her.

"It's a hunch. You can't exhume a body based on a hunch." Quinn eyed her holding the picture, but didn't say anything.

"What if I'm right?" she asked softly. She placed the picture back. "What if she was killed? If so, there's a murderer wandering around out there maybe targeting his next victim."

196

"His victim? Or *her* victim? Because you think Wade's stalker has been planning this for a while, don't you?"

"I don't know. If she has, then I think maybe when she learned Wade and Justine were going to marry, it pushed her into action." She pursed her lips, then blew out a low sigh.

"But he didn't start getting those gifts until recently."

"I know. I don't have all the answers because the only person who can give them to me is doing her best not to get caught. I just feel like we're missing something and Justine's death may be a part of that. I don't want to let something slide just because it's a long shot." She narrowed her eyes. "I want Francisco to do another autopsy on Justine."

"What about Justine's family? How are they going to feel about it?"

"I bet they'll want answers."

"Answers to questions that might not need to be asked. You could be opening Pandora's box all over again. This is serious stuff here, Liv."

She ground her molars and paused before letting the words release from her lips. "I know that, Quinn. I'm not a novice. I'm not a cop anymore either—at least not in the normal sense of the word." She narrowed her eyes and locked gazes with him. "But I haven't lost my cop instincts and I really think I'm right about this." At his continued silence, she resisted reacting. Instead, she rose and took a step toward him, placed her hands on his desk, and leaned in. "Who sends a suicide note via text?"

"Someone who wants to be found fast?"

She grimaced. "Okay, I'll give you that one. But to say 'I'll miss you'? Is that something a person who is so depressed they're going to end their life would say?"

Her intensity must have finally penetrated that thick skull of his, because he sighed. Then gave a slow nod. "I don't know.

I've never had anyone close to me commit suicide. But I see your point." He tapped the open file folder on his desk, then shut it. "Guess this can wait a bit. All right, we can fill out the paperwork."

"Good."

He lifted a brow. "Good?"

"And thanks." She shot him a smile and headed for the door. "I've got your number and you've got mine. Stay in touch."

He grunted. "Yeah, I've got your number."

After she finished her conversation with Quinn, Olivia made a quick trip home to water her plants and check her mail. She looked around her barren house and felt a pang of loneliness. For the first time in a long time, she'd met someone who made her wonder if her future could be different than the one she'd mapped out for herself. One where she controlled the shots, trusted no one, and worked enough hours that she didn't have to think about how empty her life was at the end of the day.

For a brief moment, she let herself envision a life with Wade and Amy. Her heart pounded at the thought and her breath caught in her throat. Then she pushed the vision away. She'd pretty much told Wade she wasn't interested. But the truth was, she was very interested, she was just scared.

Swallowing the sudden lump that had risen into her throat, she pushed all thoughts of domesticity away and called Katie to let her know she was on the way back to the Savage home. "How are you feeling? You need a break? Need to grab some sleep?"

"I'm fine right now. We're just waiting on you to get here so we can take the boat out."

"Charlie and Lizzie are on board for the duration. They should be there by now."

"Not yet, but I'll keep my eyes open."

"Good. Thanks. I want everyone there while Wade and Amy are out on the lake. After they're safely back inside, we can send a few people home to get some rest. Haley is staying through lunch and Charlie will cover for you when you're ready to leave. If Charlie gets there before I do, make the introductions. Also let Wade know about Lizzie in case he feels like he needs to smooth the way for Amy, prepare her for the additional bodyguard."

"You got it."

Olivia hung up and walked out the door. When she pulled to a stop at the top of Wade's horseshoe-shaped drive, she saw a red Ford truck sitting in front of the house. Charlie was here. She sat in her car while she dialed Sarah's number at the lab.

She was getting antsy waiting on the results. She needed to know about Maddy's crime scene. Had they processed the car yet? And the bear left on Wade's porch, along with the knife recovered from his house. Not to mention she wanted to know if there were any fingerprints on the GPS tracker found on his car. She slapped a hand against the steering wheel and knew if Quinn had heard anything, he would have called, but she wanted answers. Now. She had to call, even though deep in her heart she knew it would be fruitless.

"Don't have anything yet," Sarah said in greeting.

"Why not?"

"Because I have other cases ahead of the one you want answers for," Sarah said with an unamused grunt. Olivia sighed. "But I bumped yours up," she promised. "I'm getting to it."

"Okay, thanks."

"I'll call you as soon as I have something."

"This is Maddy, Sarah," Olivia said quietly. "We need something to help us find the person who did this to her. And Wade."

"I know, Liv. Soon, I promise."

Olivia knew she wasn't the only phone call Sarah would get today begging for lab results. Too many crimes, not enough lab workers or time. She climbed from the car and walked up the steps to rap on the door.

Charlie opened it. In his midtwenties, Charlie Lee was good-looking enough to take a woman's breath away. Fortunately, Olivia was immune. However, she had to admit it amused her to take note of the jealous glances she received from other women whenever she and Charlie went out in public together. "Hey, handsome."

Charlie hugged her. "It's been a while."

"Yeah. I know." Although his tone had been neutral without any accusation, Olivia couldn't help the tug of guilt. "How is the family?"

He lifted a brow. "They're fine." Which she would know if she bothered to call. She heard the unspoken words, but again, there was no accusation. She grimaced.

Wade stepped into the foyer. He blinked when he saw her. "Hey."

"Hi."

"Have you eaten? Joanna and Martha are in the kitchen. There's plenty if you're hungry. Charlie, you're welcome to stay."

Her stomach growled as though on cue. She smiled. "Guess that's your answer, thanks."

Charlie grabbed a small bag by the door and gave her and Wade a nod. "I appreciate the invitation, but I'm going to scout the other side of the lake and make sure everything is a go to take the boat out." He gave her a quick kiss on the cheek.

"Stay in touch," she said.

"Of course." And then he was out the door.

Wade eyed her. "Thought you were going to get some sleep. I can tell you didn't."

She grunted and walked toward the kitchen. "Careful with all that flattery, Wade, it could turn a girl's head."

He caught her hand and spun her around, his eyes intense, determined. "Has anyone turned your head?"

And just like that, nerves attacked her. She swallowed hard, careful to keep her expression neutral. "Why do you ask that?"

"You're so closed off," he said quietly. "Do you ever let anyone in?"

She thought about offering a flippant answer, but stopped it before the words left her lips. He deserved better than that. "No, not often."

"Why?"

She sighed. "I think you probably can figure that answer out. People are unpredictable, they change with the wind. One day they want you, the next they don't." She gave a slight shrug. "I suppose when you get hurt enough, eventually you push away the source of that hurt."

"People."

"Yes."

"What was his name?"

"C.J. Garrison. We dated for about two months before I broke it off when I realized he just couldn't handle my work in law enforcement. But he's not even the reason I have a hard time opening up to people. I think it's just my past and the way I had to grow up. From one foster home to the next. The only reason I think I turned out halfway decent is because of the Lees."

"I'm sorry." He glanced at the door Charlie had just exited. "And your family? Why do you push them away too?"

She stiffened and pulled her hand away from his, just now realizing he was still holding it.

"What's Charlie to you?"

So, he'd heard the exchange. She sighed. "Charlie is Shana's brother—and mine too, he says. But I've never really . . ." She shrugged. "I don't know."

"You've never really accepted them as your family," he guessed.

She fidgeted. Uncomfortable and wanting to run away from the conversation, but unwilling to do so. Which she found strange.

"I see." He stared at her for a few more seconds, then looked away before nodding. "Thanks for telling me."

Olivia rubbed her eyes, then felt his hands on her shoulders.

He steered her toward the kitchen. "I don't know about you, but I'm ready to eat and then hit the water."

She nearly wilted in relief. She didn't have to tell him anything and yet she found she wanted to. It was a new sensation. A bewildering dilemma and one she wanted to spend some time thinking about. When she wasn't trying to figure out how to keep her client alive while staying off the water.

The watcher lifted a hand against the sun and smiled. Right on time. Wade, Amy, and Katie headed for the boat. Would they find it? The little gift that had been left? Maybe. The watcher shifted on the seat and ran a probing gaze down the shoreline. Cops were out in abundance. That Olivia sure had a lot of friends willing to do her favors.

A short laugh escaped. If only she knew it didn't matter how many people she had watching and protecting and working to find Wade's stalker—they'd never figure it out.

If only she knew.

It was time for Wade to die. It looked like today would be the day.

[27]

Olivia stood on the shoreline. It was hot and she was sweating, but the discomfort was worth putting up with to have the best vantage point of the surrounding properties from her spot near the dock. The water lapped at the edge of the manmade beach. She held the binoculars to her eyes and swept the area behind the boat. She caught sight of several of her people keeping watch.

Two other volunteer officers stayed in a smaller craft right next to Wade's but could be on Wade's boat within seconds if they were needed.

Her phone rang and she pressed the button on the Bluetooth device in her ear. "Hello?"

"It's Quinn."

"How's it going?"

"I'm up at the hospital with Maddy."

Hope sprouted. How she'd wanted to go visit, but she simply couldn't take the time away from Wade. "How is she? Is she awake?"

"Not yet, but the doctors say she's not as far under as she has been. She could wake at any time, so that's good."

"Any activity around her room? Like someone trying to get to her?"

"No."

"Huh. Interesting."

"We'll keep watching. Either the person doesn't think she'll wake up or she's not worried about it."

"If it's the latter, it means Maddy definitely didn't see who attacked her."

"Yeah."

"What else do you have?" she asked.

"Justine's family immediately agreed to the exhumation. I went by their house myself and talked to them. Told them what you suspected. Justine's mother broke down and sobbed, saying she knew it wasn't a suicide."

"Wow."

"I'll submit the paperwork and mark it top priority for Francisco. We should get approval either tonight or first thing in the morning."

"Great. That's great. Thanks, Quinn. Keep me updated."

"Sure." Olivia disconnected the call and kept watch on Wade's craft. She ignored the sweat rolling down the middle of her back. *God, we haven't talked in a while and I know it's my fault, but just . . . keep them safe. Please.*

⦙⦙⦙⦙⦙⦙⦙⦙⦙⦙⦙⦙⦙⦙⦙⦙⦙⦙⦙⦙⦙⦙⦙⦙⦙⦙⦙⦙⦙⦙⦙⦙⦙⦙⦙

The events of the weekend threw a pall over the day for Wade. He wanted to keep checking in with security, make sure they were alert and watching, but he knew Olivia was doing that and everything else she could to keep them safe. Every once in a while he'd catch a glimpse of her pacing the shoreline. Still, he couldn't help watching the surrounding area a little more intently. But Amy needed the relaxation as much as he did, and he was determined to enjoy the time with her. On the other hand, he couldn't stop thinking about Olivia.

She'd told him some pretty personal stuff, and as a result, some of her barriers had come down. And while he could see that scared her to death, he was glad she'd been able to bring herself to do it. He looked forward to more conversations with her, more learning what made her tick, more exploring the attraction he knew was mutual. If they could both knock the remaining barriers down. Did he really want to open himself up to the possibility of getting his heart broken again?

Maybe.

He glanced around. Olivia had called in the big guns and security was tight. Katie and Haley were with him and Amy. Olivia stayed on the shoreline attached to a radio, her eyes on the area. She'd called in several of her off-duty friends who relished the idea of picking up a few extra bucks for some protection duty. Two other bodyguards, Lizzie and Charlie, had shown up, and Wade found himself liking them as well. He felt like he and Amy were in good hands. They'd kept them alive this long anyway. Joanna sat next to him and sipped a soda. "Thanks for letting me come along."

"Sure. Always happy to have you."

"Too bad Martha had that headache. She thinks she's coming down with a sinus infection. I told her the sun would do her good, but she didn't seem to think so." Joanna shrugged and stood. "I'm going to get in the water with Amy." She grabbed a float and tossed it overboard, then jumped in with elegant grace. Wade heard Amy giggle and the two start up a conversation.

Haley appeared from the cabin below in shorts and a T-shirt. She was an attractive woman, but Wade couldn't help wishing it was Olivia on the boat with him. Haley settled in the chair next to him. "Katie's at the back of the boat watching behind us."

"The stern."

"What?"

"That's what the back of the boat is called."

"Oh." Haley laughed. "I've never been around boats much but should have known that, I guess."

He smiled. "I'm just being picky." Amy's wet head appeared before she turned around and jumped off the ladder back into the water. He kept his eyes on Amy but voiced his question to Haley. "I notice the accent. It's very pretty. Irish?"

"What. Callaghan didn't give it away?"

He smiled. "Yes, but a surname for a woman doesn't necessarily mean she was born with that name."

"Very true, but I was. I grew up in Ireland."

"How did you wind up over here?"

She shrugged. "My mum married an American when I was seventeen. He brought us here."

"You like it here?"

"Yes, I do. I miss Ireland, of course, but I've been an American for the past fourteen years, so it's home too."

He nodded. "Do you mind if I ask you a question about Olivia?"

"You can ask."

He heard the unspoken, *but I might not answer.* "Why doesn't Olivia like water?"

Haley took a sip of her water and then placed it in the chair's holder. "That's probably a question you should ask her."

"I haven't had a chance, but she said she and water just didn't get along." He flicked a glance at her and saw her grimace.

"No, they don't."

"And you're not going to tell me why?"

"It's not my place. If she wants you to know, she'll tell you."

He lifted a brow. "Of course. I didn't mean to pry. I didn't realize it was a confidence."

Haley sighed. "It's not so much that it's confidential, it's . . . Olivia is a very close-to-the-vest kind of person. Sometimes I don't know what's okay to talk about and what isn't."

"So you don't say anything."

"Exactly."

He smiled at her. "She's blessed to have a friend like you." Haley relaxed a fraction and took another sip of her water. Amy turned a flip off her float. "Way to go, kiddo." Joanna clapped and wiped the water from her face. She shoved her sunglasses back on her head. Amy pushed her hair out of her eyes and grinned at him. He gave her a thumbs-up, then glanced at Haley. "You read up on me, my family, and my past before you took this job, didn't you?"

"Of course."

"So you know about Justine."

"Yes." He heard the soft sympathy in her voice.

He turned his gaze to see Olivia pacing along the shoreline, her steps never faltering, her watchful gaze moving from one area to the next. They were out in the middle of the cove, surrounded by shoreline and green sloping grass with patches of trees and shade strategically placed on the various properties. "Olivia seems to think Justine's death was murder. What do you think?"

Haley hesitated as though weighing her words. He waited her out. "Olivia is one of the smartest people I know," she finally said. "If she has a reason to suspect murder, then I would listen to her."

He nodded and watched Amy and Joanna climb back onto the boat. Wade held out a towel and Joanna wrapped his daughter in it, then took one for herself. "I was afraid that might be the case," he said softly.

"I'm thirsty, Dad," Amy said.

"There are drinks in the fridge. I just put some in there yesterday."

"Cool." Amy headed down to the galley.

Joanna wrung her hair out, then settled a towel around her shoulders. "I'm just going to make a couple of phone calls. I have messages I need to leave for tomorrow morning."

She followed Amy below and Wade closed his eyes for a brief moment, relishing the August sun on his face. He so rarely took the time to relax that he often felt guilty about keeping the boat. But when he was out on the water, he was very glad he had it.

"Hey, Dad, where'd you get these chocolates? Can I have one?"

Wade looked up to see Amy standing in front of him, holding a box of candy.

Exactly like the one his stalker had gifted him with several weeks ago. He let his feet thump to the floor and stood holding out a hand. "Give me those."

She lifted the lid. "Can I have one first?" She took one out and moved it toward her lips.

"No!" He grabbed for it.

Then Joanna was there, knocking the piece from her hand. Amy startled and dropped the box. Chocolate rolled across the deck of the boat. Amy burst into tears as she whirled to go back down into the living quarters.

"Amy, stop! I'm sorry!"

Joanna went after her. "Amy, stop."

Amy froze, then whirled and wrapped her arms around Joanna's waist. Katie took the box from him and a glove from the bag she'd brought on board.

Wade went to his daughter and gently pulled her from Joanna. He turned her to face him and grasped her by her upper arms. "I'm sorry I yelled."

Amy sniffed and glared at him. "I just wanted a piece of chocolate."

"I'm not sure where the chocolate came from, but I didn't put them there." She shot him a confused, hurt look and he sighed. "I'll explain later."

Using gloved hands, Katie had replaced all of the spilled chocolates into the box. "I'll keep this with me and just check below real fast," she said.

She disappeared down the steps and Amy swiped the tears from her face and shook her head. "I get it. You think it's that woman who's stalking you, don't you? You think she left them?"

"Maybe."

"Oh." She shifted from one foot to the other. "Or Aunt Martha put them there."

"Maybe. But maybe not. I don't want you to eat them until I find out for sure where they came from. They weren't there when I loaded the fridge with drinks yesterday."

"You think something's . . . wrong with them?"

"I hope not."

"They're just like the other ones she sent. They're your favorite."

"I know." He ran a hand down her wet hair and drew her out of Joanna's arms and into his own.

She buried her face in his chest. "I ate the others and nothing bad happened," she mumbled.

"Yeah, but that was before she started causing all this trouble."

"Right."

He looked at Joanna. "Thank you."

"Sure," she said softly. "I didn't recognize the box, but I

could see how distressed you were at the thought of her eating one. I just reacted."

"I appreciate that. We may have both overreacted, but I'd rather be safe than sorry."

"Of course."

Katie came back and gave him a nod. "Everything is fine down here. No more surprises that I could find."

Wade nodded and gave Amy a gentle push toward the stairs. "Go get dried off and we'll head back in so Katie can get those chocolates to the lab."

Katie lifted a brow at him. "You read my mind."

"Sad, isn't it?"

Katie's voice came through the earpiece loud and clear. "Someone planted a box of chocolates in the refrigerator."

Olivia flinched. "Planted them? Wade didn't put them there yesterday when he was getting the boat ready?"

"He said they're the same kind he received from the stalker the first time she sent something. And no, he said he didn't put them there."

"All right," Olivia said. "Bring them in. We'll check with Martha and make sure she didn't put them there. If not, then we'll get them to the lab and have them analyzed."

"When do you think she planted them?"

"If it was the stalker, I'd say it was last night when I caught her looking in the window and chased her down here by the boathouse. I'm guessing she stopped here first and slipped that box in the fridge, then decided to see if she could take a peek in the window."

"Only you saw her."

"Yes."

"We're coming in now."

The boat cut through the water smoothly, a slow glide that made her want to be one of the occupants. "I see you. We'll get them settled inside and then you can take the chocolate in to Sarah. I'll see if Quinn or someone wants to come process the boat." Olivia knew the other security personnel could hear every word. The officers she'd hired stayed put in their positions. Each one reported in that their area was clear. Olivia watched the boat dock and vowed she'd conquer her fear of water one day soon.

But first things first. Keeping Amy and Wade safe took precedence. The boat disappeared into the boathouse. Shortly after, Amy came out wrapped in a towel, flip-flops on her feet, and a mutinous expression on her face. As the girl approached with Katie right behind her, Olivia held her ground. "You okay?"

"I'm fine. I just wish you'd get the person causing my dad so much stress. He's becoming impossible to live with."

Olivia looked past the drama and saw the fear in the girl's eyes. Katie and Joanna hovered in the background while Olivia talked to Amy. "I understand and we're hoping all this will be over soon. Just keep telling yourself anything he says or does is because he loves you."

Amy's stiff shoulders relaxed a bit. "I know. It's just . . ."

"Just what?"

She sighed. "Just unnecessary. Just because some woman has issues, we have to pay for it. It's completely unfair."

"I totally agree with you on that."

Amy lifted a brow and stared at her for a minute. Then a small smile tilted her lips. "Well. Good. Thanks."

"You're welcome."

She rubbed the edge of the towel over her face. "I'm going to get a shower and change."

"I'm going to wait on your dad." She looked at Katie. "Will you check with Martha about the chocolates? See if she knows anything about them being on the boat?"

"Sure thing."

Amy and Katie disappeared. Wade was already walking up the hill with Charlie and Lizzie nearby. Joanna trailed behind them, toweling her hair, her face pale. Wade caught Olivia's eye and frowned. "This is getting downright scary."

"I agree."

"So what are we going to do?"

"That's really up to you, isn't it?"

[28]

TUESDAY

The rest of Monday had passed in a quiet blur, for which Olivia gave thanks. She'd delivered the chocolates to Sarah at the lab and the woman told her not to hold her breath. Which was why she was surprised when Sarah called and said she had some results if Olivia wanted to find time in her schedule to visit the lab.

Tuesday dawned overcast and muggy. Humidity and Olivia's hair had an ongoing battle. The humidity usually won, so she didn't bother fighting this morning. She simply pulled her strands into a loose ponytail, dabbed on a minimum of makeup to cover the darkening circles under her eyes, and grabbed her keys. Once in her car, she called the hospital to check on Maddy and was relieved to hear her friend and co-worker had shown even more improvement. She was responding well to the antibiotics and her wound was healing with no sign of infection.

213

Her next call was to Katie, who'd pulled night duty with the Savage family.

"All was quiet," Katie reported.

"Let's hope it stays that way. I'm on the way to the lab to see Sarah. I'll let you know what she found."

Fifteen minutes later, she pulled into the parking lot of the lab and sent Sarah a text:

Olivia
I'm here.

Sarah
I'm waiting for you.

Olivia pushed through the glass doors and presented her identification to security. He buzzed another set of doors and she made her way to the elevator and stepped inside.

At the fourth floor, the doors whooshed open and Olivia came face-to-face with Sarah. "A little impatient?" Olivia asked.

"Not at all. Follow me."

"I know where your office is."

Sarah shot her a sour look. "You take all the fun out of mysterious."

"I'm tired of mystery. I want answers."

"Then follow me."

"You couldn't just send me a picture?"

"Nope."

Olivia shut up and did as requested. She spotted Quinn and Bree standing just outside the door to the lab.

"This way, people," Sarah said. Olivia noticed she wasn't her usual chipper self. She did indeed have an air of mystery around her, but her smile was missing and her shoulders remained stiff under her white lab coat. Concerned, Olivia exchanged greetings with Quinn and Bree while Sarah marched ahead.

"You know what this is about?" Olivia asked in a low voice.

They both shook their heads as one. "We just had a summons too," Bree said.

Once inside the lab, Olivia and the detectives stood to the side while Sarah went to the table to the right and picked up a small brown bag. "I autopsied the headless teddy bear that was left at Mr. Savage's house."

"You don't do autopsies."

Another black look from Sarah. "Humor me."

"Sorry." Olivia drew in a calming breath. "And?"

"I found this." She snapped on a pair of gloves and reached into the bag.

Olivia tensed. Sarah pulled out a small piece of paper and opened it. "'You shouldn't have done that. I would have given you everything. Now you'll pay,'" she read.

"Whoa." Olivia sucked in a deep breath. "Well, that's a direct threat if I've ever heard one."

Quinn nodded and narrowed his eyes. "It's a threat, but it doesn't surprise me."

"But this might," Sarah said. She held up a piece of paper. "I had a rather wild hunch and tested the blood found on the teddy bear."

"And?"

"I got a match."

Olivia called on every ounce of patience within her. She loved Sarah, but sometimes the woman's penchant for drama annoyed her. "To whom?"

"Madelyn McKay."

Olivia felt her stomach drop. "What?"

Now that her bomb had been dropped, Sarah was all business. "The note was soaked in her blood. I had to work to see if there was anything else on the paper. Once I got the blood out—don't ask me how, even I'm not sure how I managed to do it without destroying the words—I was able to see what it said."

"That's sick," Olivia whispered. She rubbed her brow and turned away to get control of her anger. Getting mad was fine, keeping a clear head was more important.

Bree blew out a breath. "Well, she's definitely made her point, hasn't she?"

"I'll say."

"What about the note from the night Wade was attacked?" Bree asked.

"Same person did it," Sarah said. "Same type of lettering, same paper, same glue." She shrugged. "You could try to figure out what store it came from, but I wouldn't bother. It's just simple white printer paper, a newspaper bought off a local stand or grocery store, and Elmer's glue."

"So nothing real traceable," Olivia said.

"Right. And no prints. The person is being super careful and using gloves. No hair fibers, no nothing. It's squeaky clean."

"Okay," Quinn said, "I think our best lead right now is the caller. Let's see if we can track her down. Today."

His phone rang and he snagged it from the clip. "Hello?" He listened and Olivia watched his face. His brows dipped, and his jaw tightened. "Right. We're on the way."

Bree shifted, already turning her body toward the door. Quinn hung up and shot an apologetic look at Olivia. "We've got a missing persons case we've got to head over to. Wade's caller is going to have to wait."

Olivia nodded. "Fine. Go. I'll take care of things here." Quinn and Bree left. Olivia rubbed her chin, weighed her options, then sent a text message to Katie.

Going to check something out. How is everything on your end?

"What are you going to check out?" Sarah asked, looking around Olivia's shoulder to read her text.

"Nosey."

"And proud of it. How else do you think I stay on top of everything around here?"

Olivia couldn't stop the small smile that tugged at her lips. Then she frowned. "Anything on the knife from Wade's house?"

"Actually yes. I got a print. I ran it through IAFIS, but came up empty. Whoever threw it—if it's her print—isn't in the system."

"Okay. Thanks."

"Of course."

"Anything about those chocolates from the boat?"

"Not yet."

"Wade was just on the boat Sunday, stocking the refrigerator," Olivia said. "He didn't put the candy there. So it had to have been put there Sunday night."

Sarah sighed. "I believe you, but it's just not a high priority since no crime was committed—at least that you know of."

"I know, I get it. I'm just itching to find out if the candy is as innocent as it appears."

"I'll try to bump it up if at all possible."

"I'd appreciate it."

"I know." She fell silent for a moment, then looked back at Olivia when she didn't move. "Now what are you up to?"

Olivia tapped her lip, thinking. "First I'm going to call the restaurant where Valerie Mathis works, and if she's there, I'm going to see her. If she's not, I'm going to ride over to her house and see if she's home."

"And if she is?"

Olivia pursed her lips and thought. "I'm not sure yet. I'll assess the situation and make a decision accordingly."

"She's not your case."

"But Wade Savage is."

....

Wade had watched Katie drive away with Amy while Martha frowned at him. Haley stood at the door, her hand on her weapon, her tension letting him know she was alert and ready for anything. Once Katie was out of sight, she turned.

"Where's Olivia?" he asked her. The question had haunted him ever since Haley had stepped foot in his home. She wasn't supposed to be here, Olivia was. The fact that he cared bothered him. The fact that he was attracted to the woman scared him to death. He wasn't in the market for romance. Ever. Never again.

"With the detectives, Quinn and Bree."

"Right." He paused. "Why?"

Haley held up her phone. "I'm getting occasional updates. The gist of it is this: Sarah Baldwin is a crime scene investigator. She processed your house and Maddy's attempted murder. She texted Olivia and requested that she and the detectives meet her at the lab this morning first thing."

"For?"

Lizzie shrugged. "I don't know. That's all I've gotten so far."

He shook his head. "Okay, I appreciate you keeping me updated on everything."

"No problem." She studied him. "Olivia will be here as soon as she can."

Martha gave a small snort and shot him an amused look.

He felt the heat start to rise from the base of his neck and wondered why he was so easy to read. He narrowed his eyes at her and she turned away. "Joanna's coming over. We're going to be planning Amy's thirteenth birthday party."

Wade winced. "I should be helping."

Martha waved a hand. "We've got it covered. Don't worry, you can put your name on the card and the gift." She headed out the kitchen door to her apartment and Wade sighed. He wanted to be a part of the planning, but sometimes with Martha, it was easier to cave than to insist. But he'd still talk to Amy and find out exactly what she wanted to do for her birthday and work around Martha and Joanna if he had to.

"Thirteen," Haley said. "That's a special one."

"Don't I know it. In some ways it seems like just yesterday I was teaching her how to ride a bicycle. Before I blink, I'll be handing her the keys to the car."

Haley glanced at her phone. "Olivia's headed for Valerie's house."

"She is? With Quinn and Bree?"

"No." Haley frowned. "Alone."

"What?" He tensed. "If Valerie is my stalker and the one who attacked Maddy, isn't that dangerous?"

"Yes." Haley tapped a response and slid the phone back in her pocket. "But she can handle herself."

"But that's not—" His phone rang, offering him a welcome distraction. He glanced at the screen. Cameron Short. "I need to take this."

"Of course." Haley left and Wade tapped the screen. "Hello?"

"Wade, how are you doing?" Cameron asked.

"I've had better weeks, thanks. How are you?"

"I guess you have. I hate that you're going through this."

His friend's compassion helped. "Thanks." His thoughts weren't far from Olivia. He offered up a short prayer for her safety.

"Maybe this will cheer you up," Cameron said. "We've got

six more fundraisers on the calendar. All venues we've never been to before. All with deep pockets and sympathetic hearts. We're going to be able to help a lot more families."

"Excellent. Put them on my calendar and I'll . . ." He'd what? Be there? Not if his stalker had her way. Or stalkers—as in plural. Unbelievable.

"What is it?" Cameron asked.

He sighed. "My life at the moment. Look, put them on the calendar as tentative dates. I'll have to see where I am with this whole stalker business."

"Wade, if I start setting these up, we can't cancel."

"I know." He closed his eyes and ran a hand down his cheek. "When is the first one?"

"There's this Thursday night, of course. We can't cancel that one, but if you have to back out of being there, I'll figure something out."

"I'll be there Thursday night," Wade said. "Olivia is checking on security."

"I'll do that too. We'll have to spend some of the profits on the security, but—"

"No."

"What?"

"No, we won't spend a dime more than budgeted on security. Any extra will come out of my pocket. I refuse to take services away from the children just because some psycho has decided to come after me."

"All right." Cameron's drawn-out answer told Wade the man was thinking. "Maybe we can get some volunteers. Off-duty police and that sort of thing."

"Maybe. You work on it from your end and I'll do the same."

"Be careful, Wade. Don't take unnecessary risks. Amy needs you."

"Yeah." He didn't need the reminder, but kept his mouth shut. Cameron was right. Wade didn't plan on doing anything that would take him away from his daughter. But he didn't plan on hiding away in his home either. Surely there was some kind of middle ground? He dialed Olivia's number, not sure why he felt so compelled to know she was all right. When she didn't answer, he hung up and stared at the device for a moment.

"Wade?"

He looked up to see Martha standing in the doorway. "Yeah?"

"What is it?"

He told her where Olivia was going and shook his head. "I don't think that's smart. I'd go over there if I knew the address."

"You stay put and let her do her job."

"Her job is protection, not chasing down attempted murderers and stalkers."

"Well, if she catches a possible killer or stalker, she won't have a protection job anymore, will she?"

He stared at his sister-in-law, not appreciating her reasoning. "Catching the person causing all of the trouble and grief would be good, yes."

"But?"

He sighed. "But what if the killer catches *her* first?"

[29]

"She never showed up to visit her family, Liv," Haley said. Olivia pressed the Bluetooth device tighter into her ear and gripped the steering wheel as she maneuvered the streets of the cute middle-class neighborhood.

She figured it had been built back in the early eighties. Trees lined the entrance, giving it a soothing and welcoming feeling. Olivia decided it would be a great place to live and made a mental note to check out any houses that might be for sale. "And they weren't worried?"

"No, apparently she texted her sister and said something had come up at work and she wouldn't be able to leave until sometime next week."

Olivia followed the GPS directions until she came to a two-story home on a quiet cul-de-sac. She parked, looked in her rearview mirror, studied the area around her, and frowned. "That's weird."

"Why?"

"Because I just got off the phone with the manager of the

restaurant where she works and the woman told me she's not working this week."

"That doesn't sound good."

"I know. I need Valerie's cell phone number."

"I can probably get it for you, but it may take me a few minutes."

"Okay, you try on your end and I'll see if I can get it too. Text it to me when you have it."

Within sixty seconds Olivia was on the phone with the manager of the restaurant once again. "I know you said she wouldn't be back until Wednesday, but I have something super important to talk to her about. I also know it's probably against the rules, but would you mind giving me her cell number?"

"You're right, I can't do that."

Olivia decided to crank it up a notch. She didn't want to drive all the way downtown to get the number, which she knew she could do. All it would take would be a quick flash of her official-looking identification she used when she worked jobs for the police department.

Or she could just wait until Quinn or Bree was ready to talk to the woman and tag along. But she was antsy, with an itchy feeling that wouldn't leave her alone until she'd talked to Valerie. "Look, she never showed up to visit her family. She said something had come up at work and she would have to stay home."

"What? That's not true! I'm telling you she's not on the schedule."

"I know. Something's not adding up and I'm concerned. I just want to check on her." Not a lie. She was concerned.

She sensed hesitation on the other end of the line. The woman was weakening. "Or you can call her and give her my number," Olivia said. "I'm open to whatever it takes to get in touch with her."

"Now you've got me worried. I'll call her. Hold on while I switch to another line."

"Thanks."

Olivia heard the click and waited. Impatience made her want to fidget. Instead, she stared at Valerie's house and waited.

"She's not answering," the manager said a few short minutes later.

"Then let me try. I'll call until I get her." More hesitation from the manager. "Look, I promise not to tell her how I got the number, but if she's in trouble . . ."

"Fine. Fine." The woman rattled off the number and Olivia quickly jotted it down on a receipt. "And remember, if I wasn't worried, I wouldn't have given it to you. She's not just an employee, she's a friend."

"I know. Thank you so much. Oh wait!"

"Yeah?"

"What's your name?"

A sigh. "Ginger."

"Ginger, do you know if Valerie had a boyfriend or was seeing anyone? Had she been acting different or missing work lately?" The woman didn't answer and Olivia wondered if she'd pushed too hard. "Never mind. I'll ask her when I see her."

"Why do you want to know?"

"Just a hunch."

"You sound like a cop."

"I used to be one. Now I work for another agency."

"And you need information on Valerie for this agency?"

"I'll be honest with you. Like I said, I'm not a cop. You don't have to tell me anything at all. The only reason I'm asking questions about Valerie is because I'm concerned about her welfare. She said she was going to visit her family and she didn't. She said she had to work and she didn't. That bothers me enough for me to look into her whereabouts and make sure she's all right."

"I see." She paused and Olivia waited hoping she was going to share more. "Your hunch is right on," Ginger said.

Thank you. "Why?"

Another, longer sigh filtered through the line. "Valerie's been working the morning shift for a year now. She recently started being late all the time. That wasn't like her. When I asked her about it, she told me she'd met someone—or was interested in someone."

"Did she say who?"

"No. But—"

"But?"

"She said the reason she was staying up so late was to listen to some guy's radio show and that's why she was having a hard time getting to work on time."

"So she was interested in the guy doing the show?"

"I guess. She never came right out and said it was him, but she sure doesn't want to miss listening to his show."

Why the woman decided to open up and share all of this information was a mystery, but Olivia decided not to question it. She just appreciated it. "Did she say anything about sending this person some gifts?"

"Gifts? Like what?"

"Concert tickets, expensive jerseys, candy."

"No way." She gave a short laugh. "Valerie is practically broke. She lives in a pretty nice house that her grandfather left her, but it's not paid off and the mortgage payment eats up her little paycheck. I know for a fact her credit cards are maxed out. She can barely afford to keep her lights on, much less buy anyone expensive gifts. Her brother even had to send her the money for the visit this week."

"When was she supposed to get there?"

"Yesterday. Will you let me know what you find?"

"Of course. Thank you so much."

"Sure."

Olivia hung up and dialed the number. It rang four times, then went to voice mail. Olivia disconnected and considered how she wanted to approach this. She wasn't a cop anymore, but she knew how to handle an investigation. But since this wasn't her investigation, she couldn't go in and just start asking Valerie questions.

Maybe if she sat there long enough, the woman would come out to get her mail, go for a jog, or something. Assuming she was even home. She was supposed to have visited her sister, but never showed. Her family thought she was working, but she wasn't. Olivia found that more than a little concerning. Although it could just be the woman wanted some time alone and had told a couple of white lies in order to make that happen.

Or she could be making it convenient to stalk Wade without having to worry about work or family checking up on her. Establishing an alibi? But such a poor one? Surely she could come up with something better than that. It would be too easy to prove she wasn't at either place.

Olivia got out of the car and walked up the front porch steps. She rapped her knuckles against the door and waited. Silence echoed around her. A car drove down the street and slowed as it passed hers. She turned and waved. The person waved back, then kept going.

Olivia pulled her phone from her pocket and tried Valerie's number again. It rang in her ear—and from inside the house. She tried the door and found it locked. But the phone kept ringing.

Olivia unsnapped the strap that kept her weapon in the holster. She had no reason to believe anyone would cause her harm, but old instincts died hard.

Assume the worst, hope for the best.

She moved off the porch and to a window, trying to see inside. The blinds were drawn and she couldn't even see around the edges except for the light filtering from the living room. So she was going to be gone, but left her living room lights on?

Olivia held her weapon in one hand, her phone in the other. She pressed the button to redial Valerie's number. Again she heard the phone ringing from inside the house. She cut the connections and dialed Quinn's number. It went to voice mail and she figured he was busy with the missing persons case. She tried Bree on the off chance she could answer.

"Yeah, Liv, what's up?"

"I'm at Valerie Mathis's house. I can hear her cell phone ringing from inside but no one's answering."

"Maybe she forgot it."

"Maybe. Lights are on in her living room too."

"You think something's wrong?"

"I do. Nothing's adding up. I'm going to get inside and see if she needs help." Olivia frowned. "She might be hurt."

"Or she might not be there. Don't put yourself in possible danger."

"There's no danger. I think she's incapacitated in some way or not here. Don't worry, I won't be stupid."

"Why doesn't that comfort me?"

"Seriously, if she's hurt, she might need help fast."

Bree sighed. "Be careful."

"Right." Olivia hung up and stepped around the corner of the house. The grass hadn't been cut recently, but it wasn't overgrown or neglected. She walked around to the back. The windows were covered. No seeing in there. She kept moving until she came to the side carport. She moved inside and tried the door that led to the kitchen.

The knob turned.

·····································

The stalker waited in the shadows. Watching. Following Olivia had proved to be a worrisome task. She constantly looked over her shoulder, keeping a watchful eye on her surroundings. Like she *expected* to see someone. But she hadn't noticed anyone following her.

When Olivia had sat outside the house and just talked on her cell phone, the stalker thought she might decide to leave without going inside. And that would be fine. But no. Olivia had gotten out of her car and was going in. So now Olivia would have to die. The car door opened, then shut with a quiet click.

·····································

Olivia stepped inside Valerie's kitchen and wrinkled her nose at the odor that greeted her. She shut the door behind her and her belly churned. She knew that smell.

She swallowed and automatically reached for the Mentholatum that she used to carry while on duty. She slapped an empty pocket. Right, she didn't need that anymore. Usually.

"Valerie? Are you here?"

No answer. But then she hadn't really expected one.

She hesitated. So. Wait on backup or go see what—who—was making the house stink? In her heart, she figured she knew the answer to the second part of her question, but her mind wanted to deny it until she saw the proof. Could be an animal had crawled into the house and died. Nothing sinister about that at all.

She could only hope that was the case.

She moved through the kitchen and into the den, breathing through her mouth as she moved, trying not to gag. Using the hem of her shirt, she flipped the den light on. Nothing looked disturbed. She moved toward the hallway, pausing at the base of the stairs that would lead to the second floor. She heard nothing from above.

Her phone buzzed. She looked at the screen. A text from Bree.

Bree
You all right?

Olivia
According to the stench, there's a dead body in this house. Looking for it now.

I'll send backup.

Let me make sure it's human. If it's Valerie. I'll need the ME and most likely CSU. If it's a dead animal or something then, I'll let you know.

When she got no immediate response from Bree, Olivia figured the woman was probably notifying someone to stand by and be ready to roll out to Valerie's house.

Olivia checked the living area, a bedroom, and a bath. Nothing set off her alarm bells. She turned back to the steps and started up.

One at a time, the butterflies did the frantic dance inside her stomach at the thought of what she was going to find. Every horror movie she'd ever watched played through her mind. Every crime scene she'd ever covered flashed in Technicolor slides behind her eyes.

She couldn't help her antsiness. She took comfort in the feel of her weapon against her palm.

At the top of the stairs, she stopped. The odor was much stronger, the pungent scent of death and decay made her want to hurl. But she couldn't leave now. If there was a body, she needed the right people here to process it. Could be an animal, she reminded herself.

Olivia pulled the collar of her shirt up over her nose. It didn't help much. A slight creak from somewhere in the house made her pause.

Was that a footstep? She held still, breathing shallow breaths, and listened. Her grip tightened on the butt of her weapon. She went back down to the bottom of the stairs, stopping on the last step that would take her into the open foyer. She peered around the corner. Left. Right. Nothing. Another thirty seconds of listening convinced her it was just the house making noises. Probably.

She turned and started up the stairs again. When she reached the top, she found herself in the middle of a hallway. To the left were two bedrooms with a connecting bath and to the right a closet, then probably the master bedroom. Her pulse beat a fast rhythm and she could hear the pounding of her heart. Why was she so keyed up? She'd seen dead bodies before. Smelled them too. Had been one of two rookies who hadn't passed out, vomited, or left the room in a hurry during the autopsy she'd viewed while in the academy. Still . . .

Her phone buzzed and she pressed the button. "Yeah," she spoke in a low voice, no more than a whisper. She cleared her throat. "Hello?" she said in a more normal volume. Her voice sounded loud, disturbing in the tomblike quiet of the house.

"Olivia?"

Wade's voice almost made her pause. She hadn't expected to hear him on the other side. "Yeah."

"I've been trying to call you. Are you all right?" he demanded.

"I'm fine. I'm not sure Valerie is, though." She paused. "Is Haley with you?"

"Of course."

"Let me talk to her a second, please."

She waited while he made the switch. "What's going on?"

Olivia told her.

"Have you found the body?"

"Not yet." A low creak reached her ears and she froze. A footfall on the hardwood stairs. Then another. Coming up toward her. Okay, that was not the house settling. She lowered her voice. "I think someone's in the house with me, Haley. I'll call you back."

"What? Get out of there. Stay on the phone with me."

"Going to call Bree."

"Olivia!"

She hung up and dialed Bree. It went to voice mail. She tried Quinn. Voice mail.

Great. She put her phone on vibrate.

Keeping a firm grip on her weapon, she moved to the master bedroom. The closed door mocked her. She placed a hand on the knob and turned.

Her phone vibrated. The door opened but she kept her back to the room, facing the stairs where the threat seemed to come from. She held her weapon ready, her nerves humming in spite of her mental orders for them to calm down. "Hello?" she whispered as loud as she dared.

"Liv, you all right?"

Bree.

Olivia watched the stairs, expecting to see someone appear at the top any second. "I'm still in Valerie's house."

"You need help?"

"I think someone's in the house with me."

"The dead body?"

"No, a very much alive one."

"Liv, get out of there." Her low voice full of concern made Olivia's blood pulse faster.

"Can't. I'm upstairs with no way out but down the stairs someone is coming up. Just checking to see when that backup's going to be here." The adrenaline rushing through her made her shaky.

"Lock yourself in a room and stay there. Backup should only be about ten away."

Keeping her eyes on the hallway in front of her, the phone in her back pocket but still connected to the Bluetooth and Bree, she backed inside. A shadow highlighted against the staircase wall. A large shadow in the shape of a human.

Olivia sucked in a deep breath, fought the wave of nausea the action brought with it, and shut the door. "There's someone on the stairs." She was nearly mouthing the words, her whisper was so quiet. She hoped Bree could hear her.

"Where are you?"

"In the master bedroom off the back of the house."

She twisted the lock, then turned and froze as her eyes landed on the floor behind her.

The nausea tripled and she fought the need to lose the contents of her stomach. A woman lay on the floor next to the bed, the covers twisted around her. Her mouth and eyes gaped. Olivia gasped and gagged.

"Olivia?"

"Found the dead body. Where's that backup?"

Bree paused, said something to someone, then came back to Olivia. "Five minutes."

Olivia turned away for a brief moment before the need to survive kicked in. Footsteps fell on the thin carpet outside the room. The knob rattled but the lock held.

Olivia held her breath and listened, her gun trained on the door. Whoever was on the other side didn't speak or call out. Neither did she.

"Olivia?" Bree's voice came through the earpiece in her ear. "Shhhh."

Bree fell silent.

Within seconds Olivia heard retreating footsteps. She figured the person was going to look for something to help gain entrance and Olivia didn't plan to be there when the door opened. But first . . .

She removed her phone from her back pocket. "Hold on a sec."

"You all right?"

"For the moment." Olivia shot pictures of the body and the room. She tried not to focus on the fact that the woman on the floor had been a living, breathing person. A person with dreams and hopes. A person who didn't deserve to die like this.

Anger started to burn away the shock of seeing the evidence of such violence. She'd seen a lot of horrible stuff as a police officer and she'd never gotten used to it. She'd learned to hide her reaction, mask her horror that people were capable of inflicting such evil on other humans, but she never got used to it. She'd promised herself she'd quit if she ever became indifferent to seeing scenes such as the one before her now.

Urgency pushed her and she snapped shots from every angle she could before she knew she had to leave.

Finished with the pictures, she moved to the French doors to see out. No tree to climb out on and shimmy down. Just a wrought iron balcony overlooking the backyard.

The sharp smell of gasoline overpowered the dead body smell and she turned toward the odor, frowning. Wha—

Smoke curled under the door and understanding hit her. "He's set the house on fire, Bree. He's smoking me out."

[30]

Wade sat in the passenger seat of Haley's car and made a conscious effort to relax his jaw. "How much farther?"

"About a minute."

"Why isn't she answering her phone?"

"I don't know. She's probably busy taking care of whoever's in the house with her."

He shot her a perturbed look she missed because her eyes were on the road. "She said there was a dead body."

"Yes."

"You don't seem concerned."

Her fingers flexed on the wheel. "I'm concerned."

Wade sent up prayers for Olivia. When Haley had asked about a body, his heart had dropped to his toes. Then Olivia said someone was in the house with her and he grabbed his keys.

Of course Haley had no choice but to take him with her. She'd snatched the keys from his fingers, told him to get into her car, and she climbed into the driver's seat. Now the clock was ticking and Olivia wasn't answering her phone. "So does she have help by now? Are the cops there?"

"I sure hope so."

"Can't you call Bree or Quinn?"

"Olivia said she was calling Bree. If Olivia needs me, she'll call me back. I don't want to be a distraction."

The muscles at the base of his neck and across his shoulders felt like they might snap. He rotated his head to no avail. He wouldn't be able to relax until he knew Olivia was safe.

<hr>

"Can you get out?"

Olivia was shocked at how quickly the smoke filled the room in spite of the fact that she'd moved fast and crammed a bedsheet into the crack of the door. The bedroom door was hot to the touch. No going out that way. She wasn't worried about contaminating the crime scene at this point. She just wanted to get out alive. Flames had eaten through the bedsheet and now licked along the floor where the gasoline had soaked through.

Sirens screamed in the distance and relief filled her even while it was short-lived. Help might be on the way, but she had to help herself too. She twisted the knob on the French door. It didn't move. She shook it, rattled the knob, pushed. Nothing. For the first time since she'd realized she wasn't alone in the house, panic started to creep in. Through the haze, she tried to see if there was a latch or something she needed to release in order to open the door.

There. At the top. A sliding lock. She reached up and pushed, but again to no avail. Stuck. She wanted to scream in frustration, but refused to waste the breath. Each time she inhaled, she brought smoke into her lungs.

Lungs that were starting to burn.

She coughed, stepped back, and brought her leg up. She gave the area near the handle a hard kick. The door shuddered, but didn't open. Flames crawled along the carpet and started on the bed coverings.

She spun and grabbed the lamp off the end table, then whirled back to aim the heavy base at the glass doors. With a grunt, she slammed it into the glass.

The door shattered outward onto the deck. Fresh air rushed in and hit the flames. Heat and smoke surrounded her. Dizziness assailed her and she stumbled, coughing. The flames now licked at the drapes of the window to the left of the French doors.

She looked back, wondering if she had time to wrap Valerie's body and drag her out of the room. She wanted to preserve the evidence but didn't want to die trying. The heat smothered her. Smoke choked her. The bed was already burning. No time.

She kicked out more of the glass to make room for her to slip through. The smoke followed her out onto the small deck made of wood and wrought iron. No bigger than six feet by five, there were no steps leading down and the wood beneath her feet was old and warped. And dry. If it caught fire, she'd have only seconds. Fresh fear hit her. She had nowhere else to go.

Except over and down.

Sirens screamed to a stop at the front of the house. She faced the backyard. Bree was still connected via the Bluetooth. "I need help getting down and I need it fast."

She looked down again. The small deck was on the second floor, which wouldn't be such a terrible drop if it wasn't for the fact that the house backed up to a sharp incline leading down to a creek with woods on the other side.

She'd break her leg. Or her neck. The smoke thickened around her. The flames spread further. The stench of burning flesh reached her. She closed her eyes for a split second while she swallowed against the nausea rising in the back of her throat. Poor Valerie.

Better to break bones or fry? "Come on, Bree, I need a ladder."

"Hang tight."

She looked down, coughing, dizzy, and still nauseous. The fire arched around her. "Hang tight," she whispered. "Afraid that's what I'm going to be doing." Sparks shot at her and she hissed as they landed on her exposed skin. The dry wooden floor of the porch caught fire, the flames licking up the dry wood. Fast. The porch shuddered beneath her. "Uh oh."

"What?"

Olivia didn't have a choice.

She swung a leg over the wrought iron railing. A loud crack sounded over the roar of the fire and she flinched. Her right cheek stung like she'd been attacked by a swarm of bees.

"Olivia!"

"Bree—"

The wooden floor collapsed and her tenuous grip on the wrought iron shifted as the structure sagged with the combination of the dropping wood and her weight. She clung, but her left hand slipped off—and her right wasn't far behind.

Haley froze. With the windows down, the chaos surrounding the situation was loud and clear. Another fire truck squealed to a stop and firefighters in their gear crawled down from their trucks like ants on a mission.

A loud blast echoed through the neighborhood. The firefighters stopped and looked at each other.

"What is it?" Wade asked.

"That was a gunshot!" Haley said.

Wade stared in horror at the flames licking through the roof toward the back of the house. He got out of the car and Haley yelled something at him.

He ignored her. "Is Olivia in there?"

She grasped his upper arm. "Get back in the car."

He jerked away from her. "Is she in there?"

"I don't know!"

A black sedan rolled behind Haley's vehicle. Bree and Quinn got out. Bree didn't bother to shut the door, but took off toward the back of the house like she'd been shot from a cannon. Wade followed after her. He thought he heard Quinn shout at him, or maybe it was Haley, but he didn't look back. Olivia had been talking to Bree on the way over. Wherever the detective was going, he was sure to find Olivia.

Bree rounded the corner of the house. Wade followed her. A sharp drop-off to his right. He looked left.

And gaped. "Olivia," he whispered.

"Oh my g—" Bree shot forward with Wade right behind. "Hang on, Liv!"

"I'm trying!" Olivia dangled two floors up, one hand grasping the wrought iron railing, feet trying to find a foothold around the part of the railing that would lead her to the ground. If she could wrap her legs around it, she could ride it like a firehouse pole. But she couldn't quite reach it.

Another crack sounded, kicking up the dirt in front of him. Bree hollered and dropped to the ground. Wade flinched, but stood his ground, never taking his eyes from Olivia. If she dropped, the momentum might carry her down the rocky hill. She hung low enough that if she dropped to the ground just below her and didn't roll, she should be fine.

Haley barreled into him and shoved him behind her.

"I'm going after the shooter!" Quinn shouted.

He heard Quinn's footsteps head to the woods where the gunshot had come from. Bree was on her phone screaming for someone to get around to the back of the house with a ladder.

"I'm really not happy with you," Haley said in his ear to his right. He noticed she'd placed herself between him and the direction the bullets had come from. She tried to move him in the direction of the car, to safety. Guilt stabbed him. "Haley, please protect yourself. I'm not moving to safety until Olivia's out of danger."

"How is getting shot going to help her?"

"It won't. But look. If she falls—"

Haley finally saw what he saw and swallowed, glanced in the direction Quinn had disappeared and nodded.

"Yeah. We can't let her fall. Where's that ladder, Bree?"

Wade moved closer, his heart thundering, prayers lifting from his lips as he focused on Olivia. If she let go or lost her grip, he was going to catch her. Or at least break her fall and keep her from rolling down the hill and into the creek. Rocks, sticks, broken branches, and tree stumps littered the drop-off. If she fell onto one of them, she could be impaled. Just like her friend.

He knew she'd already thought of that. Probably why she hadn't let go yet. His pulse thundered in his ears. He waited for the sound of another crack, the feel of a bullet to pierce his skin, but he wouldn't move.

"Got the ladder! Everyone out of the way!"

He met Olivia's eyes. Desperation and pain stared down at him. Along with a harsh determination. Flames licked around her. The heat had to be intense. Wade could feel it and it almost drove him back. How was she holding on?

And then she wasn't.

She tumbled toward him. He let his body relax and accepted her hit. He wrapped his arms around her as he went down. The force of the impact from both Olivia on top of him and the ground beneath blew the breath from his lungs.

He lay there stunned, his world fading to gray, sounds dulling, his lungs straining. And felt himself start to roll down the hill. He thrashed his legs. Anything to stop the momentum.

Then he jarred to a stop, heard the chaos, felt Olivia pulled from his grip. "Watch her hands, she's got burns," he gasped.

"Sir? Are you all right?"

He was finally able to drag in a full breath. He coughed and struggled to sit up. No sharp pains so he figured he hadn't broken anything. "Olivia? Is she all right?"

"Let's get you away from here."

"Olivia?"

"She's being treated, now come on," Haley urged him. He felt her tug on his arm. "Can you stand up?"

"Give me a second." The world quit spinning and his eyes settled on the firefighters aiming the hose at the blaze that had taken out most of the back of the house. Sparks flew, debris fluttered down, and smoke curled around them. He coughed and allowed the paramedic and Haley to help him to his feet. "Did they catch the shooter?"

"Bree and Quinn have gone after him," Haley said.

"Him?"

"Or her. Whoever it was."

Wade nodded, but his eyes sought Olivia. And found her on a gurney being led to the back of an ambulance. She had a sheet pulled all the way over her head.

[31]

"No!"

Olivia blinked and coughed, heard the one-word cry of desperation through the roaring in her ears. Or was that the roar of the fire? She felt the softness beneath her, but the bouncing was making her sick. Finally, the movement stopped. The sheet was pulled back and an oxygen mask slapped over her face.

She shoved it away and winced at the pain in her palm.

The mask came back. "Leave it there a bit, will you? You've inhaled quite a bit of smoke."

She didn't recognize the voice, but decided to obey for the moment. Get her scrambled thoughts in order. Take a physical inventory. It didn't take long to figure out everything hurt.

"Olivia?"

"She's not dead, Wade," she heard Haley say. "They pulled the sheet up to keep the debris from falling on her."

No, she wasn't dead. Had she passed out? Maybe for a split second. She'd fallen, though. She definitely remembered that. The pain had been too intense and she'd let go.

She forced her eyes open. Wade. She heard the commotion,

the firefighters yelling, the water pulsing. Clarity returned. She sat up with a gasp, shoved the mask off once more. "He shot at me!"

Wade laid a hand on her arm. "Bree and Quinn are after her."

The paramedic took her right hand in her gloved one. "Keep the mask on for now." She nodded to the hand. "Do you mind if I take a look?"

Olivia finally acknowledged the pain and looked down. Blisters coated her palm and fingers. She grimaced. At least it wasn't her gun hand.

While the woman doctored her hand, Olivia took another pull on the oxygen. She coughed when it hit her lungs. The paramedic didn't blink, just slathered some ointment on her wound and started wrapping her hand in gauze.

Olivia looked at Wade and swallowed hard. "Thank you."

He nodded.

"You put yourself in danger."

"I couldn't just stand around and do nothing."

She pursed her lips. "Yes, I know." And she did. She might be his bodyguard, but his male protective instincts wouldn't allow him to stay in a comfort zone while people put themselves in danger for him and those he loved. Unfortunately.

It wasn't a new twist. She'd come across this before with men, of course, but Wade put a whole new meaning to the phrase "actively involved."

For those on the outside looking in, it might appear that Wade was acting foolishly. But she understood his type of personality and knew it was just part of his genetic makeup, his DNA. And something she'd have to take into consideration from now on. Instead of working against him, trying to fight him into submission, she'd have to include him in whatever plans they made. Or he'd include himself.

She looked behind Wade. Bree and Quinn walked toward her. She didn't have to ask. The looks on their faces were enough. "Do you know where she went?"

Quinn shook his head. "She had a vehicle waiting."

Bree's lips tightened and she shook her head. "I've called in the location. Law enforcement has the vehicle description. They've already released a BOLO. Hopefully someone will spot the car soon."

Olivia stared at the burning structure. She figured the neighbors on either side had been evacuated, the others stood on their porches and rubbernecked.

The medical examiner had arrived. Francisco Zamora looked like a cover model more than an ME, with his curly black hair and perfectly complected olive skin. He stood a fraction under six foot three and didn't let his profession spoil his good humor.

His eyes caught hers and he walked toward her. "You all right?"

His light Hispanic accent soothed her raw nerves. Kind of like being in Wade's presence. She frowned. "Peachy."

"I see that. Glad I'm not going to find you on one of my tables."

Her frown slipped into an outright scowl. "Trust me, I'm more glad than you are." She sighed and with her good hand worked her cell phone from her pocket. She looked at it with a grunt of satisfaction. Her slam into Wade hadn't damaged it. "That LifeProof case was worth every penny." She handed the device to Francisco. "Text yourself the last two dozen or so pictures. I'll have to hand them over to the authorities shortly."

"You took pictures?"

"Yes."

"When the house was burning?"

"Hm."

He lifted a brow. "I don't know whether to be impressed with your bravery and quick-thinking or appalled at your stupidity."

"I know which one I prefer." She lasered him with a fierce glare. "Whoever is doing this is not going to get away with it. I had time to take the pictures." Regret flashed. "I didn't have time to drag her body out."

"Glad you knew the difference."

Wade stood silent, his tight jaw indicating he was listening—and probably biting his tongue. He met her gaze. "How did the person know you were going to be here?"

"She didn't. She must have followed me."

"You weren't watching your back?"

"Of course I was. I never saw anyone that set off my alarms."

He rubbed his nose and nodded. A black van pulled into the fray. Olivia recognized the CSU vehicle. "Sarah's here."

Francisco looked back at the burning house. "Doubt she's going to have much to work with."

Olivia scowled. "Yeah."

Francisco handed her phone back to her. She slipped it into her pocket. The paramedics started to close the doors. With her still on the stretcher inside the ambulance. "Hey, wait a minute."

The young woman paused. "We're ready to get you to the hospital."

"I don't need a hospital. I have a job to do."

"Yes you do need a hospital," Haley said. "I've got Wade covered, Katie's on Amy. You need to get checked out. When you're finished, text me and we'll go from there."

"I've got a burn and some smoke inhalation." Olivia held up her bandaged hand. "Got this covered. Nothing much they can do for the other."

Haley's eyes narrowed. "They may need to monitor you.

There's no telling what you breathed in. We don't need you thinking you're fine and then collapsing."

Olivia opened her mouth to protest, then snapped it shut when Wade climbed in beside her. He nodded to the paramedic. "Let's go."

<hr />

Six hours of waiting was taking its toll. Wade watched from the chair that had been positioned outside Olivia's room so Haley could keep an eye on him—and afford Olivia some privacy while the doctor checked her out. His gut burned. He felt like a child in time-out. But since he was working on his attitude and cooperating with those who had pledged to protect him at all costs, he kept his mouth shut and didn't ask if he could enter the room. Not yet. He needed to think anyway. Being in the room with Olivia would just be a distraction.

He leaned back to stare at the ceiling. The girls were fine, according to Martha, and occupied in Amy's room watching a video. Martha had said something about preparing a dish to take to a friend who'd had surgery. Haley was pacing like a caged tiger, checking and rechecking her phone with never a change to the scowl on her face. Since the initial report, no one seemed inclined to tell him anything more about Olivia's condition, so he simply sat and thought.

Someone had thrown his life into turmoil all because of what? She'd fixated on him? Decided he didn't deserve to live because he hadn't responded positively to her advances? Had targeted people he loved because he wouldn't concede to her twisted desires?

He mentally reviewed the women in his life and couldn't come up with one who might be capable of instigating the incidents he'd managed to live through.

Should he run? Find a place to hide out and pray the woman gave up? He shut his eyes. "What would that do to Amy, Lord?" he murmured.

The idea of running went against everything in him. He'd always stood his ground and fought for what he believed in. But what if the cost of fighting was too high? He sighed and rubbed his temples. He simply didn't know what to do.

He glanced at his watch, then pulled his cell phone from his pocket. He had one more person he could touch base with. He pressed the fifth number on speed dial.

"Savage Counseling Center."

"Hi, Linda."

"Wade, how are you doing?"

"I'm hanging in there, thanks. Any trouble canceling the appointments for the rest of the week?"

"No, everyone seemed to understand and I've already gotten them rescheduled for next week. You're going to be putting in a bit of overtime, though."

"That's fine. I'm praying all this is over by next week. Actually tomorrow would be nice."

"Wade—"

He frowned at her hesitation. "What is it, Linda?"

"You're not in any *real* danger, are you? I mean, this person wouldn't *really* kill you, would she? She just wants some attention or something, right?"

The concern and worry in her voice warmed him. Some days he felt so alone and then in the blink of an eye he was reminded he wasn't. He did have people in his life who cared. And while he *knew* that, it was nice to have it reinforced. "I'm not sure, but we're doing our best to make sure nothing happens to me or my family."

"Oh me. Please be careful."

"Of course."

She cleared her throat. "All right, I'll send you the revised schedule and those patients who may be running low—or out—of their medications."

"Thanks, Linda."

"Stay safe."

He hung up and blew out a slow sigh, his mind spinning.

He looked up to see Haley finishing a conversation with a nurse. She turned and walked over to him, much of the tension drained from her face. "They're releasing her."

Olivia had passed all tests, had her bandage changed on her hand, and was waiting—albeit impatiently—to be released from the hospital. The doctor had grudgingly agreed to let her go with specific instructions on symptoms to watch for that would require her to return to the hospital for more treatment of the smoke inhalation.

Fifteen minutes later, while Haley was on her phone just out of hearing range, Olivia stepped from the room. Wade's eyes immediately went to her even as he stood. She had a red welt across her cheek. "What's that from?"

"A bullet, I think."

He winced and lifted a hand, then stopped as though to drop it. "That was close."

Olivia gave him a slow smile. "Thanks."

"For?"

"For not asking if I'm all right."

"Except for that welt, I know you're all right physically."

"You're wondering about my mental state?" The idea seemed to intrigue her.

"Maybe a little. You almost died."

"But I didn't."

"Thank God."

"Hmm. Maybe."

He lifted a brow. "You don't believe in God?"

"I believe in him, I just don't like him very much."

Wade frowned. Now she had him curious. "What's not to like?"

She looked away. "Not now."

Haley stepped up and slid her phone in her pocket. Wade snapped his lips shut. But he'd bring the subject up again soon.

"So what's next?" Haley asked, her gaze bouncing from him to Olivia.

"Now we lock down Wade's house like Fort Knox," Olivia said, "wait for labs to come back on the woman who was killed in Valerie Mathis's house—just to confirm it was actually her—and map out a plan for the next few days."

"What kind of plan did you have in mind?"

"One that keeps Wade alive and puts a stalker behind bars."

[32]

Olivia's hand throbbed, but she refused to cave and take one of the painkillers that might dull her reaction time. Amy was safe at school with Katie and Lizzie to protect her should Wade's stalker try to get at her again. Charlie was on his way over. In the meantime, she needed to think. To plan. Last night had been quiet, but she didn't fool herself into thinking the woman—and man?—had disappeared. She figured they were just in the eye of the storm.

She knew Wade didn't want to rock Amy's world, she got that. She also got that he wasn't being deliberately difficult. He was naturally an independent, do-it-himself kind of guy who had to be in control. Figuring out he wasn't was hitting him hard. But at least he wasn't stupid. He recognized he was out of his element, and was willing to meet her *almost* halfway.

Olivia paced Wade's den and hung up the phone. It had been an intense and in-depth conversation with the head of security for the event, but worth the time she'd taken to have it.

Security was actually very good for the dinner Wade still

planned to attend tomorrow night, so that made her breathe a little easier. Local law enforcement would be in attendance as well as private security hired by Wade's father. Bruce wasn't taking any chances and had given carte blanche as far as doing what they needed. Katie and Charlie would remain with Amy, along with the officer assigned to the house, while Olivia and the rest of her employees worked the dinner.

When she'd arrived first thing this morning at Wade's home, he was already locked in his office making phone calls to patients, calming some, reassuring others, adding a personal explanation as to his absence.

Martha had rolled her eyes and muttered something under her breath about his workaholic tendencies, then shook her head as though to rid herself of the worry over something she couldn't change.

"He really cares about his patients, doesn't he?" Olivia said.

Martha's irritation vanished in a flash and her face softened. "Very much so." She had shot a fond look at the closed door, then turned her attention back to Olivia. "Joanna's on her way over," she said. "No need to jump out of your skin when she rings the bell."

"Thanks for the warning," Olivia murmured.

Martha sighed. "You know, I told Joanna as much time as she spends here, she should just move in with me. That apartment above the garage has two bedrooms."

"And she won't?"

"No. She laughed and said being roommates might destroy a lifelong friendship."

"She could be on to something there."

"True." Martha slipped past her and into the kitchen. "Amy's birthday is coming up. I sure hope you catch this crazy person before her party."

"I hope so too."

Martha had clicked her tongue and started concocting some delicious-smelling breakfast while Olivia got on the phone.

Now she mulled over another topic. Justine.

"Everything all right?"

She looked up to find Wade in the doorway.

"All right as far as what?"

"Just . . . are you all right? How's your hand?"

She held it up. "It hurts."

He frowned. "I'm sorry."

"I'm not. If you hadn't caught me, I'd probably be a lot worse off."

"Yeah."

She studied him. "You shouldn't have been out there, you know that, right?"

"Um-hm."

"So why were you?"

He tilted his head and cocked a brow. "I was with Haley. I knew you were in danger and I couldn't just sit by and do nothing." He walked toward her and held her gaze. The look there caused a skip in her pulse. What was he thinking? "I know it's your job to put yourself on the line for your clients," he said, "but that doesn't make you any less vulnerable than the average person. You can still get hurt."

"I know that." She didn't look away as he came closer. She just . . . couldn't. Instead, her heart picked up speed. Her stomach fluttered. She felt ensnared. Trapped. But in a good way. A new way. An emotionally terrifying way. Her mind screamed, *Run!*

But her heart ordered her to stand still.

He lifted his hand and cupped her cheek. She stared up at him, saw the intent on his face, and couldn't back away. Didn't *want* to back away. They'd been attracted to each other from their first meeting. He knew it and she knew it. Maybe it was time to stop fighting it. His head lowered, slowly, fraction by fraction. Olivia didn't move.

"Wade, could you—"

Olivia spun away, unable to believe she'd stood there as long as she had. She cleared her throat and pulled her phone from her pocket. When she turned back, she saw Martha's stunned gaze on her brother-in-law. Then she shot a puzzled, accusing look at Olivia.

"Yes, Martha, what is it?" Wade asked.

"Um . . . ," her gaze darted between Olivia and Wade, who'd taken only one step back from Olivia, "I . . . uh . . . just wanted to know if you'd get the big mixing bowl down from the top shelf of the pantry. I never use it, but thought I'd mix up some pancakes and so . . . yeah."

"Of course," he said to Martha, although he never took his eyes from Olivia.

Wade didn't look in the least embarrassed. A tad shocked, maybe, a little bemused at his behavior, but definitely not embarrassed. He'd given them both something to think about. When he followed Martha from the room, Olivia let out a slow breath. Okay, she'd think about what almost happened later. Not now. Somehow he'd shattered the thick walls she'd spent years building. All in the space of a few days. Now she felt exposed. Vulnerable. Stupid. And a tiny bit thrilled. Because deep down, she wasn't sure she had the capacity to feel anything remotely like interest in a man. Not because she'd been hurt by one in her past, but because she'd been hurt, period. Trust didn't come easily for her. And now . . .

She blinked.

Later. Back to work.

"Focus," she whispered.

One more thing preyed on her mind, taking over the moment she'd just shared—or *almost* shared—with Wade, and she punched in a text to Francisco.

> **Olivia**
> Would you let me see the autopsy report for Justine Harmon?

> **Francisco**
> Why?

> Just because. I'm curious.

Her phone rang. She answered. "Please?"

"Anyone can fill out a request," Francisco said, sounding slightly out of breath. "You should have an answer in a few weeks." He gave a grunt.

"Are you doing push-ups again?"

"Yes. The paperwork can be found online."

"Francisco . . ."

A sigh reached her. "Fine, I don't remember the name so I probably didn't do the autopsy. I'll pull the file, but you have to come here to read it. If I'm not going to go through proper channels with a written request, yadda yadda, I'm not leaving a paper trail."

"I understand. I'll be there as soon as I can get there."

"I'll have it ready."

"How many?"

"I did ten thousand three hundred nonstop pushups this past weekend."

"Awesome."

"Not awesome enough if I want to break the world record."

"You'll do it, you're incredibly close. I'm on the way." Olivia hung up and stared at the floor for a few seconds. She heard Martha and Joanna in the kitchen, but wasn't sure where Wade had disappeared to. She went to find Martha and stopped outside the door when she heard her name.

"He did what?" Joanna asked.

"Almost kissed her. I think," Martha said, her voice low. "I'm not sure, but that's what it looked like."

"That's . . . odd."

"He hasn't shown any interest in a woman since Justine and now her?"

"Maybe you're wrong. Maybe it was just . . ."

"Just what, Joanna?" Martha snapped.

"I don't know."

Olivia felt her cheeks burning. There was no way she could walk into the kitchen and face those two women. Not yet. She went back into the den and called Charlie. "Hey, how far away are you?"

"About ten minutes."

She told him her plans, then called Bree. "What's up?"

"How much of a background check did you do into Martha Taylor?"

"The sister-in-law?"

"Yes."

"A pretty comprehensive one. Went all the way back to her high school years. Hang on a sec." Olivia waited. Wade stepped back into the den, saw she was on the phone, and turned to leave. She held up a finger to stop him. He waited. Bree came back on the line. "There's nothing that stands out. No red flags. She got into some trouble as a teen, but nothing since she turned eighteen and went off to college. Worked her way to the head of public relations for the hospital, then went to work for Wade."

"Okay. Thanks."

"Why?"

"Just . . . something happened this morning that made me want to take a closer look."

"Anything I need to be concerned about?" Bree's voice sharpened.

"No. Not yet. I'll keep you updated."

"You do that." A pause. "How's Maddy?"

"Quinn hasn't been keeping you updated?"

"Somewhat. Every time I ask about her, his mood turns dark and stormy enough to rival Hurricane Katrina. I'm giving him some space and getting my information from other reliable sources."

"Gotcha. Last I heard she was still in a medically induced coma, but healing."

Wade leaned against the doorjamb and watched her, his eyes tracking her movements, his gaze just as intense as it had been earlier.

". . . good news. Let me know if you need anything else."

Olivia blinked and turned her back on Wade. "I will. Thanks." She hung up and rubbed her eyes, thinking. She was going to be much later getting to the morgue than she'd planned. She turned to face Wade. He hadn't moved, just lifted a brow.

"What is it?" he asked.

"Just a few minutes ago, I overheard a conversation between your sister-in-law and Joanna."

His relaxed posture didn't change, but his eyes sharpened. "And?"

"Martha was under the impression that you were going to . . . uh . . . kiss me."

"I was."

The heat immediately invaded her cheeks and she swallowed. "I thought so." She pushed the embarrassment away. "She told Joanna, and I could hear the anger behind her words."

Wade frowned. "Why would she be angry with me for kissing you?"

"She wouldn't be. Unless she felt threatened in some way."

A silence stretched between them. He glanced over his shoulder toward the muffled sounds coming from the ladies in the kitchen. "You're not suggesting . . ."

"I don't know. I thought it a pretty strong reaction from someone who claims to have no romantic interest in you."

The lines on his forehead deepened and his nostrils flared as he thought. "I think you're wrong, but I'll talk to her."

"No, don't. If she's the one, then we don't want to tip her off that she's a suspect. Just play it cool." Her phone buzzed and she answered. It was the officer watching Wade's house. "Yes?"

"Charlie Lee is approaching the house."

"Thanks."

Wade opened the door for Charlie and shook his hand. Charlie went into the den and Wade headed for the kitchen. He found Joanna and Martha huddled together at the table. He bought himself some time by grabbing a bottle of water from the refrigerator. When he turned, he found their eyes on him. Martha's accusing, Joanna's narrowed and cold. He sighed. Really? *Play it cool, remember?*

"Okay, ladies, what is wrong with me taking an interest in someone?"

Martha blinked at him, all traces of ire or accusation gone from her gaze. "Nothing, of course."

"Then why are you both giving me the stink eye?"

Martha dropped her gaze. Joanna looked over his shoulder. Martha finally shrugged. "It's not important, Wade. Who you're interested in is your business, not ours."

"Yes, that's true," Joanna said. "But . . ."

"But?"

Now her gaze was concerned. "Do you really think you should be developing feelings for anyone while you have a stalker after you? Especially feelings for the person who's been hired to protect you? What if she gets distracted? What if she's in danger and you decide to try to protect *her*? What if something happens then?"

Wade blinked. He'd already been placed in that situation and he realized he'd do it again if necessary. But he kept those thoughts to himself. He eyed both ladies. Was that all it was? Or was there something more behind their words? He pinched the bridge of his nose and closed his eyes. He couldn't believe he was even entertaining those thoughts. He'd become suspicious of everyone in his life.

"And what if the stalker finds out you have feelings for Olivia and decides to go after her?" Martha asked. "But even more concerning than that, what if Olivia's distracted with her feelings for you enough that Amy gets put in danger?"

Wade paused and sucked in a deep breath. At first he was tempted to just brush aside their concerns, but at the mention of Amy . . . "All right, I'll think about what you've said."

Martha nodded and exchanged a relieved look with Joanna. "Good."

Because distraction could spell disaster for them all.

[33]

Olivia stepped into the morgue and followed the sounds of the grunts coming from the office to her left. She'd visited the morgue enough times during her two years as a detective with the force that Megan, the receptionist, simply waved her on back. Wade got a strange look, but since he was with Olivia, Megan simply shrugged.

"You should have stayed home," she told him.

"Not a chance."

She found Francisco on the floor of his office. "How many today?"

"A thousand."

"Did you figure out the problem?" she asked, indicating the body on the table. Francisco did push-ups for a lot of reasons. One of those reasons was when he was confused or trying to work through a problem.

"Yes. She was strangled from behind. Not a difficult problem to figure out. The fingerprints on the front of her throat were pretty much a dead giveaway."

Olivia rolled her eyes. "No pun intended, right?"

"Of course it was."

"This is Wade Savage."

"Pleased to meet you," Francisco said from the floor.

"Likewise." Wade didn't seem to find it at all strange to be talking to the medical examiner while standing over him.

"Anything on Justine Harmon?" she asked.

Francisco popped to his feet and motioned to the laptop on his desk. "Take a look."

He wiggled the mouse as Olivia slipped into the plush leather chair. Francisco had bought the chair himself, saying the hospital-issued one hurt his back. She could see why he liked this one. Wade moved behind her and she found she was very aware of his presence. Not just the fact that he was there, but that she was *glad* he was there. Glad he'd insisted on coming. Glad that Charlie had been willing to follow them and act as a lookout in case they were followed. She didn't want to be glad. She frowned. *Focus.*

Justine's file was already on the screen and she pushed Francisco's hand from the mouse. "I'll take it from here, thanks."

"Right. You're welcome."

She looked up. "Sorry. I appreciate you letting me do this."

"I know you do. Otherwise I would refuse. I'll just be making a Y-incision in room 4. Text me when you're finished." With one last glance at Wade, he left.

Olivia focused her attention on the words in front of her while Wade read over her shoulder.

"The first part of the report just talks about what she looked like coming in, what she was wearing," Olivia said. She clicked through the pages. "What I want to know is at the end of the report. Here." She pointed. "See where it says, 'Opinion'?"

"Yes."

"Okay, time of death is reported to be between 11:30 a.m. and

1:00 p.m. due to body temperature, rigor and livor mortis, and stomach contents. Cause of death is a single gunshot wound to the head. Manner of death is reported as a suicide. No special remarks were made by the medical examiner."

"And why is it important that we know this?"

She heard the pain in his voice and minimized the screen. "I'm sorry, Wade. You shouldn't have come."

He cleared his throat. "Yes, yes I should have." Then he frowned. "Wait a minute. Can you pull that back up?"

Olivia hesitated, then complied.

"There," he said and pointed. "Where it gives the time of death. How accurate do you think that is?"

"Pretty accurate. Why?"

He pulled his phone from his pocket and tapped the screen. Then he held it out to her. "Because if the autopsy time of death is right, then Justine would have had to send me her text after she was already dead."

Wade stared at Quinn as he paced the morgue floor. The detective had been visiting Maddy's family at the hospital on the fifth floor when Olivia texted him. He'd come right down and not said a word about Olivia reading an autopsy report. Now he had his gaze fixed on Wade's phone, which showed Justine's text. Then his eyes bounced back to the screen that clearly showed her time of death.

"Well?" Olivia asked, her tone low, not rushed, just curious.

"I would say this makes me go 'huh.'"

"'Huh' as in we need to check into this a little more or 'huh' as in 'so what?'"

"The first."

"Good.

LYNETTE EASON

"I'll get that exhumation request expedited and we'll go from there," Quinn said.

"Are we all set for the charity dinner tomorrow night?" she asked.

"All set. Security is as tight as I've seen with the private sector involved."

Olivia gave a short nod as though she'd expected no other answer. "Excellent."

Quinn took a screen shot of Justine's text. "All right if I send this to myself?" he asked Wade.

"Of course."

Quinn did, then gave Wade a penetrating look. "Did you ever doubt it was a suicide?"

"I did, but never really considered murder. I thought at first it had to be an accident, but with the text . . . ," he nodded at the phone and then gave a slight shrug, ". . . I figured I just didn't know her as well as I thought I did."

Quinn nodded. "All right, I'll be in touch." He turned back. "Oh, meant to tell you, I talked to Erin Abbott."

"And?" Olivia asked.

"She took the weekend off like you thought. She's covered as far as an alibi. We checked her key card, and Friday, it was used last around 11:04 p.m. She placed a call from her room for breakfast at 8:15 a.m. and it was delivered at 8:47. So it looks like she was in the room the entire night. Same thing for Saturday night as well."

Wade shook his head. "I hate that she felt like she had to lie to me. I would have gladly let Stacy stay no matter what Erin wanted to do."

"Well, there really was a conference that she was registered to go to," Quinn said. "She said she decided not to at the last minute. I don't think she's your stalker. Admirer? Yeah. A little

261

phone happy with the calls to the station? Sure. Stalker? No. Probably not."

"She never gave her real name when she called," Wade said. "I never knew it was her."

"She seemed embarrassed about the whole thing, to be honest."

"I won't bring it up," Wade said. "If she wants to talk about it, fine, but otherwise . . ." He shrugged.

Quinn nodded and held out a hand to Wade. "I may have misjudged you. I thought you were just a rich daddy's boy playing at having a career. You're not. I was wrong and I apologize." Without giving Wade a chance to respond, he left and Olivia rose.

Wade didn't move, just stared at the floor as he processed the fact that Justine might have been killed. "Why?" he asked.

"Why what?"

He lifted his gaze to meet hers. "Why would someone kill her?" He saw the intense compassion in Olivia's eyes and it was nearly his undoing.

She rested a hand over his. He gripped her fingers. "I don't know," she said. "Maybe she had enemies you weren't aware of."

"She had people who got mad at her sometimes if they didn't like what she had to say in a counseling session or if a child confided abuse and Justine had to recommend removal from the home. But . . . murder?"

Olivia sighed. "I know it's hard to process. I'm sorry."

Wade didn't think about his actions, he just pulled her into an embrace. A loose one so that if she didn't want to be there she could easily slip away.

But she didn't. He held her against him, taking comfort in her presence and the compassion she extended. "I miss her," he whispered.

"Of course you do."

"She would have liked you. And you her."

"I'm sure."

He felt a slight tremor run through her. "Can I tell you something that's going to sound awful?"

She looked at him out of the corner of her eye. "Okay."

"Justine and I had a different kind of relationship, as I've already explained, but I asked myself a question the other night."

"A question?"

"If I'd have met you first, would I have looked twice at Justine?"

Olivia caught her breath and he could see she wasn't sure if she wanted to hear the answer or not.

"Justine was a truly wonderful person and I liked her. Even loved her. As a friend. But . . ."

"But?" Olivia whispered.

"We lacked something." He tilted her chin so he could look down into her eyes. Wary eyes. Thinking eyes. "Something that I think I feel with you."

"Wade—" She pulled back and stared at him. "I can't respond to that right now." She stepped all the way out of his embrace. "In fact, I shouldn't even . . ." She waved a hand. "You know."

"I know. But I want to make sure that you know I care about you." He cleared his throat and thought about Martha and Joanna's concern that he could be a distraction for her. "It's okay. Just concentrate on getting this person who's stalking me. We can talk about—" he mimicked her hand wave—"whatever, later." He kept his tone light, a teasing mockery.

She gave him a slight smile and shook her head. "Fine. Let's go back to your place and discuss security for tomorrow night."

"I'd rather talk about why you're so scared of the water."

Her eyes darkened, lips tightened. "I'd rather not."

"You'd trust me with Shana, but not with that?"

She blew out a sigh and he thought he saw a glint of frustration in her suddenly cool blue eyes. "It's not a matter of trust, it's . . ."

"What?"

"Nothing. Let's go."

[34]

As soon as they walked in the door, Wade went straight to his office and closed himself in. Olivia checked the knob and found it unlocked. Which was what she wanted. She had to be able to get to him if she needed to. For now, she allowed him his privacy. She knew he was frustrated with her lack of willingness to bare her soul, but she also knew he would come around and realize he had to give her some time. And the fact that she'd already come to know him that well startled her.

Releasing her grip on the knob, she moved into the large den that overlooked the lake and pushed aside one of the drapes she'd requested be kept closed at all times. No sense in giving a sniper an easy target.

Olivia couldn't get the conversation with Wade out of her mind, but she had to find a way to shove it to the side. She'd already told him about Shana, did she really want to open up yet another piece of herself? A piece she'd never really come to grips with? Her biggest fear was water. It made her nauseous to even think about the past, but she was considering telling Wade about it. What had gotten into her?

She had to get ready for the charity dinner and make sure no one got through security who didn't belong. She didn't have time to be thinking about romance or anything else except the job. People could die if she lost her focus. And that wasn't going to happen.

She called Haley, who answered on the second ring. "How are the background checks going with the people on the list to attend the dinner?"

"So far so good. A few minor things, but nothing that sets off serious alarm bells. The good thing is, it's a small event. No more than fifty people."

"Yes, he likes to keep most of them small and intimate, to be able to interact with the attendees and give them the personal touch."

"We should be done with this in a couple of hours."

"Let me know if anything stands out."

"Of course."

Olivia hung up and swallowed two ibuprofen she dug out of her front pants pocket. The throbbing in her hand was getting on her nerves. Just one more thing to ignore.

A footstep fell behind her and she spun to see Wade come into the den. "I'm sorry," he said.

"For?"

"Prying. Pushing. It's none of my business. I'll stay at arm's length."

She sighed. "No, I don't want you at arm's length." It took a lot to admit, but it felt good to say it. She was tired of being alone and Wade was the one man who'd sparked her interest in a long time.

He looked stunned at her admission and she couldn't help but feel a bit sorry for him. She knew she was sending mixed messages and it was time to stop. To trust and take a chance by letting Wade past the barriers. She let the words tumble from her lips. "I haven't liked water since one of my foster siblings tried to drown me when I was ten years old."

Wade paled. "Tried to drown you?"

She shrugged and looked away while she gathered her thoughts to put them into words. "Before my parents were killed, I used to love the water. We hung out at the pool every summer, took trips to the beach. My dad used to call me his little fish. Then my parents died and I went to my first foster home. I liked it there. The mother was sweet and doted on me. I assume it's because she didn't have a daughter and wanted one. The couple's biological son—and only child—Nate, was jealous of the attention I was getting from his mother. They had a pool. One afternoon I was outside kicking the soccer ball in the net, and he came out, grabbed me, and shoved me in the pool. When he realized I could swim, he jumped in and held me down. I passed out. When I woke up, I was in the hospital."

Wade stared at her. "Who found you?"

"The foster mother. She did CPR and called 911."

"What happened to her son?"

"From what I remember and overhearing the adults talk about it, he was fourteen and had never had any kind of incident like that before. I was their first—and last—foster kid. I don't know where he is today, I've never checked. I just wanted to forget about him back then and I still do."

"But you haven't been able to."

"No, of course not, but you would think I'd be able to move past it." She clenched her fingers into fists. "I can't even wade in the ocean or take a hot bath. It's crippling and I hate it, but I can't seem to do anything about it." Her heart thundered in her ears at the confession, the memories the telling invoked, but a sense of cleansing started to take place as well.

Wade shuddered. "Why was that so hard to talk about?"

She rubbed her temples "It's just another incident in my past I try to forget about. Talking about Shana is different. Hard, but different. She wanted me to do something with her death. Make a difference in people's lives. Help people. Having someone hate you enough to try to kill you leaves a permanent scar."

"Yeah. Tell me about it."

They shared a small smile. Of course he knew how that felt. "And . . . ," she sighed, "the incident left me with a permanent fear of the water. I tried to swim after that, but every time I got close to the water, I'd freak. You know Amy's panic attacks?" He nodded. "Water does it to me every time."

"Understandable."

"But frustrating. I don't like letting fear rule me."

"You like to be in control."

She straightened a picture on the mantel, then looked him in the eye. "Yes. I like to be in control. But you already knew that."

"Yes. I knew it, I just didn't know why." He moved closer and ran a finger down her cheek. "Your life spun so out of control when your parents died that when you finally got old enough, being in control is what's enabled you to survive," he murmured.

She lifted a brow and moved away from him, his nearness making her wish for things she shouldn't wish for. "Are you analyzing me?"

"Maybe." He studied her even as he let her go. "Or maybe I just know how it feels to want to be in control, to hang on so tight to whatever it is that you have some say-so over, because if you let go, you might splinter into a million tiny pieces."

She turned a shade paler with each word. He was right on target. Everything he said was like he'd opened up her heart and read the *Understanding Olivia Edwards for Dummies* manual.

Her phone rang and she snagged it from her back pocket,

grateful for the interruption. The screen ID'd Bree as the caller. "Yes?"

"Hello to you too."

"Sorry. What's up, Bree?"

"Thought I'd fill you in on some information."

"Go for it." She put it on speakerphone. "Wade's here listening too."

"That's fine. The woman in the house was definitely Valerie Mathis. Quinn checked her financials and your friend, Ginger, was spot-on accurate about her sad state. She was broke and struggling to pay her bills. None of her credit cards show any charges that could be related to the gifts Wade got."

"Then why kill her?"

"She was a threat. She was interested in Wade and the killer somehow knew that. Also, Sarah's still working with trying to find any trace evidence, but frankly she doesn't have a lot left to work with."

"I didn't think she would."

"We got a hit on where the bears were purchased, though it didn't come from Valerie. Quinn took a picture of the bear and asked people around the station who had kids and teens. One cop said he'd seen one on his daughter's pillow. He called her and she said she bought it at a small store at the mall. They're a pretty popular item. We questioned the cashier—even two others who work there—but all said the same thing. That they sold so many they'd never be able to remember who bought one. There's another small boutique that sells them as well, but same story."

"Great. What about the GPS tracker?"

"That was a run-of-the-mill device that can be purchased from just about any electronics store. It could also be purchased online."

"So what you're saying is, there's no way to trace it."

"Exactly. And there were no prints on it."

Olivia rolled her eyes. "Well of course not. Why make it easy for us at this point?"

"I know. Sorry."

"It's not your fault. Thanks for the heads-up."

"Sarah said she did run a preliminary test on the chocolate. I've already called Quinn, but it looks like the candy was laced with cyanide."

Wade froze, his face paling. Olivia knew he was thinking how close Amy had come to eating a piece. What if she'd decided to just sneak a few pieces and never mention finding the candy? She shuddered at the thought. "Enough to hurt someone?"

"Enough to kill someone. And fast."

Wade felt sick when he heard those words. He pictured Amy almost putting the chocolate in her mouth. What if she'd decided to sneak it? Eat it down below deck and not mention it to him? The thought made him shiver. He had to do something, he couldn't continue to stay in his home. And he either had to send Amy away or go with her.

The revelation wasn't sudden. He'd been thinking about it for days. And he'd almost waited until too late.

Olivia had taken another call on her speakerphone, and he heard her say, "Hang on a minute, Haley." She put a hand on his arm. "Are you all right?"

He leaned against the mantel to steady himself. "You know that vacation you want me to take?"

"Yes."

"When do we leave?"

She blinked. "What about the charity dinner Thursday night?"

"Cameron can handle it. He'll tell the truth about what's going on and I'll have to trust God with the rest. We'll get someone to speak. Someone who's been impacted by the charity and the funds previously raised, who wouldn't be where she is without Breaking Free." He shook his head. "I don't know why I didn't think of it before." He paused and sighed. "I realize I've forgotten one of the most important things."

"What have you forgotten?" Olivia asked.

"It's not my charity."

"It's not?"

"Nope. It's his." He pointed his finger heavenward. "He's used a lot of people in my life to make sure Amy and I stay safe. My father, you and your team, the officers who've been willing to work overtime to watch out for us. It's time I start being thankful for everyone instead of resentful. It's also time I put my family first. Amy could have died Monday. I can't stop running different scenarios through my head, and I know if something happens to her or anyone because I was being bullheaded, I couldn't live with myself." He kept his gaze on Olivia. "Sometimes you have to let go to hang on. In this case, I've got to relinquish control. So . . . if you think we need to leave town, I'm ready to go."

The sound of Haley clearing her throat came from the speakerphone. "All right then. I'll start putting it together. Be ready to leave in an hour."

Olivia jerked and Wade blinked. They'd both forgotten Haley was on the phone. Olivia nodded. "Good. We'll be ready."

Wade set his jaw. "I'll tell Amy. She won't like it because we'll have to cancel the birthday party that was planned for Saturday, but we'll have to deal with it."

"I'll come with you. You can blame it on me if you need to." She gave him a faint smile.

"No." He frowned. "The only person getting the blame for this situation is the one causing it."

They found Amy playing a video game with Katie. Amy was winning, so they waited until she'd navigated the maze and crossed the finish line. "Woo-hoo!" Amy whooped.

Katie shook her head and laid her controller on the sofa cushion. "That's five for five. I'll never be able to beat you, my girl."

Amy smiled, her expression shy and smug at the same time. "No, you probably won't."

Wade laughed even while pain bloomed in his heart. "Amy, I have to tell you something."

Her happiness faded and her anxious "what's going to happen now" look tightened her features. "Okay."

"We have to leave for a little while. We're going to take a vacation."

The anxiety faded. Interest replaced it. "Oh. I thought it was going to be something bad. Where are we going?" She hopped up. "Can we go to Disney World? Can I take Stacy?"

"No. I mean we have to go now. Leave today."

His daughter's eyes widened. "What? Why? When are we coming back? My birthday party is on Saturday." She frowned. "We'll be back for that, right?"

"Ah . . . maybe, but we might have to reschedule it."

Tears welled in her eyes. "But all my friends are coming. Stacy and Anna and Sherry and—" She swiped her eyes. "Is this because of that stalker?"

"Yes," Wade simply said.

Amy worried her bottom lip with her top teeth as she studied him. "But I don't want to reschedule it," she said softly.

Wade sighed and dropped his chin to his chest, said a prayer for wisdom, then looked Amy in the eye. "Honey, this person is getting way too close. The chocolates on the boat were poisoned."

"What?" Her eyes went wide and her face paled. He saw her swallow hard. "I almost ate one," she whispered. "But then I didn't want to feel guilty if you'd put them there to give to someone. You're always letting someone use the boat, so that's why I asked."

"And I'm so glad you did."

Her lower lip trembled. "Would I have died?"

"No, no way. You would have probably gotten really, really sick and been in the hospital for a while, but no, you would have eventually been fine." He asked forgiveness for the probable lie, but he wasn't going to tell her the truth and bring on nightmares. He just wasn't. One day he might share the truth, but not now. "So that's why we have to go. This person has access to us and I don't know what else to do but go away until she's caught."

"What if she's never caught?"

He nodded. "That's a good question. I don't have an answer right now. I just know we have to go."

Amy hung her head and scuffed her foot against the dark hardwood. "It's not fair."

"No, it definitely isn't fair."

Amy crossed her arms and stuck out her lip. "I want to go on record as not liking this."

"Duly noted," Wade said.

The watcher pulled the headphones off. So Wade was planning to leave. Amy almost eating those chocolates had scared him enough to run. It had been a risky move, planting the candy. They hadn't been for Amy, but it could have worked as a positive in the plan should she have eaten them. Amy's death would have left Wade more vulnerable, more open to staging his death as a suicide. It was believable. Already heartbroken over the death of his fiancée, the death of his daughter would send him over the edge. The watcher smiled. The listening device planted in the den had come in handy on more than one occasion. Now to implement the last part of the plan and collect the payoff.

[35]

"He's leaving," the voice said.

"Leaving? What do you mean?" she asked.

"They're taking him away in less than an hour."

"Where?" She panicked. "They can't leave! How will I see him? He'll never know everything I've done for him!"

"I have a way for you to stop him, so listen up."

In the bathroom, Amy grabbed what she considered essentials for a trip overnight. Her emotions were all over the place. Anger at the canceled party. Okay, maybe not canceled, but most likely postponed. Worry that someone really might hurt her dad—even kill him—and she'd be alone. She'd wanted to talk about it with her father and had even tried to get him to come upstairs with her to help her, but he'd been on the phone and gestured for Katie to go with her.

Katie had complied without a word. And while Amy liked Katie, she wished her father had come so she could ask specific questions about the kind of clothing she needed to pack. For instance, did she need a swimsuit?

Her phone buzzed and she smiled when she saw it was from Stacy.

Stacy
Hey, can you get past your watchdogs and meet me outside in the trees at our spot? I got your text that you were leaving and I want to say bye.

Amy dropped her toothbrush into the overnight bag, then snatched her phone up.

Amy
I don't know. Maybe. I'll try. Can you stay there for about ten minutes?

Stacy
Yes. Better hurry tho. My mom doesn't want me over here until u catch the wacko.

Okay, hang on. I'm coming.

Where r u going? Do u know?

No, but Olivia and my dad arranged everything. This stalker person has everyone crazy so we're going on a little vacay until they catch her.

What bout ur party?

Rescheduling it.

Ugh.

Tell me bout it. Now stop texting so I can get out of here.

K. C u in a minute.

The fact that the wacko—as Stacy called her—had left poisoned chocolates on the boat scared her. The fact that she almost ate one terrified her. She didn't know what to think or who to trust. Other than Stacy, of course. And her dad, Olivia, and Katie. And Aunt Martha and Joanna, of course. But that was about it. Amy grabbed her small makeup bag and added that to the pile. Now what?

A knock on the door grabbed her attention. "Amy?" Katie asked. "Are you about ready?"

"I just need a few more minutes, okay?"

"Sure. But we need to get going, so don't take too much longer if you can help it."

"Okay." She rolled her eyes. She knew that her dad's stalker was a dangerous person. She'd learned that fact in the bathroom at the church. Not to mention the poisoned chocolate. She needed to say goodbye to Stacy, though. Who knew how long she would be gone? But she probably needed to clear it with someone. She opened the door. "I want to tell my friend Stacy goodbye. Will you go with me?"

Katie looked concerned. And understanding. "I don't think we have the time, but I can check on it for you."

"Thanks. I'm almost ready."

She could hear Katie talking through the door. The woman must have been standing just on the other side. "All right," she heard her say. "She's not going to like it, but all right."

Amy sighed and kicked her overnight bag. She couldn't even tell her best friend goodbye. Anger rose in her. Anger at her father's stalker. Anger at her father for wanting to leave. Just . . . anger at the unfairness of it all. Well, stalker or no stalker, she was going to tell Stacy goodbye. She slipped the overnight bag over her shoulder and opened the door that led into the guest bedroom.

"Amy? You coming?"

"I've got to find a couple more things and then . . . um . . . use the bathroom," she called. Then walked to the door of the

guest room and looked out into the hall. Empty. She moved to
the back staircase and hurried down it. At the bottom, the door
led out onto the back porch and the patio with the outdoor
kitchen.

Her phone buzzed. She pulled it from the back pocket of
her jeans. Stacy again.

Stacy
U coming?

Amy
Working on it. Chill.

K.

Amy slipped up to the brick oven and glanced around it.
Security personnel patrolled the grounds, but thanks to the trees
and other shrubbery along the edge of the property, she could
probably stay hidden well enough to meet Stacy. The problem
was getting from the porch to the nearest tree. She waited until
the closest security member had his back turned, then darted
across the lawn.

Heart pounding, she glanced back. No one shouted, no one
said a word, no alarms had been sounded. She'd done it. Now
the easy part. She ran as fast as she could behind the tree line to
the copse of trees between her property and the neighbor's. She
slipped into the clearing and dropped her bag on the ground.
Why had she brought it anyway?

"Stacy? Are you here?"

No answer.

"Stacy, come on. Don't play games, I don't have a lot of time."

A bush to her left rustled and she turned toward it. But Stacy
didn't come out from behind it. Amy stamped her foot even
as a niggling of doubt raised its head. She probably shouldn't

have snuck out. She'd never done anything like that before, but she'd never been in this kind of situation before either. Her heart picked up speed and her breath started to strangle in her throat.

"No," she whispered. "Not now."

Where was Stacy? Her uneasiness grew and she moved backward, eyes still on the bushes. Stacy wouldn't play games like this. Amy pulled her phone out and texted Stacy.

> **Amy**
> Where r u? I have to go!

> **Stacy**
> Behind you.

Amy turned, expecting to see Stacy. Instead her eyes widened when they landed on the woman who stepped out from behind the tree. Amy walked toward her. "What are you doing here? Did you follow me? I just wanted to say goodbye to Stacy."

Instead of speaking, the woman simply lifted her hand. In it she held a small canister. "Don't worry, Amy, I'll make sure you don't suffer." Her finger pushed the top and a spray of something caught Amy full in the face. She gasped, choked. Dizziness hit her. Her legs gave out and she dropped to the ground. Her phone tumbled from her fingers. Vaguely, she felt someone lift her, hands under her knees and shoulders. Strong hands. Not the woman's.

But she couldn't get her eyes open long enough to focus. Then she felt herself being slid into the back of a large vehicle. She tried to rise, but was just too tired. Even the fear that started pounding through her couldn't keep her awake any longer.

Wade finally hung up the phone. It was past the allotted hour, but he now had everything arranged. Cameron was more understanding than Wade had expected, given the man's drive and passion for the charity. He thought the idea of using someone impacted by the charity a great idea and promised to line it up. "Even though it is incredibly short notice," he'd muttered.

"I need you to do this, Cameron. Amy could have been killed. I can't trust that this person won't get to her again."

"I know. I know." A heavy sigh filtered through the line. "Of course you have to protect Amy. And yourself. Fine. Don't worry about a thing. Stay safe and be in touch when you can."

Olivia appeared in the doorway of the den. "You ready?"

"Yes. Just one more phone call."

"I'll get Amy and Katie. Charlie and Lizzie are in the cars. Charlie will be driving the one in front. Lizzie's in the one behind."

"All right."

Olivia's phone rang. She paused and answered it. "Hi, Quinn." Her brows went up and she shot him a look. "Uh-huh. Okay. Thanks for letting me know."

"What is it?" Wade asked when she hung up.

"Francisco finished Justine's autopsy."

"And?"

"And he agrees, it wasn't suicide. She was murdered. Something about the angle of the bullet entrance not being consistent with a self-inflicted wound."

Wade stumbled to the nearest chair and sank onto it. "I almost don't believe it."

She crossed the room and placed a hand on his shoulder. "I'm so sorry, Wade."

"No, I'm sorry. Sorry I didn't push for an investigation when I first learned of her death. Sorry I let her down and let myself believe she could do something like that." He shook his head.

"Can I do anything for you?"

"No. I'm shocked and not surprised all at the same time, you know? Why didn't the first medical examiner who did the original autopsy catch that?"

"Who knows? Maybe he wasn't being careful. Maybe he just did a cursory examination. I'll make a report of it to make sure he knows he made a serious mistake, but for now, let's focus on what we need to do."

He cleared his throat. "Right. I'll just make my last phone call and be right out. We can talk in the car."

"Sure."

Olivia turned and Wade stood. As she stepped out of the den, he walked to the mantel and stared at the picture of him and Justine, taken just a few days before she'd died.

Been murdered.

He felt his phone buzz and looked at it. A text message from Anonymous.

> I have Amy. Walk out of the door and down to the boathouse. I'm watching you. If you speak to anyone, Amy dies.

Wade went still. He stared at the text, unbelieving. Was this a joke?

> Who are you?

Another buzz brought a picture of his sweet girl tied to a chair, her tear-streaked cheeks flushed, eyes drooping, sleepy looking, but on the person who'd taken the picture. Wade's heart stopped for a full five beats. His legs immediately went weak. He stumbled to the chair again. But no. He couldn't sit. Couldn't waste time. Couldn't throw up.

He walked back to the mantel and gripped it, leaned his

forehead against the edge, and took a deep breath. When he looked up, resolution ran deep and fast.

Help was mere steps away. Could he get a message to one of them? Olivia was outside on the porch talking to one of her employees. He looked around for a pen and paper, but saw nothing.

Anonymous
What are you waiting for?

He looked at Amy's picture on the text again and paused. He knew that place. He knew where she was being held. But how to pass on the message? He looked back up to the family pictures on the mantel, picked up one, then the next and the next. Amy was in most of them. He and his parents in another when he was just an infant. He closed his eyes and fought the urge to scream, to rail against the unknown person doing this to him and his family. And knew he'd do whatever it took to rescue his child. But he had to find a way to leave a message. An idea formed.

His phone buzzed again.

Anonymous
You haven't left the house. I'm watching. Go out the back door to the boathouse. Now. Your security is tight. Don't get caught or Amy dies.

Wade
How?

Figure it out. Now go.

He had no choice.

His phone buzzed again. He looked at it. This time it signaled a call from Olivia. A text appeared at the top of the screen.

Anonymous
Don't answer it. Put the phone in your pocket
and keep going.

His fingers flew over the keys.

Wade
If I don't answer, she's going to come looking
for me.

Anonymous
Fine. Make it good. I can hear everything you
say. Amy wants her father to come rescue her.

After only a fraction of a second of hesitation, he pressed the
button to answer the call. Could the person really hear? With
technology these days, he couldn't afford to take any chances.
"I'm coming."

"Where are you?"

"Just had a few more things I needed to put together. A few
instructions about Thursday night, but I'm finished now. Just
stopped in the den to . . . reminisce a little."

"We don't have time for reminiscing. I'm coming to get you to
escort you to the car." He heard murmuring in the background.
"Wade, Katie can't find Amy. Is she with you?"

"No." He cleared his throat.

Another buzz. He lowered the phone to read the text.

Anonymous
Be careful what you say.

"Olivia? She's around there somewhere. Check her closet.
Sometimes she likes to hide there when she's feeling anxious."
The words left a sour taste in his mouth, but he couldn't say anything that would cause his stalker—and Amy's kidnapper—to
do anything rash. Like kill his daughter. Fear pounded through

him. He wondered if Olivia could hear his thundering heart. He walked toward the back door of the house and paused to watch as security made their rounds.

"Okay, meet me at the front door, but don't go outside yet."

Too late for that.

Finally, when he could see no one who might spot him on the path to the boathouse, he moved. He swiveled his head from side to side, taking care not to be seen by any of the security as he darted down the hill, slipping behind a tree now and then to scope the area. He didn't even feel stupid. Amy was waiting on him, scared and desperate. He wouldn't let her down this time. "Dad's coming, honey, just hang on," he whispered under his breath as he waited for the guard in black pants and black T-shirt to move away. Wade had the advantage of knowing where to look and was able to skirt the edges of security until he reached the boathouse. A flash across the lake caught his eye, and he figured the person giving him directions had some high-powered binoculars trained on him.

He slipped inside the building and shut the door behind him.

Felt the same stinging sensation he'd experienced in the parking lot of the radio station. This time he didn't bother to fight it. He simply sat down and waited for the darkness to close over him.

[36]

Olivia paced the front porch and finally gave up, went back inside to hurry Wade up, and found Katie coming down the steps. "She's not there, not upstairs, not in the closet, not in her aunt's apartment above the garage, not anywhere."

A sick feeling started in the pit of Olivia's stomach. "She has to be. No one saw her leave or I would have heard about it."

"She said she was going to the bathroom and would be right back. I was helping her pack so I finished zipping up her suitcase. When she'd been in there awhile, I knocked on the door. She answered that she'd be out in a minute."

"Wait a minute," Olivia said. "She wanted to tell Stacy bye."

"Yes, she asked. I never had a chance to tell her that she couldn't because we had to leave immediately. I knocked several more times, then I went in. And she was gone. The door to the other side, going into the guest bedroom, was open."

Olivia pictured the setup. Amy's room shared a bathroom with the guest room Olivia had taken her nap in after the radio station explosion. "Why would she leave?" she muttered.

"She wouldn't. Someone had to take her," Katie said.

"But they would have had to come in the house to get her, and we both know no one got in." Olivia paced, thinking. "She simply had to leave on her own."

Katie frowned and shrugged. "But why? What could compel her to walk out the door when she knows the danger?"

"Her friend. It had to be. She snuck out to go meet her."

"Then we have to find her—and fast. Let's go tell Wade."

Olivia took off down the hall with Katie following her. Olivia's phone buzzed. It was Haley wondering where they were.

> Olivia
>
> Amy is missing. Start looking for her. Tell the others to start searching and call in the dogs. She can't be far yet.

> Haley
>
> On it.

Olivia burst into the den. Only to find it empty. She stopped and frowned. "He's not here." She knew she was stating the obvious, but couldn't seem to stop herself.

"And the doors leading out to the porch are wide open," Katie said.

Olivia's bad feeling grew to mammoth proportions. "He was supposed to come straight from the den to the front door, get in the car, and go. We would have passed him if he were coming to the front door."

"We need to search the house."

"No we don't. He's not here and neither is Amy."

Katie stared at her and Olivia felt a wave of nausea and horror sweep over her. "She's done it," she whispered. "She's got them. I don't know how she did it, but she did. And we've got to find them. Fast."

Wade woke slowly. At first he let his mind stay blank. Then the text picture of Amy's scared and tearstained face came to mind, and his heart thumped while he breathed a prayer for her safety. *Please, Lord.*

He took inventory. Hands tied or taped in front of him. Still sleepy. Warm. No, hot. Too hot. He maneuvered himself around until he could feel his back pocket. He gave a grunt of disgust when he found it empty. Whoever had drugged him had taken his phone.

Amy. He had to get to Amy. Where was she?

He looked around even as he strained against his bonds and fought the effects of the drug. Where was *he*? His eyes landed on the far wall and his heart stuttered in his chest. A table was pushed up against the wall. But that wasn't what caught his attention. It was the rows and rows of pictures. From the top of the table to the top of the wall. A huge collage consisting of hundreds of pictures.

Of him. All of him. He squinted and thought he saw one of him with his wife from years ago. Only she had a red X slashed across her face.

He swallowed as he took it in. Disbelief pounded in his mind. "Amy," he whispered.

A surge of adrenaline burst through him and he tugged once again. But he had no strength, no control over his muscles for now. He ceased his useless struggle, blinked, and lay still. He knew how this would play out. He would be groggy for another couple of hours. Then it would be time to fight.

Olivia paced the den, thinking. Law enforcement officers had swept the grounds and the house. Katie had called in two FBI agents she'd worked with in the past. Neighbors had been questioned and a BOLO released to the press. Olivia knew Wade would hate the attention he'd face if he came home. When. When he came home. He and Amy. They would come home.

God, please . . .

Yes, she was even willing to start praying again if that would do any good.

Bruce Savage sat on the couch staring into space, his face drained of color, the pallor making him look ten years older than the last time she'd seen him.

The door opened and one of the officers entered with a bag and a cell phone. "We found these in a little clearing. Do you recognize them?"

Olivia took the phone encased in the plastic bag. "This is Amy's," she said softly. She pressed the button and started going through her messages. The very first ones jumped out at her. Texts from Stacy. Olivia pulled her personal cell phone from her pocket and dialed Stacy's number.

The number rang four times and went to voice mail. She hung up and walked over to lay a hand on Bruce's shoulder. "I need Stacy's mother's number. Do you have it?"

Bruce blinked. Then nodded. "Yes." He handed her his phone. She looked up the number and dialed it.

"Hello?"

"Hello, Mrs. Abbott, this is Olivia Edwards, Wade Savage's bodyguard."

"Yes?" A distinct cooling. Olivia supposed she could understand that. She'd been questioned at length and caught in a lie. A lie that had nothing to do with Wade, but still she had to be embarrassed.

"Is Stacy there?"

"No. She's not." And I'm not telling you where she is. Olivia heard the silent statement loud and clear.

"Mrs. Abbott. Amy and Wade have disappeared. Do you think you could cooperate with me?"

"Disappeared?" The coolness was gone. "Why didn't you say so? What happened?"

"We're not sure. That's what we're trying to figure out. The officers found Amy's phone with several text messages from Stacy's phone about meeting her at their special place."

"Right, the little clearing in the woods." She sounded much more willing to talk now. "Stacy's in her room. Hold on a second." Olivia heard her call for Stacy to come here. "Honey, do you have your phone? Did you text Amy to meet you at your place?"

"No."

"Can I see your phone?"

"Um . . . I can't find it. It disappeared while I was at church."

"What?"

"I'm sorry, Mom. It was in my purse, but when we got home and I looked for it, it was gone. I didn't want to tell you. I was hoping I could find it before you found out. But it hasn't turned up yet."

"What have I told you about—"

"Mrs. Abbott?" Olivia interrupted.

"Yes?"

"It's not Stacy's fault. I think someone stole her phone for the whole purpose of using it to lure Amy away from the house."

"Oh. Oh my word. I can't believe that." She truly sounded like she couldn't. "Okay then. I won't fuss at her."

"I have to go now. If you or Stacy should hear anything from Amy, will you call me right away?"

"Yes, of course."

Olivia gave the woman her number, then handed Bruce's phone back to him. She filled him in. "Where's Martha?"

Bruce rubbed his face. "She . . . uh . . . she . . . I don't know.

She was feeding all the officers, and I think when she realized they weren't going to find Amy and Wade right away, she went to her apartment. She was crying when she walked out." He shook his head and stared at the wall again. The poor man was in shock. He stood and walked over to the mantel. "Did you or anyone else mess with the pictures?"

Olivia frowned. "No sir. Not that I know of."

He flipped one up that had been facedown. "This is one of Wade's favorites. Why would he lay it facedown?"

Olivia walked over to look at it. "That's the one that he has on the desk at the radio station. He told me it's one of his favorites."

Bruce nodded. "It's one of the last pictures taken of him and his mother together. He wanted to buy the property to build this house on, but the owner wasn't interested in selling."

"So he got the next best thing."

"Yes."

Alarm bells jangled in her mind. "I didn't notice the picture when I was talking to him earlier in here, but that doesn't mean it wasn't turned down."

Bruce frowned. "It's definitely strange. I noticed it right off, but just ignored it. But I'm thinking that it might be a serious mistake not to take note of it."

"Could it be a message?"

Quinn stepped into the room. "We've got a subpoena for Wade's phone. Text message transcripts, et cetera. Until then, we'll keep looking. I'm heading out. It's been six hours. Bruce's phone is rigged so that if he gets a ransom call, it'll be recorded and traced. Officers are monitoring it. Right now, we can keep looking, but we're in the 'wait for someone to contact us' phase."

Bruce's face almost crumpled and Olivia placed a hand on his arm. He drew in a deep breath and closed his eyes. She knew he was praying.

Quinn gave her a short nod. She knew what he was thinking. If they didn't find Wade and Amy soon, they might not find them at all. At least not alive.

Bruce stood beside her, his worry a palpable thing, but his now unflappable expression intrigued her. She kept watching him, curious. It had been her experience that most people who found themselves in such a tense, emotionally charged, adrenaline-inducing situation flipped out. They got angry, laid blame, tossed out orders, went hysterical, and required sedation. But not Bruce. He stayed silent, his lips moving every so often in what she decided was prayer.

She left him alone and just stood beside him, thinking, offering him her support and letting him know she was there.

She found herself almost praying that his prayers worked, but she felt too unsure, too disconnected from God to even feel like she had the right to pray. She'd pushed him away and had purposefully kept him out of her life. She felt too ashamed to ask him for help now.

Olivia knew her career change had been the right choice, but watching the officers do their job earlier had her on edge and wishing she were a part of them. But she wasn't. Not really. Not anymore. Her friends on the force supported her and respected what she did, but she was no longer on the team. The team that stormed buildings and rescued kidnap victims.

"Do you believe in God, Olivia?" Bruce asked her.

She sucked in a deep breath and let it out slowly. "Yes." What made him bring that up?

"Do you believe he has a purpose in everything?"

"That one I'm not sure about."

"I am."

"Really?" He truly wanted to talk about this now? "What purpose could there be in my parents dying in a plane crash?

What purpose is there in your wife dying or Wade's wife dying? What purpose is there in this whole situation?"

"I don't know, but he does, and I guess that has to be good enough for me."

She shook her head. "I don't think I'll ever have that kind of faith."

"Well, maybe when you've lived as long as I have, you will. But keep in mind it's not something that just happens by osmosis. It's like any other relationship. You have to work at it. You have to get to know God on a very intimate level in order to have the kind of faith that will withstand the storms life throws at you. It's a good thing that we only have to have the amount of a mustard seed. Sometimes that's about all I can find." He shrugged. "You won't find even that much, though, if you treat him as the enemy or simply a passing acquaintance."

That struck a chord. "Is that what I've done? Pushed him away so that he's only a passing acquaintance now?" Of course it was. She'd admitted it to herself just a few minutes ago.

"I think so. But he'll take you back anytime you're ready. He doesn't hold grudges, just open arms."

Olivia stared at him. His son and granddaughter had most likely been led into a trap by a killer and here he was comforting her, offering her a spiritual hope that she'd figured was lost forever. It nearly shattered the last barrier she'd managed to keep up around her heart.

Bruce picked up the picture that had been laid facedown. "What are you trying to tell me, Son?" he whispered.

Amy sucked in a deep breath and blew it out slowly. She swiped the tears from her face and stared at the ceiling from her position on the bed. She'd awakened to find herself in a room that looked almost identical to the one in her house. In fact, when she'd first woken up, she'd thought that was where she was. She'd figured she'd just had a bad dream and no one had sprayed anything in her face and no one was stalking her dad.

Then she'd gone to open the door and found it locked. Then the window that had cement blocks in place of the glass. When she'd realized she was trapped, she'd pounded on the door and screamed until she was hoarse. And no one had come. She stared at the vent above her head and slowly sat up. Would it work? Could she do it? Was it big enough?

She looked around. Only one way to find out. Amy scrambled off the bed and grabbed the chair that had been pushed under the desk. She shoved it on top of the bed and under the vent.

"Okay, God, when I am afraid, I will trust in you," she muttered. "And use the brain you gave me."

Once she got the chair placed like she wanted, she gently climbed onto it and reached up to touch the vent. Fortunately, there was only a little clip that held it closed. She opened it and swallowed at how small it was. She wasn't sure she would fit.

But she had to try. She grabbed the opening and stepped up on the back of the chair to get higher. The chair wobbled and she almost lost her balance. Sweat pricked her forehead and made her palms slippery.

But she wouldn't give up. She just had to get high enough to get to the flat part.

And she couldn't do it with the chair.

She let herself back down onto the bed and pulled the chair off. She went to the door and listened. She thought she heard voices and backed up until her knees hit the bed. Then realized they weren't coming closer. Her eyes landed on the desk.

Wade breathed deeply, finally somewhat clear-headed and alert. Waiting. Listening. His heart thundered in his ears and his chest hurt. His breathing quickened and he tried to drag in another gulp of air. But he couldn't.

He couldn't breathe!

The elephant on his chest pressed harder. Tighter.

Breathe! He needed to breathe. His left arm tingled. He was having a heart attack.

He panted and finally caught a breath.

The tightness eased and it dawned on him he was having a panic attack. All of his symptoms mimicked Amy's. He shuddered. His poor child. *This* was how she felt?

He forced himself to stay still, to keep his eyes closed while his mind spun.

A door opened and shut and he tensed. The seconds ticked by slowly.

"Come on, Wade, I know you're awake."

He stiffened, the hairs on the back of his neck spiked and goosebumps pimpled his arms. "I'm awake." He recognized the woman's voice and froze.

"I've waited a long time for this, Wade."

He sat up and closed his eyes until the nausea passed and the room settled back down. Then he opened his eyes and looked straight into a woman who'd been his friend for the past fifteen years. Or so he'd thought. "How could you, Joanna? Just . . . why? And where's Amy?"

"Like I said, I've waited a long time for this. Amy is fine. For now." Her fingers loosely clasped a weapon. A gun. Seeing her hold it—on him—almost didn't compute. But . . . worry for Amy washed through him. "Is she here?"

"Yes. Waiting on you."

"Take me to her." He kept his fear and anger in check, his tone even, not wanting to do anything to anger her or spur her to do something in haste. Like kill him. Which would probably happen if he unleashed the words hovering on the edge of his tongue. Would it set her off? Would she shoot him in a fit of rage?

"In a bit. I want to talk to you first."

"Before you kill me?"

She scowled. "I never wanted to kill you. I just wanted you to . . . notice me, to see me. I met you first. You should have been mine."

Wade blinked. How had he been so blind? Sure, Joanna had flirted with him when they were younger and he'd probably flirted back, but it hadn't been anything serious. To him. Obviously she'd felt different. "Wait a minute. If you never intended to kill me, why all of the craziness? The bombs on the radio station doors, the poisoned chocolates in the boat. Those would have killed me." Or Amy, but he left her out of it for now.

"I know. I . . . didn't have . . . um . . . anything to do with those things. I didn't like that, but he said it would make you notice me—"

"He?"

"—to believe when I said I loved you because I was willing to go to such extraordinary lengths to make you see how much I cared about you," she said as though he hadn't interrupted. "I saved Amy from those chocolates!"

"Chocolates you put there!"

She looked insulted. "I didn't put them there."

"Then who did?"

"That's not important. I believed him, though. I believed

him when he said you would eventually see me for who I am and that you would be so impressed . . ." She trailed off and studied him. "But now I'm not sure. I don't know if it was the right thing to do, to let him do those things."

"Did you attack Maddy McKay?"

She blinked at him, her face blank. "Who?"

"The woman outside the radio station. She was one of my bodyguards. She was attacked."

"Oh her." She nodded and shrugged. "She watched you. She followed you. She never took her eyes off you. She wanted you and I had to make sure she didn't have you. But I didn't attack her. He did. I told him about her the night of the charity. I told him everything."

The reference to someone else again. "Who did you tell, Joanna?"

She spun away. "It doesn't matter. It's time to take you to your room. Get up."

"One more question."

She sighed. "What?"

His eyes flicked to the pictures. To the picture of his wife's face marked out. "Were you ever her friend?"

Joanna's gaze followed his. "Yes. At first. Before she met you."

"And how did meeting me change that?" He continued to pull and work his wrists trying to free his hands, but it was hard to do anything while she watched him so closely.

"Because when she showed up, you never looked at me again. Even after I took care of her, you—"

Wade stiffened, all thoughts of getting loose on hold. "What do you mean you took care of her?" he asked softly.

She fidgeted, clearly agitated. "It doesn't matter now."

He shifted, the tape chafing his wrists. He felt for a rough edge, a nail, anything, but found nothing. Panic wanted to take over. He struggled to keep his terror under control. "Joanna. Did you kill Pamela?"

"Of course not."

He watched her pace now, her steps quick and agitated. "Joanna . . ." He sucked in a deep breath. Had to draw from his training. He knew how to talk to people like her, but this was personal. She had taken his *child*. Amy was waiting for him to come get her.

"She died in a wreck, remember?"

"Yes, I remember."

"She was drinking and driving. She ran off a cliff." Her breathing increased and she continued her maddening pacing.

Wade knew Pamela drank. It had been a contention the entire time they'd been dating. He knew he never should have married her, but he'd been young and in love with the girl who'd made him laugh . . . and feel like he was the center of her universe.

Until Amy had come along.

Joanna sniffed. "She didn't deserve you. She never gave you gifts. She wanted to party and drink and . . ." She waved a hand. "It was wrong. I could see how it hurt you."

Yes, yes it had.

"And it bothered you to see me hurting?"

"Of course it did," she wailed. "But I couldn't do anything about it."

"You were my friend, Joanna. I trusted you. You were drinking with her that night," he said. "You let her get behind the wheel of the car."

She scoffed. "No, Wade, I didn't let her. I forced her to. She drank until she passed out. She mocked you and talked about what a brat Amy was and how she was stuck with the two of you." Her fingers squeezed the butt of the gun so tight he thought it might go off even without her finger on the trigger. "I drove her to that cliff, then dragged her over into the driver's seat and strapped her in. Then I put the car in neutral and pushed her over. Gravity helped with that one. I picked a downward-sloping spot." She shook her head. "I actually almost went with her. I had a hard time rolling out of the passenger seat after I put the car in gear." Her eyes widened. "I thought once Pamela was out of the picture you would finally see me. I knew you'd need time to grieve and I tried to give that to you. Then Martha moved in with you and she talked about how lost you were, how you were still grieving. So I waited. I even dated other guys so you would see I was desirable. But you never seemed to notice. Even after Justine."

Wade gaped. He almost couldn't take it all in. His mind wanted to cower and run from what she was telling him. His wife hadn't lost control of her car and gone off a cliff. She'd been murdered. And Justine . . . ?

"So you started sending me gifts through the mail?"

"Yes. I thought if you saw how giving I could be, how generous, you would be intrigued. But you weren't." Her eyes narrowed. "You mocked me on your show. You threw my gifts away." Tears filled her eyes. "How could you do that?"

"How could you terrify and kidnap my child!" He yelled the words before he could stop himself, his control slipping away bit by bit, word by word.

Joanna flinched and raised the gun.

Wade dropped his head, his breaths coming in harsh pants. He desperately reined in his fury, the desire to strangle the woman in front of him. He had to stay calm. For Amy. "So what now? Are you going to kill me because I didn't love you back?"

"Kill you? Of course not. I love you."

His head snapped up. Completely confused, he stared at her. "You're not?"

LYNETTE EASON

"No. I figured the only way you would realize—that you would *see* me—was if I just put you in a position where you had to. I think once we're together for a while, you'll see that you can love me. Just like those arranged marriages in the past. Sometimes people didn't love each other when they first got married, but eventually they grew to love their spouse." She shrugged. "Maybe one day you'll come to love me."

She was crazy. But he already knew that. The fact that she'd admitted she wasn't going to kill him helped. It meant that Amy was probably safe as well. "Can you release my hands?"

"Oh no. I can't do that. You're too strong and I'd never be able to overpower you again. You'll just have to stay here and I'll visit and bring you food and gifts and we'll talk, but I can't free you and you're not going anywhere."

"Joanna, think about it. I need my hands. I need to eat and take care of other business like going to the bathroom."

She looked stumped for a short second, then just shook her head. "You'll have to figure that out, but I'm not untying your hands."

Frustration filled him. "Where does Amy fit in this plan of yours?"

She frowned. "She'll stay in the room I've made for her. I knew you'd never cooperate unless she was here too. But as long as you cooperate, nothing will happen to her."

"You made a room for her?"

"I did. I made one for you too. Do you want to see it?" She sounded almost excited. Like a giddy child at Christmas.

Wade started to feel hopeful. If he could find a way to talk her into at least releasing his hands . . .

He nodded as though thinking about her statement.

"Who was the other person?" he asked.

She jerked. "What do you mean?"

"Who was helping you? On the video from the church, there was someone else. A man. And at the radio station, you couldn't have put those bombs on the doors. We know there's someone else involved. Who?"

"Me."

Joanna shrieked and spun. A crack sounded and Joanna fell to the ground. Wade stared, first at Joanna, then at the man who'd shot her.

And felt his world fall apart all over again.

[37]

Olivia wasn't waiting for the cops. By the time they arrived, it might be too late. If Bruce was right.

He'd finally lifted his head and held up the picture from the mantel. "That's it."

"What's it?"

"It may be a long shot, but I might know where Amy and Wade are." He looked at Olivia, then nodded at the picture. "The boathouse where the picture was taken."

She'd check the area and find out for sure before requesting backup, but she'd texted Quinn and told him Bruce's deduction. Quinn promised to stand by in case they needed backup. She, Haley, and Katie would check out the place and be in touch.

Bruce climbed in the passenger seat and slammed the door. She didn't have time to argue that he should stay home. She simply threw the car in drive and headed in the direction he pointed.

Less than two minutes later, she was halfway around the cove of the lake when she pulled to a stop across the street from the house Bruce indicated. "Wait here, okay?" she said.

"You're kidding right?"

"Bruce. I need you to stay here. If Wade and Amy are hostages, you can't get in the way—or the line of fire. Wade's got enough on his mind worrying about keeping Amy safe. Let's not add you to the mix."

At first she thought he would protest, but he nodded. "Fine."

Olivia slipped from the car. Haley and Katie pulled behind her. "Let's be subtle about this, okay?"

The women nodded and Olivia led the way down the hill. "Katie and Haley, can you clear the house? I've got the boathouse, it's smaller. I'll holler if I need you." They each had an earpiece all on the same frequency. They'd be able to hear anything—including a call for help.

Katie and Haley broke off to cover the house. Olivia went on down the hill to a boathouse that looked similar to Wade's.

Once Bruce had told them he thought Wade had placed the picture facedown because he wanted them to go to the boathouse of his childhood, Olivia had simply reacted. Now she had her weapon out and was ready for whatever she found.

She moved to the window and tried to look in, but it was covered. The water lapped against the edges of the dock, but that was the only sound she heard. She moved back to the front of the building and found the door unlocked. She twisted the knob and opened it a fraction.

Through the crack, she could hear voices.

Wade stared at Cameron. The man gave a sigh that sounded almost sad, then he tightened his lips and motioned for Wade to stand up.

Wade stayed still, listening to the water rocking against the dock next to him. There was no boat in the slip to his left. The one on his right held a small houseboat. "Why?" he finally croaked.

"Stand up and get in the boat."

"Why?" Wade demanded. "Why would you be a part of this? What's in it for you?"

"Money, Wade. It's truly as simple as that."

"What money?" Wade slowly pushed himself to his feet. Where was Amy? The nausea had passed and his head had quit spinning. Mostly.

"The money that goes to me when you die."

Wade felt the blood drain from his face. He wobbled, locked his knees, and forced himself to stay upright. His hands felt numb, tight. But the tape felt like it had loosened maybe a fraction. He kept working at it even as he stared at the man who'd betrayed him and his family. "The charity."

All charities had plans in place should something happen to the founder. While Cameron handled the financials now, with Wade gone, he would be in a position to walk away with millions. It might not take long for someone to realize something wasn't right—especially when the checks started bouncing—but by then, Cameron Short would be long gone, probably with a new identity.

"Exactly. You're the only thing standing between me, that money, and a tropical beach." He scowled. "I've worked for you and your father for years and for what? A bonus at Christmas? A thank-you and a slap on the back every so often?"

Wade stared at the man. His family had taken very good care of Cameron. Wade wanted to give in to his weak legs and slide back down the wall. He resisted. "So you . . . what? Used Joanna to lure me to this place?"

"Joanna was a poor, love-starved woman who caught my attention because I thought she would be useful. I danced with her at one of the charity events not too long ago and we had a nice conversation. She was so desperate to have you that she would have done anything I asked, convinced that I knew what I was talking about, due to our close friendship. And yes, I set her up to take the fall. She was the crazy stalker, and when you ended up dead, she would be the one everyone looked at." He glanced at her still body. "Only now she's no longer needed. I guess I'll have to make it look like a murder-suicide. Unfortunately."

"What about Maddy?"

Cameron blinked as though not placing the name.

Wade ground his molars. "The woman whose throat was cut in the radio station parking lot."

"Oh yes. That was me. I had quite a bit of that lovely drug propofol left over after Gina's death. I simply modified one of my dart guns and a few darts and it made a nice little weapon. Valerie too. Nice little waitress who talked about your show a little too much to her customers. Had to make it look like Joanna would remove anyone who was a threat, anyone who might take an interest in you."

Wade blinked.

"Or anyone you might take an interest in."

"Justine," he whispered.

Cameron sighed. "Justine was becoming a problem. Your father said you were actually thinking of marrying her. I couldn't let that happen."

"Because everything would revert to her, should anything happen to me after we were married."

"And she was already getting nosey, pushing herself into the everyday workings of the charity, asking Linda for access to the financial software so she could get a feel for how Breaking Free was doing." He shook his head. "Couldn't let that happen."

"Because you've been stealing money from it," Wade deduced. He felt sick. Cameron didn't deny it. "And the bombs at the radio station?"

"Yep. That was easy to get too. The internet is a very helpful tool. Now no more talking. Let's get this over with."

Cameron raised the gun and pointed it at Wade's face.

"Please think about this, Cameron."

Cameron shoved him with the weapon and Wade lost his balance. Without his hands to help break his fall, he crashed onto the dock and slammed his shoulder against the wood. He rolled and managed to sit up and glare at Cameron. "Was that necessary?"

"Yeah."

"At least let me see Amy. Hold her while she's scared."

"You can hold each other for eternity." Keeping the gun steady on Wade's head with one hand, he pulled the small dart gun from the waistband of his khakis. He even dressed well to commit murder. "Goodbye, Wade, it was good while it lasted."

Hope shriveled. His attempt to lead help to him and Amy had failed. He'd known it was a long shot when he'd done it, and even if someone had noticed, there was no reassurance that they would understand what he meant by it—or that anyone would even connect it to him. And there was no way Cameron was going to let him or Amy live.

Olivia glanced at her watch. The whole conversation had taken less than five minutes. She shot a text to Quinn, Haley, and Katie confirming that she'd located Wade.

She didn't know where Amy was yet, but apparently she was there somewhere. She saw that Cameron had the dart gun aimed at Wade's center mass. "Need some backup, now," she whispered to Haley and Katie.

She pushed open the door and stepped inside. Cameron's profile came into view. Wade had his back to her. Slowly, ever so slowly, she centered her weapon on the only spot she could safely hit without the possibility of shooting Wade. Cameron's head.

"No! You leave my dad alone!" Amy's cry came from above Cameron. He looked up as Amy dropped from the vent onto Cameron's head. He howled, dropped the dart gun, and pulled the trigger on the much deadlier weapon. The shot went wild, slamming into the ceiling above Olivia's head.

Wade dove headfirst into the man's stomach. Cameron went down with Amy still attached to his back. Cameron and Amy hit the deck near the edge of the water. Amy gave a pained cry and rolled away. Haley and Katie burst through the door, weapons ready.

"Stop! Let her go!" Olivia bolted over to the chaos and aimed her weapon at Cameron, but Amy was still in the way. She lay on her back and kicked out with both feet, slamming them into whatever flesh she could reach. Then she rolled to her feet and kicked out again, one lucky swipe catching Cameron in the knee.

He howled again and brought the butt of his gun around. It connected with a solid thud across Amy's forehead. She dropped to the deck, eyes shut. Wade gave Cameron a vicious shove with his shoulder and the two men went down, Wade on top of Cameron. Hands still tied together, he wrestled for the gun, but Cameron managed to keep his grip. Wade was at a distinct disadvantage with his hands still duct-taped together. And if Olivia didn't do something fast, he might die.

But Olivia still couldn't chance a shot. In the background she heard Haley and Katie yelling orders, requesting backup, but she couldn't take her attention from the trio in front of her. Amy had fallen near the edge of the dock and lay still.

Cameron's weapon went off again. Wade yelled and went to his knees, hands on his left shoulder, blood streaming through his fingers. Olivia aimed and squeezed. Caught Cameron in the right side. He dropped to his knees, scrambled back to his feet. She got him again in the chest. He jerked, but stayed on his feet. He met her gaze, then gave Amy a vicious kick that rolled her over the side of the dock and into the water.

"Amy!" Wade's terrified shout spurred her. Cameron had dropped to the deck. Haley and Katie rushed to Cameron and Olivia pressed her weapon into Wade's hand. She didn't have time to find a way to release his bonds. Amy only had a few seconds if she didn't regain consciousness when she hit the water and fight her way back to the surface.

Not knowing how deep it was, she slid off the edge of the dock, panic in every pore, but her focus on Amy. She tried to stand and couldn't. So it was pretty deep. She dove, hands out, eyes open, but unable to see anything in the murky water. She moved left in a pattern, then back right, trying to stay just above where she saw Amy fall in.

She kept moving, feeling, praying. Her lungs protested, strained, bright colors flashed behind her lids. She had to breathe or drown. She found the bottom of the lake and pushed off. She broke the surface and sucked in air, saw Haley and Katie had Wade's hands undone and paramedics were working on both men, patching the bullet holes she'd put in Cameron and trying to keep Wade sitting down.

Law enforcement had descended.

She went back down as Wade hit the water beside her, with Katie, then Haley behind him.

She moved a few feet to the left and dove deep, hands out in front of her. Her mind kept going to the day her foster brother had placed his hands on her head and held her under. She remembered her lungs feeling as though they'd burst. And she remembered she'd prayed. *Please, God, don't let me die.*

Her fingers snagged something silky, felt the strands wind around her hand, her wrist.

Hair.

She closed her fingers around the hunk of hair and pulled. Kept her eyes open. Amy's face came into view, eyes closed, face pale and still. Like death. Lungs reaching the end of their capacity, Olivia slipped her arms around the girl's body and heaved her upward. She kicked and pushed and finally broke the surface, gasping in lungfuls of air even as she aimed herself to the dock.

"Liv!" Haley cried. She pulled herself out of the water and turned to wait for Olivia.

Another hard kick brought Olivia to the edge of the dock, Amy's limp body held next to hers. "I don't think she's breathing."

Haley hauled her up out of the water and onto the dock. Olivia held on to the side and gasped. Then looked around. Where was Wade? He'd been shot, but that hadn't stopped him from going after his child. "I'm going back down for Wade."

Just as she was about to dive, he broke the surface, panic and terror on his chalky white face. "I can't find her, Olivia. I can't—"

"She's here. Haley's got her."

He gasped and swam to the edge of the dock and pulled himself out of the water with a pained grimace. Olivia gathered her strength, but couldn't seem to find the power. Then Wade's good hand wrapped around her wrist and she let him pull her out. She collapsed onto the wood but rolled to see Haley still breathing into Amy's mouth. Katie had her fingers on the girl's wrist. She glanced up at Wade. "Her pulse is strong. She just needs to breathe."

Olivia finally prayed. "Please, Jesus, let her live."

Wade watched them work, his face stony, right palm pressed against the wound in his shoulder, lips moving, but no sound coming out. Olivia moved to stand beside him, curled her fingers around his elbow, and added her prayers to his.

Amy jerked, coughed. Water dribbled from the corners of her lips. Haley flipped her on her side and thumped firmly on her back. "Good girl, cough it up."

Amy sucked in air, coughed, and spit up until she finally wheezed and started breathing on her own. Wade dropped beside her and wrapped his good arm around her. The wound in his shoulder started bleeding again, but he didn't seem to care.

Amy reached a hand up toward the goose egg on her head. "What happened?" she whispered. Then her eyes went wide. "Dad!"

"I'm here, baby girl, I'm here."

"You came."

"Yeah. But you saved us." He cupped her chin and looked into her eyes. "You were so brave and I'm so proud of you."

Her eyes widened as she spotted the blood. "You're hurt!"

"I'll be okay. It's just a scratch."

She gave him a big smile, then burst into tears. Olivia thought she might join her.

Quinn stepped up from wherever he'd been watching everything play out. She'd just noticed Cameron had been removed from the boathouse. Under lock and key and the watchful eye of attentive officers.

"How did you manage to get into the air vent, kiddo?" Quinn asked.

She swiped the tears from her face and blinked up at him. "The room where she had a desk and a chair just like the ones in my room at home. I managed to get the desk on top of the bed, then put the chair on top of that and . . ." She shrugged.

"You picked the desk up?" Wade asked.

"Sort of. I scraped it across the floor up against the bed, then lifted one end until it was like standing up longwise." She indicated with her hands how she managed to maneuver the desk. "Then I grabbed the bottom legs and used the bed as a whatcha callit to get the desk on the bed."

"A fulcrum?" Wade asked.

"Yes. That. And I got the desk on the bed upside down. Then I just had to flip it over. It wasn't super heavy."

And her adrenaline had been flowing at warp speed. That had probably given her some added strength, Olivia mused.

"Anyway, I put the chair on top of the desk, climbed up, and heard your voices. I followed them and saw Mr. Cameron holding the gun on you. I pushed on the grate thingy and it was loose. I yelled at him to leave you alone and pushed harder and fell. I didn't actually mean to fall through it, but I'm glad I did."

Wade closed his eyes and Olivia knew he was thinking about all his child had been through. He hugged her tight against him again.

Quinn shook his head. "You need to get to a hospital and get that looked at."

"It's fine." His white face worried Olivia. He might say it was fine, but she agreed with Quinn. She waved at one of the paramedics and he nodded he'd be there in a second.

Quinn shrugged and tapped Amy on her shoulder. "You're a smart kid, you know that?"

"Yes, thank you."

Quinn gave a little laugh. "Well, good. We need kids like you to grow up to be detectives."

Amy's eyes widened. "You really think I could do that?"

"I really do. You're clever, you think on your feet, and you didn't panic when you were in trouble. All great qualities in a good detective." He held out a fist and Amy fist-bumped him.

She looked at her dad. "I didn't panic, Dad," she said softly.

"Nope, and that's one time I wouldn't have blamed you if you had." Amy gave him a weary smile and leaned into him. "And you know what?"

"What?"

"I think God let you like small spaces because he knew you were going to have to crawl through one to save me."

Her eyes widened. "You think God did that?"

"I think he did."

"Cool." She snuggled back against him and Wade held her tight.

Quinn walked over to Olivia and leaned over next to her ear. "They're keepers," he murmured.

She felt the flush start at the base of her neck and cleared her throat. "Right. Thanks for offering your opinion."

He patted her on the back. "You know I'm right."

Yes. She did. "I can't believe Cameron would do such a thing. Not after all Wade's family did for him and his wife."

Quinn shook his head. "He sure wasn't at the top of my suspect list. But I just learned a valuable lesson."

"What's that?"

"Don't make the mistake of assuming that just because you do something nice for someone that that person won't turn around and stab you in the back. For some people, greed always trumps loyalty."

"That's sad, Quinn."

"Yes, yes it is." He nodded to Amy and Wade. "But don't let them get away. That's *one* mistake you don't want to make."

"Get real. I don't want to make *any* mistakes."

He snorted and rolled his eyes.

She watched him walk away and shook her head even as a small smile twitched her lips. Until realization slapped her. Family didn't have to share common blood as long as they shared a love. A love that bound them tighter than any liquid flowing through her veins. She had that in Quinn, Haley, Katie, and Maddy. And her family.

Stunned, she stared at Wade. Why hadn't she figured that out before now? Oh sure, she'd had people tell her that, but she truly hadn't gotten it until just now.

Just. This. Very. Minute.

She pulled out her phone and sent a text to her brother. Yes. Her brother.

> **Olivia**
> I love you, Charlie. Tell Mom and Dad I love them too.

His instant response came through.

> **Charlie**
> Are you dying????

She gave a choked laugh through the tears she held back. Just barely.

> No, just coming to my senses. Thanks for being a great brother.

> You're dying. Stop lying to me. I knew I should have stayed. Now you've got me seriously worried.

> I'll call you in a little while. Tell Mom I'm coming to dinner Sunday night.

> What hospital are you in?

Shut up.

OK, now I know you're OK. I'll tell Mom. See
you soon. Oh, love you too, Turkey.

She spun to face the man and girl who'd woven their way
into her heart . . .

. . . and found her lips captured in a long, sweet kiss. Wade's
hand came up to keep her head in place while he poured out his
feelings in a way that made her heart thud faster than chasing
bad guys or protecting clients ever had.

Amy's giggles finally penetrated and Olivia pulled back.
Okay, so in spite of all of her internal angst, she was willing
to admit she'd been wanting him to do that for a long time.

"We need to talk," he said.

"Yes, I guess we do."

The paramedic cleared her throat. "You can do that after
we get this guy to the hospital. He looks like he might pass out
before you get your talking done."

Wade swayed and Olivia wrapped her arms around his waist.

"Okay," he said. "I'm not going to argue."

[38]

Olivia sat on the swing she'd just helped him install on his back porch overlooking the lake. With him having only one good arm, it had taken them a lot longer to get it done. But with laughter and a bit of clever maneuvering, they'd managed. Martha had come over and offered her help and they'd taken her up on it.

She'd disappeared about ten minutes ago.

Together Olivia and Wade sat side by side, Wade's foot keeping the swing going in a gentle swaying motion. It had been so crazy over the last two days that this was the first chance they'd had to talk. "You think Martha's going to be okay?"

"She will be. In time. Learning Joanna killed Pamela was a harsh blow. Martha and Pamela had been close. Cameron's betrayal nearly did her in as well." He drew in a deep breath. "But she'll heal. We all will." He leaned his head against hers. "You jumped in the water for my child," he said quietly. He'd never forget seeing Cameron knock Amy out and into the water, with him helpless and unable to save her. Then Olivia had simply rolled herself in after Amy.

Olivia nodded. "I had to."

"You didn't even hesitate."

"I couldn't. If I'd hesitated, I might have chickened out."

He pulled her to him and she let her cheek rest against his heart. He kissed the top of her head, then pulled back. "I know we've both got our issues, but I want a chance with you, Olivia."

"Issues? What issues?"

He heard the quiet mocking in her tone and laughed. "Yeah. What issues?"

She turned serious and looked at him. "Wade, I've had my heart closed off for so long that I'm not sure if I'll ever be able to open it up completely. Shana's death nearly killed me. I don't want to ever hurt like that again. But—" she blinked the tears forming in her eyes—"but I don't want to miss out on life anymore either. I want to live it to the fullest, experience the joy that I know can come with it."

"If you open yourself up to joy, you might experience some pain along the way."

"Yeah, I know. But when you have someone by your side walking with you through the pain, then maybe it doesn't hurt so bad."

He hugged her. "I want to be there for you."

"I know. I feel the same way about you."

He dropped his arm and threaded his fingers through hers. "So. I have a question for you."

She stiffened, her gaze wary. "What kind of question?"

He sat up and took her hand. "Olivia Edwards, would you do me the honor of—"

She stared at him, eyes wide, looking ready to bolt.

"—going out on a date with me?"

Her breath whooshed out and she punched his good arm. He laughed.

"Not funny, Savage."

"You should have seen your face. It was pretty funny."

"Ha-ha." She kissed his cheek. "Yes, I'll go out on a date with you."

Her phone rang and she glanced at it. "It's Quinn." She answered it and put it on speakerphone. "Hi, Quinn. Wade's listening in, so be nice. How's Maddy?"

"Awake!" He sounded jubilant.

Olivia sat up. "She is?"

"Yep. She can't talk right now, of course. Her vocal cords still have some healing to do, but she's alert and able to type messages on her phone."

"Wonderful. I'll be sure to go by and see her in a little while."

"She was asking about you and the others."

"Will you let them know?"

"Of course."

She hung up and turned to hug Wade. He held her and she let a few tears escape. "I guess God does answer some prayers the way we want, doesn't he?"

"When the prayer matches up to what he wants." He smiled.

"It's good to be on the same page with him again. I didn't realize how much I missed him until I made the decision to make him a part of my life again. The most important part. It's so crazy how God uses bad to bring good, isn't it?"

"There's a verse about that very thing."

"What is it?"

He pulled his phone out and tapped the screen a few times. "'As for you, you meant evil against me; but God meant it for good, to bring it about that many people should be kept alive, as they are today.'"

"I like that. I like keeping people alive. I like knowing I'm doing something good with my life."

He nodded. "That's how I feel about my work with the charity. Being a psychiatrist is great and I know that I help most of my patients, but being actively involved in the charity really excites me. Making a difference in a kid's life, a parent's life. That's a natural high." He smiled and leaned closer. "I think we could do some great things together. What do you think?"

"I think we think alike. Why don't we see how the first date goes and revisit this topic at a later time?"

He laughed. "Okay, I'm not in a huge hurry."

"Well, I am." Amy popped up behind the swing and Olivia gave a surprised laugh.

⸻

"Are you eavesdropping?" Wade asked. Olivia heard the amusement in his voice.

"Of course," Amy said. "How else am I supposed to know what's going on around here?"

"You sound like a friend of mine," Olivia said.

Stacy's head appeared next to Amy's. "When are y'all getting married?"

Wade flushed and Olivia turned away to hide her grin while he shushed the girls.

Erin Abbott had brought Stacy by and quietly apologized to Wade. He'd hugged her and told her not to think another thing about it. She was so relieved she almost started crying. "Thank you."

"Anytime you need some time off, just let me know. I'm more than happy to keep Stacy." He glanced at the girls bent over Stacy's new phone. "And I don't think Amy will argue."

Erin's gaze jumped between him and Olivia, and Olivia tensed, wondering if the woman was going to be as snarky as she'd been at church, but she had just smiled. "I'll be back in a couple of hours to get her."

Now Olivia leaned her head back against Wade's arm and

closed her eyes. *Thank you, God, for not giving up on me. And for helping me conquer my fears.*

"Get out of here or I'm going to tickle you," he growled playfully.

Olivia opened her eyes to see Amy roll hers. "Puleeze, Dad. I'm almost thirteen."

"Yeah, I know."

Amy grabbed Stacy's hand. "Come on, let's go check out your new makeup and you can tell me what Jason said about me."

The girls ran inside and Wade sighed. "Life won't be perfect, you know," he said, his voice rumbling in her left ear.

"I know. I don't expect perfect."

"Well, if you plan to continue your line of work, I don't expect it will be boring either."

"Nope. Probably not." She bit her lip. "Are you all right with me doing what I'm doing?"

He shifted his wounded shoulder. "As long as you're a better dodger than I am."

She raised his hand and kissed it. "I'll do my very best," she promised. Then looked into his eyes. "I have too much to live for."

"Let's keep it that way."

Her phone buzzed and she lifted a brow. "That's the mayor. I'll have to take it."

"Go for it." His eyes reflected his pride in her.

She gave him another quick kiss and pressed the phone to her ear. "Hello?"

"We have a celebrity coming to town next weekend who's received some death threats. Are you available?"

Olivia felt peace sweep her. This is what she'd been called to do. She glanced back at Wade. This, and to be a part of a very special man's life.

"I sure am."

READ AN EXCERPT FROM

WITHOUT WARNING

BOOK 2 IN THE

ELITE GUARDIANS

SERIES

Coming Summer 2016

Chink, chink, chink.

Seated at the desk and studying the frustrating spreadsheet, Daniel Matthews had ignored the sound for the past five minutes. Until he realized it wasn't supposed to be there. It came from somewhere below him, a barely-there noise, but one that had him curious. He looked up from the computer. Everyone else had gone home for the night, leaving him alone in the building.

Hadn't they?

Of course he was alone. He'd escorted his new head chef, Marie Stewart, out the door and to her car. When she drove away, he'd returned to the restaurant and locked himself inside. He tapped his pen against the paper on the desk and thought. Okay, so if he was the sole occupant, what was making the noise? Something with the water heater again?

Chink, chink, chink.

Didn't sound like the water heater, but what did he know? He rose from the desk and walked to the open office door. Just beyond the threshold, the steps to the basement and wine cellar were to his left. The door stood open because he'd promised his closing staff he'd take care of locking up. Before he left, he planned to check the wine inventory—he just hadn't gotten to it yet. The numbers on the spreadsheet had captured his attention.

It was past midnight. He'd come down to the restaurant after putting in a full day in his fifth-floor office at the headquarters building. He might be the CEO of A Taste of Yesterday, Inc., but he still liked to keep his hand on the day-to-day operations of all of his restaurants. This one in particular, since it was his newest establishment.

The *chink, chink, chink* sounded again. He frowned and flipped the light on in the stairwell, revealing brick walls that were original to the old 1860s building. One of the few structures in Columbia that had survived Sherman's 1865 march when he and his troops had nearly burned the city to the ground.

Daniel started down. His hand slid along the rail and he tried to listen over the echo of his shoes on the matching brick steps. At the bottom, he paused, the chill of the basement penetrating the wool sweater he had on over a long-sleeved T-shirt. At the bottom, he stopped. Listened for the sound.

Heard . . . a footstep? "Hey! Is someone down here?"

He walked past the wine cellar. Just past that, rows of storage shelves greeted him on either side of the brick path that ran between them. He continued toward the back of the basement, his heart pounding a bit faster, his blood humming through his veins. As he got closer to the back, the temperature dropped. A lot. Why was it so cold in here?

A shuffle of a footstep up ahead made him pause. "Hello? Who's there?"

No answer. But he knew someone was there.

Uneasiness crept through him and he wondered at the wisdom of continuing on in his search for the source of the noise.

Chink, chink, chink.

What *was* that? The noise was louder now, so it was definitely coming from down here. More footsteps. But fainter. Daniel moved back to the wine cellar and grabbed a bottle of wine from the nearest rack. Probably not much of a weapon but better than nothing. He patted his back pocket. He'd left his phone upstairs. He grimaced. Of course. And the Beretta M9 he'd slipped from his coat pocket into the locked top drawer of his desk wouldn't do him any good. He rarely went anywhere without the gun on him, but had gotten too comfortable in his office. If he went to retrieve the weapon, whoever was down here would get away. If he confronted the person, it could be a deadly mistake. Then again, it was highly unlikely the person up ahead would know Daniel had once been a Marine. Daniel would use that to his advantage.

He gave a low grunt. So be it. Hand-to-hand combat it would be. No one was going to break into his restaurant and not expect to face consequences.

With his adrenaline surging, he made his way back toward the sound. The recently replaced exposed pipes above his head rumbled. He'd never noticed that before. True, he'd had everything checked out before he bought the place, but since it had been renovated and opened to the public, he'd spent little time in the basement.

He finally came to the end of the row of shelves. The room opened up and light from the parking lot filtered through the open basement door. He heard the roar of an engine, and a chill that had nothing to do with the basement temperature swept over him. He raced to the door in time to see taillights fade into the distance. Someone had been in the basement. But why? Who?

A gust of wind caught him full in the face and he flinched. Goosebumps pebbled his skin.

Chink, chink, chink.

Daniel spun toward the sound. His eyes landed on a body hanging from the ceiling pipe, held there with a chain wrapped around his neck. Daniel inhaled sharply and backpedaled as he stared at the grotesquely distorted features gently swaying back and forth.

Another heavy burst of wind came through the open door behind him and the extra length of the chain knocked against the exposed pipe.

Chink, chink, chink.

⸻

Katie Singleton fought a yawn as she crossed the Broad River on 76 and headed home. To her left, just off Elmwood Avenue, blue and red flashing lights caught her attention. Briefly she wondered what was going on, but was too tired to think any more about it. At least it was a good tired.

She'd just come off a job that had ended well. It had been a fun concert with a well-behaved, well-mannered celebrity who appreciated—and listened to—her security team. Otherwise known as a dream assignment. As far as she was concerned it was the perfect way to start her week of vacation. Well, week of renovation. Which was vacation to her. She'd just purchased the home she'd grown up in as a child. A 1920s Charleston-style home on Gadsden Street that was "livable," but still needed a lot of work.

She glanced in her rearview mirror, the law enforcement lights catching her attention once again as she passed them. Was that Daniel Matthews's restaurant? A Taste of Yesterday? Riley Jamison, Daniel's niece, was one of Katie's students in the self-defense class she taught twice a week at the local gym. Katie made a spontaneous decision and pulled off at the nearest street. She swung onto Elmwood and headed back toward the lights.

When she got closer, she slowed and could see the action

going on toward the back of the building. She also recognized Detective Quinn Holcombe, a man she worked with in a professional capacity on a regular basis. She rolled to a stop outside of the tape that had already been strung and caught Quinn's eye. He lifted a brow and jogged over.

She lowered her window. "What's going on?"

"Katie." He placed a hand on the hood of the car and leaned over. "What are you doing here?"

"I was on the way home from the concert across the river and saw all the lights. It looked like it was coming from here. I know Riley Jamison, Daniel Matthews's niece."

The light went on for him. "I see." He shook his head. "Apparently someone broke into the basement of the restaurant and hung himself."

Katie blinked. *Hung* himself?"

"Well, that's what it looks like. I'm not saying that's what happened."

"Murder?"

He hesitated and she knew it wasn't because he was talking out of turn. Thanks to the mayor and her work with the Elite Guardians, Katie had special credentials that allowed her to be "read in" on cases, even contracted as a professional in certain circumstances. "Maybe," he finally said. "I think so, but that's just speculation. We'll have to wait for the ME's report, of course, but . . ." He shrugged. "Matthews said he heard footsteps and made it to the door just in time to see a car drive away. Like I said, we'll see."

"Do you know who the victim is?"

"The chef Matthews fired week before last." He consulted his notebook. "Maurice Armstrong. Apparently they had words after Matthews caught him stealing from him and confronted him. Armstrong denied it, but Matthews had it on video. He told him if he ever set foot on one of his properties again, he'd turn him in and have him arrested."

"Ooh, that doesn't sound good." She frowned. "Why *didn't* he call the police and have him arrested?"

"Armstrong has a fifteen-year-old daughter he's got sole custody of. If he goes to jail, she goes into the system."

"Sounds like Matthews is not such a bad guy."

"I don't think he is. I think he's tough—he's a former Marine who served two tours in Afghanistan—but he's also got a good heart."

A man who could take care of himself then. And while his actions sounded honorable—even compassionate—were they? Or had he not reported the theft for ulterior motives? From what little she'd picked up from Riley, the girl adored her uncle. But she might have on rose-colored glasses. "Matthews—Daniel—was here alone? And he found the body?"

Quinn pursed his lips and nodded. "Yeah."

"You think he killed him and staged it to look like a suicide?"

"I think someone did. Don't have the feeling it's Matthews though." He shrugged. "We'll know more as time passes."

"If it's truly a suicide, I can see hanging himself in the restaurant as being some sort of freaky revenge for Daniel firing him. But other than that, why would anyone kill him, then decide to string up his body in the basement of a restaurant where he used to work—and was subsequently fired from?" she murmured.

"Good questions. The only answers I can come up with for now would be to make Matthews look bad. Guilty."

"Frame him?"

"Yeah. I don't know, but we'll figure it out."

"No doubt. Any security cameras?"

"On the front of the building. One on the back. We'll take a look and see what they show."

She glanced past him. "Where's Bree?"

Brianne Standish, Quinn's partner, was usually on the scene with him, only Katie hadn't spotted her.

"Her sister had a DUI, she's dealing with her—and her mother."

Katie winced. "Ouch."

"Tell me about it."

Bree had some family issues that were making her crazy, but she was coping as best she could—and she had a partner who understood and had her back. "All right, I'll get out of here. I just wanted to . . ." What? She shrugged. "I don't know what I wanted. Guess to make sure Riley wasn't somehow involved."

Another officer rushed from the building. "Quinn!"

Quinn straightened and turned. "Yeah?"

"We've got another development."

"What's that?"

"One of Matthews's other restaurants is burning over on North Lake Drive."

"You've got to be kidding me."

"Nope. Apparently, it's been burning awhile. Fire trucks are already on the scene."

Quinn tapped the hood of Katie's car. "You want to join the fun?"

Katie considered it. Did she? Could she? As an ex-ATF special agent and trained arson investigator, the thought of the fire intrigued her. Flashes from the past made her hesitate. "Um . . . no. I don't think so."

Quinn studied her for a moment. "You know you want to."

Yes. Yes she did. "Okay, I'll ride over. I know where the place is." She bit her lip wanting to recall the words. But she didn't. She caught the brief flash of surprise in his eyes before he nodded. "Good. See you there."

"Where's Daniel?"

"Still answering questions. He's pretty shaken up."

"Are you going to arrest him?" she asked.

He blew out a puff of air. "No. Like I said, I don't think he did it. But even if I did think him guilty, I've got no evidence to support an arrest tonight."

She hesitated. "Why don't I give him a ride? I can come back this way on my way home and drop him off to get his car."

"I'll tell him."

So much for starting her vacation.

ACKNOWLEDGMENTS

Thank you to my parents and my in-laws for your willingness to keep my kids so I can travel to conferences or just spend time writing.

Thanks to Andrea Doering, my fabulous editor at Revell, and to Tamela Hancock Murray of the Steve Laube Agency. I appreciate you and all you do!

And thank you, Barb Barnes, for your excellent work on this manuscript—and others. You truly make them the great reads that they become.

A huge thanks to Wayne Smith and Drucilla Wells, beta readers extraordinaire—and retired FBI agents who know their stuff. Anything that is found lacking in this area of the book is totally my fault.

Thanks to my sweet Tuesday afternoon "critters," Edie Melson, Vonda Skelton, and Alycia Morales. I value your friendship so much—and your excellent feedback on various portions of the manuscript. Love hanging out with you girls!

And thank you to DiAnn Mills, who's always up for a Skype brainstorming session! Love you, sister!

And, of course, thank you, Jesus. You are my everything.

Lynette Eason is the bestselling author of the Women of Justice series and the Deadly Reunions series, as well as *No One to Trust*, *Nowhere to Turn*, and *No Place to Hide* in the Hidden Identity series. She is a member of American Christian Fiction Writers and Romance Writers of America. She has a master's degree in education from Converse College and she lives in South Carolina. Learn more at www.lynetteeason.com.

Come meet
Lynette Eason at
www.LynetteEason.com

Follow her on

 Lynette Barker Eason

 LynetteEason

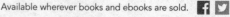